MADE
WITH
LOVE

MADE WITH LOVE

Tricia Goyer **AND** Sherry Gore

HARVEST HOUSE PUBLISHERS
EUGENE, OREGON

Cover by Garborg Design Works, Savage, Minnesota

Cover illustrations © Marvid, thailerderden10 / Bigstock

Published in association with the Books & Such Management, 52 Mission Circle, Suite 122, PMB 170, Santa Rosa, CA 95409-5370, www.booksandsuch.com.

Published in association with the literary agency of The Steve Laube Agency, LLC, 5025 N. Central Ave., #635, Phoenix, Arizona, 85012.

This is a work of fiction. Names, characters, places, and incidents are products of the authors' imagination or are used fictitiously.

MADE WITH LOVE

Copyright © 2015 Tricia Goyer and Sherry Gore
Published by Harvest House Publishers
Eugene, Oregon 97402
www.harvesthousepublishers.com

ISBN 978-0-7369-6129-5 (pbk.)
ISBN 978-0-7369-6130-1 (eBook)

Printed in the United States of America

15 16 17 18 19 20 21 22 23 / LB-CD / 10 9 8 7 6 5 4 3 2 1

To Jacinda Gore, Warrior Princess
Your beauty and grace inspired many.
Looking forward to heaven's family reunion.

One

Keep your words soft and sweet in
case you have to eat them.

AMISH PROVERB

❧

August 15

Lovina Miller opened the refrigerator and slipped her mixing bowl and pie crust ingredients inside to chill. Mem had taught her that to get the best results one had to put in one's best efforts. Mem had also told her, more than once, to get her mind out of the kitchen and be sociable for a change. It wasn't as if Lovina didn't enjoy attending the volleyball games and the church events where bachelors could be found…it was just that she had her mind on other things. On a pie shop. Of her own.

The kitchen window was open. A breeze blew in, ruffling the red and white checkered curtains—one of the few things that had moved with them from Ohio to Pinecraft, Florida.

The breeze wasn't hot and sticky like most mornings this time of year, and she was thankful. Instead, the southerly wind carried in salty air and the scent of flowers. It smelled of rain too. And maybe of promise? Lovina liked to think so.

She closed the refrigerator door and looked at the six empty glass pie plates on the counter ready to be filled with crusts.

Making the crusts was her favorite part, and filling them was a close second. But today they'd have to wait. She had an important assignment. Something inside her said not to dawdle. Could it be the Spirit of God that her grandma used to talk about? Did He really place dreams in the hearts of men and women like Grandma always said? Lovina would do anything to know. It would help her make sense of her inner urgency. The urgency telling her that today baking pies could wait.

The street outside their house was empty except for a gray stray cat that strolled just beyond their white picket fence, striding as if she owned the place.

Pinecraft was a favorite vacation destination for Amish and Mennonites during the winter. In August it was nearly empty except for the hundred or so full-time residents. There was no way Lovina could have a pie shop open by Thanksgiving when the first tourist buses rolled into town, was there? Her mind told her no, but something in her heart told her she needed to keep praying, keep looking, keep dreaming.

A shuffling sounded behind Lovina. One of her sisters was also awake. The loud yawn told her it was Hope.

Lovina turned to see her sister in Amish dress and kapp, with her hair mostly tucked in. Hope was always in too great a hurry to get outdoors to worry about spending time smoothing down her unruly strawberry blonde hair. Much to Mem's chagrin. This morning a few strands of fine, reddish blonde hair slipped from the bobby pins under her kapp and framed her face.

Hope moved to the window over the stainless steel sink, closed her eyes, and took in a deep breath, letting it out slowly. "Oh, Lovina, do you smell the gardenias this morning? They are lovely."

Lovina sniffed the air again. "Is that the flowery scent on the breeze?"

"Ja." Hope chuckled. "Those small white flowers on the bush with the dark green leaves are gardenias…like the name of our street."

Lovina nodded. "It is lovely, but not quite as good as the aroma of a pie fresh from the oven."

Hope tucked a strand of hair back into her kapp and took out a paper bag, packing a sandwich she'd made the night before and some fruit for her outing. She shrugged. "To each her own."

Lovina's mind turned back to the crusts. She'd been craving lemon meringue for a while, and Dat always enjoyed cherry. She opened the door to the small pantry and pulled out a jar of cherry filling. She tried not to compare the pantry to the cellar back in Ohio. She could nearly get lost among all the bins and shelves of jars as a girl. She brushed the top of the jar with her finger, brushing away the dust.

The pies can wait. The stirring came from within. And another thought quickly followed. *What if there's a new property for sale…one perfect for a pie shop?*

"Do you want to catch a ride to the beach? I'd love for you to join me and Betty Miller." Hope's voice interrupted her thoughts. "I don't have to be at the Shetler's house until this afternoon; little Arnie has a doctor's appointment this morning. His mom is taking him."

"I'd like to go, but I'm making crusts later…but if you're up for a quick bike ride first."

"Pst." Hope waved a hand in the air. "All you do is ride up and down these same streets. Pinecraft is only eight blocks. Do you think the perfect spot for a bakery is going to pop up overnight?"

Hope's skin had the slightest tan from being in the sun, and a natural pink tinged her cheeks. Her eyes were blue, like Mem's, and she had a large dimple in her left cheek. Everyone was always drawn to Hope's natural beauty. Lovina had noticed how the young bachelors who visited Pinecraft paid extra attention to her sister, who was closest to her in age. But Hope rarely paid them any attention. The bachelors would have a better chance at winning Hope's attention if they sprouted leaves and smelled like a rose.

The bachelors never gave Lovina the same attention—not that she expected it. She'd learned long ago not to hope that her path would lead to marriage. Most days this didn't bother Lovina. And days like today there was such anticipation inside that she knew God planned to use her in other ways. Her dream was different from that of most Amish young women, and perhaps that had been God's plan all along. Hadn't her grandmother always said that it was a *gut* thing to trust one's unknown future to a God who held each person in His palm?

Lovina released a sigh. "You never know when a new property could open up. There are places selling in Pinecraft all the time. And I need to be paying attention, or I'll miss out." She placed the can of cherries on the gold-colored Formica countertop and turned, facing her sister and leaning against the counter. "I heard that Elizabeth Bieler, over at the fabric store, is thinking about closing shop. That would be a nice place for a bakery."

Hope snorted, slipping into her flip-flops. "And where would you put an oven in that small place, in the back storage closet? Besides, Joy would pack up and move back to Ohio if the fabric store ever closed." Hope lowered her voice and leaned closer. "Yesterday I spotted her piecing another quilt, and she hasn't even finished the last. And even if something did open up how are you going to purchase it? You haven't found that rich bachelor yet, have you? None of us have. Poor Mem! We're going to be the laughingstock of the town. Five daughters and none of them married, and the oldest one twenty-five!"

Hope must have noticed Lovina's face fall because she softened her tone. She crossed her arms over her light teal dress and offered a gentle smile. Then she stepped forward and placed a soft hand on Lovina's arm. "It's a *gut* dream you have, really it is. I just wish you had left it in Walnut Creek."

Lovina shook her head. Then she reached for the dishcloth in the sink of warm, sudsy water. She set to work wiping down the countertops that were already clean. "It's not like that. It's not like you can pack a dream in mothballs and store it away in the corner of someone's barn. I choose to have faith that if God placed this dream on my heart, then He has a purpose for it."

Hope nodded, but Lovina saw pity in her gaze. Hope didn't understand. Hope was always too caught up in the moment, in the living green things blooming around her, to think too much about the future. This usually wasn't a problem, unless it was Hope's turn to cook dinner, which sometimes meant nothing got cooked and they ended up dining at Yoder's restaurant.

"Ja, well, since everything I try to plant in this place dies I might as well enjoy the beach this morning. Have fun on your bike ride. And if you don't find a place for your pie shop maybe you'll find a handsome bachelor." Hope winked, and then she picked up an apple and took a large bite. "Then again, even if your smile and the aroma of your delicious pies drew him in, those fancy ideas of yours would most likely cause him to run the other direction."

Lovina narrowed her gaze, and she placed her hands on her hips. "Watch out, Hope. You better keep your words soft and sweet in case you have to eat them. I'm not the only one with big dreams, am I?"

Hope lifted an eyebrow. "A community garden—one that can actually grow food in this sandy soil—is a much smaller dream than a pie shop."

"Does it matter the size of the dream if one can't shake it?" Lovina found herself saying. "And if I could shake it I would. It would be easier to find a nice Amish man and settle down like all our friends."

Lovina padded over to her flip-flops by the back door and slid them on. She tried to ignore the heat tingling in her cheeks. She was close to her four sisters—they did so much together—but rarely had she shared what was deep down inside. Now she knew why. Her sisters didn't understand. She doubted anyone in her family would. Why had she ever verbalized the near-impossible dream?

"See you after my bike ride!" Lovina called over her shoulder as Hope went to the back porch to retrieve her beach bag and a towel.

Lovina's flip-flops squeaked as she walked to the carport for her bicycle. She couldn't imagine wearing flip-flops in Ohio, especially not in public. But things were different here. And to her, "different" didn't matter just as long as she could still dream. Her pie shop wasn't something she wanted to give up on. Not now. Not ever.

Pie brought people a moment of joy. Sharing it brought people together. In the busyness of life, people took time to sit face-to-face. To talk and to laugh. A heat swelled in her heart. Joy overwhelmed her at the thought of a pie shop of her own.

But was she fooling herself? Was Hope right? Should she have left her dream packed in the attic rafters, back in Ohio?

She jumped on her bike and started to ride. The fresh ocean breeze brushed her cheeks. The pavement before her was damp from last night's soft rain, and the sun reflecting off it almost made the road look deep blue too...the color of ripe blueberries. The front door of one of the white cottages on Gardenia Street was open, and a trailer was parked out front, filled with supplies. The whine of a drill came from inside, and though the heat of summer had barely given way to the slighter coolness of fall, work was already getting done to make preparation for winter residents.

Their neighbors Marcus and Becky Yoder had arrived with a driver from Indiana on Saturday. Becky's aging parents would be along with them for the remainder of the season when they returned in December. The house was in sore need of a new air-conditioning unit. It wasn't something Lovina's family was accustomed to on their farm in Ohio—or electricity for that matter—but every home in Pinecraft had it because of the unbearable heat in the summer months. She was surprised how quickly her family adapted to this one major change.

It still seemed strange that this was home now. Would it ever feel that way deep in her heart?

She turned off of Gardenia Street, heading toward the Tourist Church, although there wouldn't be any buses arriving today or for the next few months.

Lovina's family had made the journey from Ohio to Florida every season for the last five years until her father's health made it impossible to maintain their farm. Her father had been premature as a baby and always had weak lungs. The doctor had told Dat if he wanted to live to see his sixtieth birthday a warmer, moister climate would do him good. They sold their house but had kept most of their land, leasing it out. With the money from the sale, and the monthly lease payments, they wanted for nothing…well, that wasn't completely true. Lovina had her dream that nipped at her heels like an active puppy.

She pedaled faster, scanning the sides of the road to see if any new properties had been listed for sale. Last night she'd made a list of what she was looking for, and she'd prayed about it. Really prayed. If God owned all the cattle on a thousand hills couldn't He lead her to the perfect spot for a pie shop?

They'd already been in Pinecraft five months, much to her mother's chagrin. There weren't nearly enough eligible bachelors to go around, not that Lovina worried about that now. Once she got her pie shop up and running then she'd start looking—and praying—for the right man.

Lovina rode by the park and paused slightly, noticing a great blue heron. His S-curved neck held a bulge, as if he'd gotten dinner stuck in his throat. Would she ever get used to this place with its strange creatures, fancy flowers, and jewel-colored birds? Would she ever stop missing the sound of Amish buggies on the roadway? More than that, would she ever find the perfect place to open a pie shop?

There had to be someplace close that wouldn't take too much work. It was only then—after she found the perfect location—that Mem and Dat would even consider her proposal.

It wasn't every day she asked her parents to sacrifice their whole life savings.

Must-Haves for the Perfect Pie Shop

- Two large bay windows
- 12-ft ceilings for an open, airy feeling
- Close enough to home to walk or bike to, even in the rain
- Storefront needs to face south or west for all-day sunshine streaming through the windows
- Room in front of the shop by the window for making pie

~

Two

The only time to look down on someone
is when you're bending over to help.

AMISH PROVERB

〜◎〜

N oah Yoder held his hat in his hands, picking at some invisible lint on the rim. He stood at the door of the simple cottage. Mr. Hosteler had some work on his shed that needed to be done after the last big storm. Noah knew he was giving the man the best deal in town, but from the folds of the older man's wrinkled brow—and the narrow gaze of his eyes—Noah could tell he wasn't going to get the job.

"I'm sorry, Noah. I'm sure you'd do good work, but…" The man's voice trailed off and he diverted his gaze.

Noah held his breath and waited for the man's excuse. He'd heard them all before. Some claimed they were going to wait on their remodeling projects. Others never got back to him and then hired another work crew. Some mumbled minor excuses that made no sense. Noah's stomach tightened and those old insecurities came back again. He remembered the furrowed brows and the whispered words when people thought he was out of earshot. Five years had passed since he'd been that rebellious youth, but the memories of the pain he'd caused stayed with him.

Mr. Hosteler stroked his beard. "The truth is, Noah, I trust you, but those boys you have working with you…well…" He let his voice trail off, but from the concern in Mr. Hosteler's gaze the message was clear.

Noah nodded. Finally, someone had said it. Amish teens, unruly and troublesome like he had been, were frowned on by those in Pinecraft. Noah understood the worried stares of the residents whenever they walked around town. Yet he also wished the people here would give them a second chance. Or actually a first chance! If someone didn't help these teens—didn't believe in them—where would they end up? Noah thought of his best friend, Leonard Hooley. Would Leonard still be alive if someone had reached out a helping hand instead of turning their backs?

Noah kicked at a rock on the ground, wondering if he should take the job alone. No, that would never do. He'd get some money and work within this Amish community, yes, but what would the boys do all day when he was working? He shuddered at the thought.

It had taken some convincing for his Aunt Verna to let his cousin Mose move down to Pinecraft. And Mose's friends Atlee and Gerald tagged along. Wasn't it enough that he offered to help out one boy? Now he had three to watch over. Troublemakers all of them.

Then again, he knew their wills could be bent with prayer, patience, and hard work—their hard work. He'd learned himself that the best way to learn to believe in yourself was to discover the jobs God gave you to do and work at them with all your might.

Yet how could he help the teens if no one would give them the chance?

"Mr. Hosteler, your shed needs work, and I'm giving you a good deal. I promise, sir, that I won't leave those young men to work on their own. It's a training opportunity. That's why I've come down here…to give these young men a chance at a new life." He wanted to continue. He wanted to add, "…just like I was given a second chance." Yet the words refused to emerge. Mr. Hostetler didn't need another excuse not to hire him.

"If it were up to me, I might try it. But my wife has other ideas." The older Amish man leaned in close. "It was her sister Merna whose house was broken into just last week."

Noah nodded. "I understand."

Mose, Atlee, and Gerald hadn't admitted to breaking into the woman's home, but Noah had been taking things to Sarasota Salvage at the time—the one time he'd left them alone. And it did seem odd that the only things that were taken were two peach pies.

Noah took a step back and placed his hat on his head. He'd never be able to convince the man now. Why would you ever invite someone you didn't trust onto your property?

He took slow steps as he made his way back to the road and strode toward his uncle's house. He'd thought God had directed him to Pinecraft, but for what reason? To have the door slammed in his face again and again and again?

Noah glanced around the streets of the small village. The morning dawned clear, but in the distance, clouds moved in. He kicked his boot against the rock in the street. It shuffled across the road and hit the Lost and Found box. He'd first seen the box after just a few days in town. It represented this place in a way, everyone taking care of each other. Of course, trust like that was given freely until one broke that trust. It was what his nephew Mose had done back home. Was Noah a fool to think he could help the young man? Was Mose a lost cause? He'd caused far more trouble in their hometown of Arcola, Illinois, than stealing peach pies. Then again, so had Noah.

Noah heard the sound of a bicycle and stepped to the side. A bicycle cruised by slowly, and he smiled at the pretty, dark-haired Amish woman as she passed. Yet her eyes didn't glance his direction. Instead, her gaze scoured the buildings, as if searching for something. He wanted to call to her. He wanted to see if she needed something or had maybe lost something. Did she know about the Lost and Found box?

The woman gazed intently at the house at the end of the street. It was his uncle's house. *Does she know my family?* Noah wasn't sure if he'd ever seen her in the two months he'd been here. He would remember if he had. How could someone forget such a pretty face as that?

Noah quickened his steps and approached his uncle's front gate. It was only then that he realized she wasn't looking at the house, but instead the property behind it. It was a large warehouse or some type of theater. In the months he'd lived there Noah had never seen anyone go in or out. He'd been meaning to ask Uncle Roy who owned the place. Chills moved up and down his arms as he considered what treasures had been left behind inside the warehouse.

The clouds moved over the sun, casting a long shadow, but the woman didn't seem to notice. Instead, she parked her bicycle and strode up to the warehouse.

An Amish man was picking up trash and cigarette butts near the building. The woman hurried over to him. They talked for a few minutes, and then the man pulled out a small piece of paper from his pocket, wrote something down, and handed it to her. When the woman turned, her smile lit up the horizon even more than the sun had just minutes before.

What had she asked the man? What had made her so happy? Noah wished he could find out.

Instead, he had to walk inside those doors to tell Mose and

the other teens they still didn't have any work within Pinecraft. Instead, he'd have to call some of his construction worker friends to see if there was anything that looked promising in their salvage piles—things he and the teens could gather up, repurpose, and resell.

How am I going to help these teens get reconnected within the Amish community if I can't even find one simple job here? It seemed the Englisch didn't mind that the teens were rough at times. They almost expected it. And Sarasota Salvage had been a willing buyer for the numerous treasures they'd rescued from construction sites and dumpsters.

Still, a burden within Noah's heart wouldn't be shaken. From the first moment he got the idea of moving down here with the guys his desire was to reconnect them with an Amish community in a safe place. Had he heard wrong? Since Pinecraft was known to be more liberal, with their electricity, air conditioning, and Amish and Mennonites from various communities living side by side, he'd thought this was the perfect place to bring the young men. To help them start over. He'd just had no idea how far one's bad reputation carried. Like geese, news of the wayward teens—and most likely his own former ways—had found their way south in record time.

There had to be something out there for them. There had to be someone willing to give him—give Mose and the others—a chance.

He walked by the mailbox and then paused. Noah couldn't remember if he'd checked the mailbox yesterday. He was waiting for his last check from Dat for some items he'd sold at auction. And then…well, they'd be out of money after that.

Where would that leave them? They couldn't stay without helping out Uncle Roy with the expenses. And the way these guys ate the money would be swallowed up by groceries alone.

He opened the mailbox and found two bills and a long white envelope addressed to him. He quickly opened the envelope and breathed a sigh of relief at the check inside. His dad had done well selling Noah's items, and it was more money than he'd expected. Also inside was a folded-up letter and a photo. He lifted up the photo to get a look and his heart sank.

It was a photo of the gift shop, just outside the city limits of his hometown. His heart skipped a beat as a flood of memories came rushing back. The small building was painted white, and four wooden rocking chairs sat out front. There was a handmade OPEN sign in the large picture window, and inside quilts and other gift items were displayed. A window box held colorful flowers.

Still standing by the mailbox, Noah opened the letter and read.

Dear Noah,

Greetings in the name of our Lord and Savior Jesus Christ!

It is a beautiful day here at home. It's the day that the Lord has made. The garden is growing much better this year than last. I think it's because of the watering system that you helped me put in before you left. It's much easier for me to make sure all the rows are watered well. The only problem is that I'm already tired of canning tomatoes, and there is no end in sight.

We had church at our house on Sunday and every room overflowed. There is talk of splitting our district again. Us ladies were laughing that the newly marrieds would take us past our threshold by next spring. Six of the young women are new mothers, all in the last month!

Joe's Verna was here asking on Mose. I could see the pain in her eyes at her worries of him. I never understood the parable of the Good Shepherd leaving the ninety-nine to go after the one until after

I became a mother. Verna has a dozen children yet to tend after, but I'm sure she'd catch a bus to Pinecraft if it was season already. I assured her that if anyone knew how to handle wayward boys it would be you.

Speaking of such things, the lady from Amish Gifts and Crafts asked me to give you this photo. She planted flowers in the window boxes and was right pleased with them. It was a nice touch.

I'll stop there before I think too much on matters past. What's done is done. What's gone is gone. It seems to me that what one learns can be used to help others, as you are doing. And although the heartache does not ever completely go away, I'm thankful that it eases with time.

But enough of that. I hoped for this note to be a cheery message, not a sad one. Write when you can and let us know if all is well with you and the boys. I must get the food out for our sewing frolic. I made skillet pear ginger pie since it's Nancy's birthday and it's her favorite. I will close now to get this into the mailbox before the driver comes.

Love,
Mem

Noah folded up the note and put it back into the envelope. He let out a heavy sigh. He didn't know what bothered him more—that whenever people looked at the gift shop, no matter how beautiful it looked now, they'd always think of him and the destruction his foolish choices had caused. Or the fact that they trusted he'd be able to help these teens. Who had he fooled more, them or himself?

He approached the house, and he heard their laughter. Nearly every morning they were playing one prank or another on each other. Yesterday Gerald had got the other two by taking their old milk carton and filling it with water mixed with white paint. Atlee hadn't noticed until he'd filled a glass and taken a long drink. Then—to make things worse—he spewed it all over the living room area rug. They'd tried to clean it up, but some of the white smudges remained.

He'd thought he'd be able to help the guys, change them too. He'd imagined they'd find work, find a purpose, and find God. How foolish had he been.

Noah ran his fingers through his hair and then removed the check from the envelope, tucking it into the pocket of his work shirt. He folded the envelope with the letter and picture until it was so small and thick that he couldn't fold it any more. Then he placed his hand on the doorknob. In the back of his mind he'd told himself that even more than the work he'd done on the Amish gift shop, his work here in Pinecraft would redeem the past. Now it was clear that it wasn't going to happen. Was God even listening to his prayers? Or had his deeds from the past put up a dividing wall that he'd never be able to scale?

Then he opened the door and took a deep breath. Laughter rose from the guys inside, but instead of bringing joy it caused him to cringe. They were most likely playing another prank, and his efforts hadn't seemed to matter. The young men seemed no closer to considering their faith and being willing to change their ways.

Noah threw the wad of envelope into the trash, and then he moved to the kitchen, placed his hands on the counter, and leaned forward, closing his eyes. He'd gotten himself into this mess. Now Noah needed to figure out what to do next. Whatever it was, it would take a miracle to make any difference. And he'd nearly run out of faith that one was coming soon.

Noah's Mem's Skillet Pear Ginger Pie

Use your favorite flaky pie dough for double crust. Make extra for filling a deep-dish skillet. For the best pie make 1½ batches of your favorite recipe and bigger circles than usual for a pie pan.

8 or 9 Bartlett pears

1 cup brown sugar

2 tablespoons all-purpose flour

1½ teaspoons cinnamon

1 teaspoon ginger

pinch of salt

¼ cup heavy cream

1 egg beaten with 1 tablespoon milk

1 teaspoon raw, cane, or light brown sugar

Preheat oven to 375°. Lay one pie dough circle into a 10-by-12-inch cast iron skillet. Peel and slice pears and place in a large mixing bowl.

In separate bowl combine brown sugar, flour, cinnamon, ginger, and salt. Pour over pear slices and toss to coat. Lay mixture in skillet and then drizzle heavy cream over the mixture. Top with second circle of pie dough. Press edges to seal crust. Cut several slits in the crust, using any extra crust for decorative fall leaves. Lightly brush crust with egg and milk mixture and then sprinkle with raw sugar. Wrap foil around outer edge of crust to avoid burning; remove foil about halfway through baking process to brown.

Bake in preheated oven for 40 minutes or until pear mixture is bubbling. Let cool enough to set and serve with your favorite ice cream. Super yummy when drizzled with a caramel topping.

Three

Kissin' don't last. Good cookin' do.

AMISH PROVERB

❧

Anna Miller sat down on the porch swing of their cottage on Gardenia Street with a small pile of mail she had yet to go through. As she dressed this morning, she'd heard Lovina and Hope's voices in the kitchen, although she could not make out their words. And nearly as soon as they were out the door her other daughters followed. Joy to her part-time job at the quilt shop and Faith to check her schedule at Yoder's, with Anna's youngest daughter Grace tagging along. She smiled, guessing that they'd probably share a large cinnamon roll while they were there, chatting over coffee and eyeing Jacob Bieler, Elizabeth Bieler's nephew who'd taken a job as a dishwasher.

A bird's song filtered down from one of the tall palm trees, carrying down Gardenia Street. The air was thick with humidity. In the distance large, dark clouds threatened to bring rain. Even though it wasn't quite mid-morning, the air was warm.

Anna pulled the collar of her dress away from her neck, wishing for a cool breeze. She knew her wishes would be in vain. She couldn't hope for cooler weather for a few months yet. And just when the weather became perfect the buses would start arriving from the Amish communities up north, filled with the snowbirds ready to enjoy the best part of the year in Pinecraft.

If it weren't for the warm weather helping her husband, John, she'd push to return to Ohio. Yet where she wilted, he flourished. He'd even taken a long walk around the neighborhood this morning. Seeing her husband well was more important than all her discomfort, all her longing for home, and all her worries about her daughters.

Back in Walnut Creek, her friends were most likely just getting settled down after Harvest Fest in Berlin and looking forward to the Quilt Show and other fall activities. Personally her favorite was Oktoberfest at Heini's Gourmet Market. For the last few years her daughters had worked during the festival, earning extra income. And it certainly didn't hurt that her daughters got to know some of the young men who also worked at Heini's.

Last year Lovina had even gone on a few dates with one of the cheese makers. Unfortunately their family had moved to Pinecraft before Lovina had time to get to know the young man. They'd written a few letters, but those dwindled and then stopped. Her oldest daughter was focused on only one thing now—a pie shop of her own.

Anna wasn't sure what had gotten into the girl. She'd been such a good child for so many years. She'd never wavered from the faith. She'd been the biggest help around home. Was Lovina feeling growing pains like all of them after their move—just in a different way?

Anna closed her eyes and tried to picture their farm in Walnut Creek. Even though the days would be warm, the nights would be cooling off. In a matter of weeks the fall leaves would be changing colors.

She smoothed her dress and apron over her legs and scanned

the roads, looking for Lovina's bike. Why would her daughter be out on such a morning like this? Did she want to get caught in the rain? Had Lovina even noticed the clouds in the sky? Anna sighed. Most days Lovina's head was in the clouds. Yes, her body was present in Pinecraft, but her mind was somewhere else.

Ever since she was a young woman and they'd visited Patty Cakes Bakery in Charm, Ohio, Lovina had talked about a pie shop of her own. Lovina had no idea that anyone, especially her mem, knew about the scrapbook she kept under the linens in her hope chest filled with recipes and photos of décor. Lovina had "hidden" it under her bed once, and Anna had found it when cleaning for church.

Seeing it had caused Anna's gut to tighten into a hundred knots. Lovina's ideas and plans were much fancier than Anna liked, but that was not the problem. Lovina was a pretty girl with dark hair—just like John's used to be when he was young—and large brown eyes full of dreams. John had always been a dreamer and that had served him well on the farm. But where had it gotten him now? Where had it gotten them?

Chasing dreams could only last so long. It was family that stayed with you through life. It was love that stayed with you. The love of a good spouse. Anna knew this to be true.

The wind caused the branches to sway, and she sifted through the pile of mail from yesterday. She'd been so busy going with John to his doctor visits that she hadn't had time to look through it. She smiled, seeing a letter from her best friend, Regina, and quickly opened it.

Dear friend Anna,

Greetings in the name of our Lord and Savior.

I'm fairly certain as you read this letter it's not the first time you've held its envelope in your hand. You're so much more patient than I.

You were always like that, even in our school days at Ridgebottom. I, on the other hand, can scarcely make it back to the house before ripping open any letters I receive from you, my friend.

I try to picture in my mind exactly where you are sitting as you read this, but since you moved to Florida and have settled in a new home, I have to use my imagination. At least I know what the town and the ocean look like. I don't suppose the beach changes too much over the years. Or maybe it does. I remember my honeymoon in Pinecraft as if it were yesterday. The beaches in Sarasota are so lovely it's no wonder the newly-marrieds all want to head straight to Pinecraft.

I'm still waiting—not so patiently I might add—for an answer from Abe about a trip to Florida this winter. He hasn't forgotten my request. He's just so busy now that autumn is nearly here. There's so much extra work a farmer has to do to ready a dairy farm before winter comes.

I do so miss you, Anna. Being separated for the first time in forty years has been difficult. More so than I thought. Perhaps it's been easier for you. Having new surroundings to explore and a new home to set up housekeeping in would keep a body busy. I suppose you've also made new friends at church and have found your place in the community, different as it all is from Walnut Creek. My days are pretty much the same, but for new babies in the family. News of an expected little one comes every time you turn your head, it seems. I can't wait until our Sadie Mae or Mary share such news with Abe and me one day. Hopefully soon! To be a groossmammi. I get goose pimples just thinking about it.

How is John faring these days? Is the mild weather helping to ease his lung condition as much as the doctor said it would? I hope so.

And the girlies? What are they doing these days to keep busy? Did Hope find a place to plant a garden? Seasons in Florida are so different from Ohio. I laughed out loud at your last letter about the sandy plot she dug up in your backyard hoping to plant corn! At least you can buy fresh anytime you get the notion with Yoder's Produce nearby. We put up 100 quarts of Silver Queen and 50 quarts of Incredible corn. Abe likes his Silver Queen! We had plenty of help with the frolic. Several from church came, as did my sisters and Mem. It's true that many hands make light work. Afterwards the menfolk joined us for supper. We served a roaster-full of underground ham casserole. Lamar's Rachel brought green beans and Joel's Laura shared several jars of pickled beets from this year's crop. My Sadie Mae made two pans of peach delight for dessert.

Lavon and Jaylene just returned from visiting their oldest son in Montana, so she was on hand to help too. I do wish you'd find room in your heart for her, Anna. She truly is a jewel. She's so cheerful a body can't help but like her. I pray you'll feel the same one day. It wasn't her fault that Lavon chose to marry the girl new to town rather than the one he'd caught toads with down at the pond. Even you have said you're thankful for Lavon's choice—thankful that God brought you John and the girls. But enough about that.

Have you any new dresses for the upcoming winter season? I have sewing to get to this forenoon yet now that the canning is behind us. I have a dress cut for Henry's Lizzie Ann's wedding. That makes nine weddings in all this year, with all the nieces and nephews. We didn't miss a one.

Any wedding news to report on your end, Anna? Bishop Mahlon often preaches God's timing is perfect. I have to admit, I've found it to be true more times than I could count in my forty-nine years. I hope you'll apply your gift of patience in this part of your life too and not rush your girls into marriage before they're ready.

> *In His glorious name,*
> *your friend, Regina*

Anna read the letter a second time, and then she released a long sigh. She usually read Regina's letters aloud to John, and he might get a chuckle out of this one. It had been nearly twenty-eight years since Regina had held her hand and offered a handkerchief for her tears, but in the mind of a best friend the memories of twenty-eight years were just as strong as twenty-eight days.

She offered a heavy sigh, thinking of the sobs that Regina had witnessed all those years ago. Anna had believed Lavon Graber to be her first love. She'd pictured him as her husband since their days attending parochial school together. During her rumspringa they'd attended some singings and had gone on a few picnics and such, but Lavon had never given her any indication that he wanted to marry her. Lavon had set his gaze on Jaylene. And while Anna had never been close friends with the woman, she didn't have hard feelings either. Looking back, Anna knew John had been the right choice, and she was thankful that Lavon had broken her heart. Once she made her vows to John she'd never looked back. And their love had grown over time.

Now Anna hoped with all her heart that her five daughters would find lasting love at a young age. Like her mother, aunts, and grandmother always told her, the most important things in life were the love of God and the love of a man. And now she was in quite the conundrum. Her love for her husband had brought her to Pinecraft, but she worried every day that the decision would cost her daughters a chance at finding husbands.

Anna's mind focused on Lovina. What was she going to do with that girl? Her mind always seemed to be someplace else. Anna bit her lower lip and said a silent prayer for her daughter—for her *daughters*. And a minute later the bird's song pulled her from her prayers.

She thought about her own mem. Anna's mother had urged

Anna to spend time with John Miller when Lavon Graber's affections hadn't held promise. Maybe she needed to be more encouraging. Maybe a little prodding would stir the fires of romance. Even though there weren't many eligible bachelors around Pinecraft, there were a few.

Anna wasted no time. She hurried to the kitchen and took a pen from the cabinet drawer, and then returned to the wooden swing on the left side of the porch that faced the street.

She clicked the pen and then turned over the envelope. On the back of the envelope Anna listed the young men in Pinecraft:

David Raber
Eli Swartzentruber
Daniel Schmid
Paul Miller
Reuben Kurtz
Jonas Gingerich
Elmer Elzey
Ervin Lehman
Emory Jones
Milo Nolt
William-Ray Girod
Noah Yoder

She read the names once, twice, three times. And then, one by one, she also crossed them off. A few were handymen. Two of the men worked at Der Dutchman. One did woodworking and lived most of the year in Pennsylvania. None of the young men seemed like the type who'd be strong enough to capture Lovina's attention. They had to be more appealing than a pie shop, and as far as she was concerned, none of them were.

When Anna got to the last name she put two lines through it.

Noah Yoder. She'd heard Roy's nephew had come to town with a group of young hooligans. Noah's reputation far preceded him. She'd first heard his name in *The Budget*. The wayward youth had not only bought an automobile, but he'd been driving under the influence, lost control, and smashed through the front of an Amish gift store. She'd heard the store had been remodeled, but she'd been shocked when she'd discovered it was *that* Noah Yoder who'd come to town.

The young man was handsome enough, with a charming smile, which had made Anna even more suspicious. She'd watched him closely last week when he'd stopped by to talk to John. He'd offered to replace their roof for a low price. Too low in her opinion, which meant he had to be up to no good.

Anna had also heard about thefts in town. Three young men had been seen nosing around her friend Merna's place, and before you knew it a lock was broken on the back window and two pies were stolen right off the counter. Merna believed the theft would have been worse if Amish Henry hadn't ridden by and had called out to the intruders. Because it was dark he hadn't seen faces, but he'd said they must have been young, considering how fast they'd darted away. Later, as she laid in bed, listening to every noise, she'd realized that those young men had probably offered to work so cheaply so they could scope out the place. Get familiar with it so they could do some more thievery.

She was considering all those things when the first drops of rain began to fall. She was ready to go inside anyway. Coffee with a little cream sounded good.

Anna took her list and hurried inside. She stopped short just inside the door when she noticed John pouring coffee into two mugs. She closed the door behind her and smiled.

"How did you know that was what I was comin' in for?"

John grinned, wrinkles crinkling around the corners of his eyes as he did. "We've been married for coming onto thirty years. I know you always take your coffee after the sun is fully up."

"Ja, maybe because there's too much to do first thing in the morning. No one has time to sit and pause."

"Lots to do, like read a letter from your best friend?" He winked.

"Ja." Anna nodded, placing the envelope on the table, and he took it in his hands. His eyebrows lifted as he saw the names on the back and read over the list slowly.

"Nice list of names here. Future sons-in-law, I'd guess."

"Not quite." Anna sat down with a huff. "Not like I wished."

John took a slow sip of his coffee and then placed his mug on the table. "Sometimes we have too many expectations."

"Is it wrong to expect my daughters to want to get married? To attend volleyball games and such? To be friendly and outgoing?"

John chuckled and leaned back in his chair. He twisted his lips from side to side like he always did when he was thinking—when he was trying to come up with the right words. He was the steady one in their relationship. He kept her grounded, but at times like this she just wanted him to spit his words out.

"I wasn't talking about expectations for our daughters, Anna, I'm talking about expectations of the young men. Do you remember what I was like when we met? Didn't have but a few dollars to my name. I was stubborn, and I spent more time dreaming than working. If I hadn't inherited the family farm, I'm not sure where we'd be."

Anna cocked her chin, yet her grin gave her away. "Well, as I see it, not everything has changed much."

John chuckled. "You talking about the dreaming part or the stubborn part?"

Anna's smile faded slightly. John had been so ill before they moved. For many years he hadn't taken time to dream. It felt good to be speaking about such things. To see the twinkle in his eyes once again.

"Both," she said, reaching over to pat his hand.

"Yes, well, as you've discovered it takes time to grow up. I think that's the important part of finding the right person…you get to grow up together. Finding someone who makes your heart dance is a good start, and I have a feeling that one of these young gentlemen will make Lovina's heart do just that."

Anna frowned. "I don't know about all that romantic stuff. Remember, kissin' don't last. Good cookin' do."

John smiled and patted his stomach. "Around six o'clock I might agree with that, but there were plenty of young women who cooked, but you…well, you're the one I couldn't stop thinking of."

Anna waved a hand in her husband's direction. "You've gone soft in your old age for certain."

He shrugged. "Just don't sign off on any young man one of our daughters brings home. The Lord sees more of the heart than we ever can."

Anna nodded and took a sip of her coffee, and John's eyes scanned the list again. She'd just have to wait and see, wouldn't she, when and if one her daughters brought a young man home.

Her eyes paused on the last name on the list once again. Just as long as the young man wasn't Noah Yoder. Everyone had read about his deeds, and Anna didn't know if she could feel safe with him around. No, anyone but that young man.

- -

Underground Ham Casserole

4 cups cubed ham
4 tablespoons butter
½ cup chopped onion
1 tablespoon Worcestershire Sauce
2 cans (15 oz) cream of mushroom soup
1½ cups milk, divided
2 cups cheese
4 cups mashed potatoes
1 pint sour cream
bacon bits, optional

Fry ham, butter, onion, and Worcestershire sauce together and spread in bottom of 8-quart roaster. In saucepan, heat mushroom soup, 1 cup milk, and cheese together and pour over ham. Mix mashed potatoes, sour cream, and remaining ½ cup milk and then spread on top of cheese mixture. Do not add any salt! Sprinkle with bacon bits. Bake for 20 minutes at 350°.

Four

No dream comes true until you wake up and go to work.

AMISH PROVERB

⁓

Lovina rode her bicycle past the Tourist Church, noticing how empty the large parking lot looked. In the winter, buses came from Ohio, Pennsylvania, and Indiana, as many as five a day! With winter came old friends and new ones. Likewise the neighborhood park overflowed with Plain people playing shuffleboard and volleyball. Children ran around with their cousins at family reunions, but today just a few part-time residents could be seen here or there. Lovina pictured these streets full. She pictured evenings of music and singing on Birky Street. Pictured serving up pie as music was carried in on the breeze.

She smiled as she headed to the corner of Kaufman Avenue and Bahia Vista Street. Since moving to Pinecraft, she'd become a member of the Mennonite bank, Everence Credit Union, transferring all her money from her bank back in Ohio. Any bank that hosted pie contests was sure to get her business.

She parked her bike out front, straightened her kapp, and pushed open the glass doors. A smiling teller greeted her.

Lovina approached. "Is Jason Schlabach available?"

The man behind the counter nodded. "He's on a call, but I'm sure he'll be off in a moment. From the twinkle in your eyes I assume you have good news?" Lovina crossed her arms over her chest and stepped back. "I hope so."

She chatted with those coming in to make transactions, and five minutes later Jason appeared, waving her into his small office. Jason's trousers and shirt were store-bought, and he had the short hair of a Mennonite, but he had a similar look to the other Plain men in the community. Even though Jason had an important job, there was no pride in his face. Instead, his kind smile told Lovina he was honestly glad to see her.

She hurried into his office and sat in the chair across from him. A simple wooden desk sat between them.

Jason sat too. Then he leaned forward, resting his arms on his desk. He lifted an eyebrow. "So have you found a place? A place for your pie shop?"

"I do believe so. There was a sign up just this morning. I couldn't get much of a look inside but a man who lives next door gave me the owner's name." She slid the piece of paper across the desk with the owner's name and number. "The man told me the price, and it's in my price range—"

"Are you talking about the large warehouse on Bahia Vista Street?" Jason interrupted.

"Ja, do you know of it?"

"I walk by all the time. Lori Ann and I do as we take our children to the park. It's big..." His voice trailed off, and she wondered why he wasn't saying more.

Lovina threaded her fingers and placed them on her lap. "Very big, which means there will be plenty of room for a bakery. A nice large kitchen and..."

"Hold on a minute now." He held up a hand. "We've yet to see inside. We don't need to be getting ahead of ourselves."

"Ja, I know. I was hoping…" She paused and smiled.

"That I'd make the call?"

Lovina blew out a heavy breath, telling herself not to get too eager. Not to lose her head in this. Jason had told her he'd help her. When she approached him about securing a future loan he'd believed in her dream. More than anyone he'd believed, but now she worried. Concern darkened his gaze.

"It really is the perfect spot," she continued, not willing to give up until Jason agreed with her. "There are just a few houses nearby and plenty of parking. I've looked up and down these streets for months, and it's the first time there's been a For Sale sign on the lot. They must have put it there last night. You should call before anyone else does."

"I should, should I?" Jason dropped his fingers on the desk, tapping out a beat. "Last time it was for sale a few years ago they wanted too much money, but I suppose it doesn't hurt to call."

Lovina jumped to her feet and clasped her hands. "Thank you! Thank you so much!"

Jason glanced at the clock on the wall. "I'll see if we can meet someone and look at the property over my lunch hour"—he steepled his fingers and leaned forward—"but I have to tell you now of my concerns. The bigger the space, the greater the cost of remodeling. I don't want you to do anything that would risk your investment. Or put your parents' property at risk."

Lovina nodded. At the thought of asking Dat for financial help her knees grew weak. She sunk back into her chair, pressing her spine against the back rest. Her stomach tightened down as if the fresh strawberries she'd eaten for breakfast had turned to lead. She'd been so excited that she hadn't thought much about the next steps. Even if she liked the property she didn't have enough money of her own for the purchase. She could get a loan, but only on one condition…her father had to agree to cosign. And where would she get money to remodel?

"I—I'd never want to cause harm to my family."

Jason picked up the phone. "I have no doubt about that. Let me find out if we can see the place before we add in those worries to the mix." He dialed, and she listened as he set up a showing with the owner. "I'll be bringing a friend," Jason told the man. "We'll look forward to seeing you at noon."

~ ◌ ~

Lovina rode home as quick as her legs would pedal. She waved and smiled as she passed the park. A few mothers chatted as their children played, and an Amish man was fixing one of the wooden fence posts that had come loose. Two small boys stood watching him. She recognized the boys—Caleb and Abby Troyer's twins. Yet she didn't know the man. He put on a show, making it seem like lifting the hammer took all his strength. The boys laughed and then the man joined in too, touching the child's head with a soft hand.

Every time she saw tender moments like that her heart tugged, and she considered having her own family someday. Her concerns grew as she got older…but even those thoughts paled in comparison to the thought of her own pie shop.

The warm wind smelled of rain and flowers, and she spotted a group of teen boys fishing at Phillippi Creek. They didn't seem to mind the misty rain that fell. In the months she'd lived in Pinecraft she'd seen people kayaking and canoeing in the brackish water. Folks had pulled out plenty of gar fish and some even claimed shark sightings. Would she ever get used to this community? How long would it take for her heart to call this place home?

She only had a few hours until noon. She didn't know if she could stand it. Could this be the answer to all that she'd been praying for?

Once at home, Lovina gave up the idea of making pies. For the first time in as long as she could remember she couldn't concentrate on the recipes she knew by heart. Instead she went to her room, shut the door, and pulled out her notebook. It had started as a simple spiral notebook that she'd used to collect recipes she liked. Over the years it had grown as she glued in pictures and ideas for her pie shop. Now the notebook was a few inches thick, filled with all her favorite things.

On the first page was a brochure from the Amish bakery in Charm called Patty Cakes. It was a magical place, and most of the visitors came for cupcakes. It even had a toppings bar, with candy, nuts, and flavored frosting where one could decorate their cupcake any way they'd like. Lovina had always enjoyed pies more than cupcakes, but the bakery had been a special treat.

She smiled thinking about the carrot cake with cream cheese icing that Mem had bought and taken home on that first visit. Lovina had enjoyed the cake so much that Mem had traveled all the way to Charm for the recipe, and had presented it to Lovina for Christmas one year. The funny thing was that Sarah, who owned the bakery, had gotten the recipe from Esther Schlabach, right here in Sarasota, Florida! That recipe was tucked inside Lovina's notebook too.

In addition to the first brochure and the recipe card, Lovina had picked up other brochures in Amish communities and had cut more photos out of newspapers and magazines. She turned to the page with her favorite photo—a long, wooden display rack filled with loaves of bread. She loved the simple design and the rustic lumber used for the rack. Lovina ran her fingers over the glossy image and then closed her eyes. She pictured a rack just like that, filled with pies in her shop. She pictured customers both Amish and Englisch choosing pies to take home for a family meal, and others sitting at small wooden tables and ordering a slice from young Amish women with bright cheery smiles.

"Lord, is this what you have for me?" The words slipped out before Lovina could stop them. Growing up in her Amish community no one prayed out loud, but she'd become more used to it here. There were just as many Mennonites as there were Amish in Pinecraft. People prayed at community meals. They prayed at church. And when her whispered prayer slipped out, it seemed the most natural thing in the world.

Lovina didn't want to pray for God to open the doors of this building. Who was she to tell God what to do? All she knew was she could see herself there. She could see the building all set up. She could picture it. But she also trusted that God's ways were best. She'd learned that as a child. Her grandmother especially had reminded her that God's good will would be done, and none of them were to question it.

The minute hand moved slowly, and Lovina made herself a cup of tea. Dat was feeling better, and he and Mem had gone out on a walk to Yoder's. Thankfully the rain had come and gone and they weren't home to ask questions. Mem would have known something was up for certain if she hid away in her room instead of baking.

Lovina closed the notebook and then got out her hand mirror to check her hair. It was no use sitting around here. Tucking the notebook back into her hope chest, she decided to ride to the warehouse the long way. And as she went, Lovina knew she'd take time to dream, take time to pray.

Finding the perfect location was one thing, but bringing her dreams to life seemed nearly impossible. Would God really go out of the way to help fulfill one young woman's silly dreams?

She rode as slowly as she could, but Lovina still had to wait fifteen minutes for Jason and the owner to show up. Finally they arrived, Jason first and then the owner.

She cast her warmest smile to the Englisch man as he approached. He extended his hand to Jason. "Ready to see inside?"

Jason shook the man's hand and then looked to her. "Yes, we are, Mr. Johnson. This is Lovina Miller."

The man nodded her direction but offered no further greeting before unlocking the front door.

Mr. Johnson was Englisch, and from the sheen and style of his clothes it appeared he had a lot of money. Lovina wanted to ask how he came to be the owner of a warehouse in an Amish and Mennonite settlement, but she changed her mind. While most of the Amish people she knew chatted about their lives and families before conducting business, this man moved with quick steps, as if he wanted to be done and on his way as soon as possible.

Lovina followed him inside and then her steps fell short. She scanned the room and sucked in a breath, thinking back to the list of "must-haves" she'd written in her notebook: two large bay windows, high ceilings, close enough to home to walk or bike to, even in the rain. This place was all of those things.

It was dusty, filled with junk, and needed work, but as Lovina scanned the large, open room her mind was already setting up shop. She knew exactly where the work counters would go, and the tables, and the pie display. The large windows were painted white to keep people from being able to see inside, and she wondered how hard it would be to remove the paint. She knew that was just one of many things to take care of when—if—she got the place. But Lovina clapped her hands with glee when she realized the last criteria was covered too. God had met her desires down to every small detail! For once the paint was cleaned off the windows the beautiful southern sun would stream through.

Jason looked at her, and she saw the concern in his eyes as he looked around. She could almost see him adding up all the remodeling costs. And she was afraid of his total.

As the two men talked about the size of the lot and the proximity to the Amish village, Lovina moved into a back area. She flipped on a light as she took in the back office and the large storage area. She breathed the dusty, still air, but it was fresh with promise. There was an office chair next to a desk. She brushed it off with her hand and sat down. She should be feeling overwhelmed, but a strange peace settled in her heart. God had birthed His dream within her. He never had to worry about coming up with a bank loan. God owned everything. He cared for His children. He had good plans for her, and she knew that as she continued to take steps forward God would guide her way.

Lovina heard the men nearing, and she prayed simply in her mind for what steps were to come next.

She also prayed that if God had other plans He'd make it clear. But when the two men stepped into the office both were smiling. And the peace within her chest swelled.

"Lovina, I've been talking to Mr. Thomas," Jason smiled at her. "And he's ready to sell. He's thinking that maybe the price he quoted before is a little high..."

Lovina folded her hands on her lap and nodded. For some reason she wasn't surprised.

Oh, Lord, You do have a plan in this, don't You? She rose to face the men, eager to see what the day would hold.

Carrot Cake

2 cups flour
2 teaspoons baking soda
2 teaspoons cinnamon
2 cups sugar
¾ teaspoon salt
3 cups grated carrots
3 eggs
1½ cups vegetable oil

Cream Cheese Icing
4 ounces cream cheese, softened
¼ cup butter, softened
½ teaspoon vanilla
1½ - 2 cups powdered sugar

Preheat oven to 350°. Mix cake ingredients together in a large bowl. Pour into a greased 13 x 9-inch pan. Bake 50 minutes. To make icing, combine cream cheese, butter, and vanilla. Gradually add powdered sugar and beat until smooth. Continue to beat until light and fluffy.

Five

It is better to hold out a helping
hand than to point a finger.

AMISH PROVERB

N oah walked into the dusty warehouse and paused. Knuckles on hips, he scanned the room and let out a low whistle.
Voices carried from the back—two men and a woman. The pretty
woman who'd been checking out the warehouse earlier that day.

Noah had just returned from grocery shopping when they'd
showed up. He'd watched them go and debated about whether
or not to follow. If the warehouse needed to be cleaned out, or
if they needed construction help, he wanted to offer his services.

He sucked in a breath. His heartbeat quickened as he took
note of the items in the room. This place looked to hold the contents of an old theater. There were framed movie posters and theater chairs. An old industrial bistro table and a bronze fountain
looked as if they'd seen better days. There were piles of lumber, a
cast iron planter, and a stack of old doors. The room was full, and
everything was partly hidden under a layer of dust.

Since he was a child strolling through the rows of items at
his dad's auction yard, he'd found nothing more exciting than

discovering unique items, cleaning them up, and getting them into the hands of someone who understood their value.

Noah had worked in his father's auction yard since he was seven or eight years old. While most of the castaway items in this large area looked like junk, he could see their deeper value. In the months since he'd moved to Pinecraft he'd built a relationship with Sarasota Architectural Salvage. When all the construction jobs he'd hoped to get had fallen through, he'd made a little money going into homes that were being remodeled. He trained the teens to search through the large dumpsters to see if there was anything worth saving. It was amazing the things that people threw away. Such a waste. In the search for new and better most folks cast off materials that were not only still useful, but were unique and interesting too.

For the last two months they'd also cleaned out attics, dug through old garages, and helped haul out items from house remodels, finding treasure among the trash. Sarasota Salvage had come to trust him, and anytime he called they gladly sent a truck for a pickup. When they couldn't, Noah found an older, retired guy who was willing to drive them around in his truck. All that was good, but just making money wasn't the goal Noah had in mind. He wanted the teens to connect with the Amish community and to see how they could play a useful part. He wanted to earn the community's respect too.

He'd made enough to support himself and the three teens, doing what he could to scrape by. But this place…he got excited just thinking about what he could do with all the forgotten and castaway items in here. He'd get a nice check from Sarasota Architectural Salvage for just a few of the things lying around. There were a half-dozen fluted columns and some corbels leaning against one corner, and those always got a good price.

Noah continued on. Two industrial metal cabinets caught his eye. He moved toward them and resisted the urge to open their doors and peer inside. He could get lost in this place, but he didn't have the whole day to wait around. Noah glanced at his watch. It was time to check on the teens, see if they were back from Phillippi Creek, and get them working for the day. There was a local rental that needed the shed in the back torn down. It wasn't glamorous, but it was work. He didn't need to stay there the whole day, but he did have to go with the guys and get them set up.

The voices in the back continued to talk. What should he do? He couldn't leave until he spoke with the owner of this place.

He tried not to eavesdrop, but their voices echoed.

"Lovina, I agree that such a place coming on the market is rare, but…" the man's voice trailed off.

"I have enough money. With the money I've saved and the loan you promised…"

"Yes, but what about after that? How are you going to pay to remodel this place? The money from the loan won't be nearly enough."

"The Lord will provide. I am certain."

The man said something Noah couldn't make out and then the woman, Lovina, chuckled. "Oh, I see you don't like that answer." Her voice held a hint of humor. "I'm not afraid of hard work. And I have four sisters…"

The man laughed then. "I know you'll roll up your sleeves. I have no doubt your sisters will too, but it's more than you can tackle alone."

Noah took a step forward. He didn't want to startle them. He didn't want to interrupt. He had no idea what the woman wanted this place for, but if she needed help…if she needed this place cleaned out and fixed up, well, that could be an answer to his prayers. Maybe hers too.

His foot hit a loose board. A loud squeak echoed through the cavernous room. The conversation in the next room stopped, and the two men and the woman strode through the doorway.

Both men wore curious looks, but seeing his Amish dress they didn't seemed alarmed. The woman looked at him, but it was almost as if she was looking through him, enraptured by the room.

"I'm so sorry I interrupted. I'm Roy Yoder's nephew." Noah pointed behind him. "My uncle lives right close, and I've been waiting to take a look in here for a while." He turned to the man in gray slacks and pressed white shirt. The man looked to be in his mid-thirties and Mennonite, Noah supposed.

Then he turned to the Englischer. "And I assume you own this place?"

"Yes," the man continued before Noah could say anything more. He glanced at his watch. It was clear that he was in a hurry. "We were just about to leave."

"Not yet. Just a minute more?" The woman, Lovina, moved to the center of the room, closer to Noah. "I can almost see it now. We can have work tables here." She motioned with her hands. "I can be rolling pie crusts as customers walk in. Those enjoying their pie will be able to ask the bakers questions and see how it's done. And then…" She pointed behind her, and her beautiful face glowed with excitement. "The kitchen will be back there."

Pie? A kitchen? Noah removed his hat and scratched his head. Were they thinking of turning this place into a bakery?

The Mennonite man sighed and looked around. His eyebrows furrowed and sadness filled his face as if he'd just had a great dream crushed. "It's a wonderful idea, but there is no way…"

The Englischer looked at his watch again, and Noah was sure

he was going to bolt any second. He wished he had a chance to talk to Lovina alone, to take time to understand her dream, but now was his chance.

"I can make it possible!" Noah stepped forward. He turned his hat over in his hands. "My name is Noah Yoder. I've worked construction for the last four years. I have a crew that can work with me, and we can turn this place around faster than you can blink. I can draw some plans and sketch out some designs. We can do that together." A lump formed in his throat as he said that last word. He liked that idea—liked it very much.

"I'm hardworking and honest," Noah added. He swallowed as he said those words. He was honest…now. The two men looked at each other with curious glances, but they didn't interrupt. It was as if they were waiting to see if he was going to put a price on this offer. He didn't give them a chance to brush him off.

"I think this place would make a lovely bakery." Noah moved toward the large windows. Sadly someone had painted them over. "Just look at these large windows. We can replace them and the sun will stream right in."

Lovina took a step closer to him, hanging on every word.

"I work with Sarasota Salvage too. I can make a few calls," he said. "I'm sure they'd be interested in some of this—a lot of this." He swept his arm, noting the items in the room.

The Englisch man stepped forward. "Listen, I'm sure you have great ideas but I have another appointment." He stretched out his hand, and then he placed a key in the Mennonite man's hand. "Can you see this place is locked up? I'll have someone swing by the bank tomorrow to pick up the key."

"Yes, yes, of course."

The man hurried out. Instead of watching the Englischer go, the woman's eyes were fixed on Noah. So much hope filled her gaze that Noah had a sudden urge to do everything he could to make sure her dream of a bakery came true.

Like him, she was an underdog. He'd grown up Amish his whole life, and he'd never heard of a woman trying to achieve such a thing. Joy mixed with concern on her face, and he understood. There were many who most likely thought she was a fool, just as they thought him to be a fool for moving to Pinecraft with the teens.

Noah's shoulders squared with determination, and he made a promise to himself to help this woman in whatever way he could. He took a step closer to her, and then he pointed across the road toward the Tourist Church. "When folks gather to welcome the bus they'll be able to see the bakers in here working. Lovina is right. It'll draw them in. What better place to welcome new friends than here, chatting over a piece of key lime pie?"

Noah looked back at them. The pretty woman smiled, but instead of looking at him she kept her gaze fixed on her shoes.

The woman glanced up briefly. "It all sounds wonderful, but I'm afraid there aren't enough funds—to pay you, that is."

"Oh, I don't need pay." The words spilled out before he had a chance to consider his offer.

The woman's head jerked up. Her mouth circled into an O and her eyes widened. She had a heart-shaped face with dark brows and even darker brown eyes. Pretty lashes blinked once, and then twice, as if she was uncertain if she'd heard him correctly.

"You don't need pay?" The banker cleared his throat. "Did I hear that correctly?"

"Well, I won't work for free, but I do a lot of salvage work." He walked over to some old barstools. They had red-painted seats, and the paint was chipped. "Items like this might be good in your bakery, but there's a lot of things around here I'm sure you won't need."

"It's a pie shop, not a bakery," she said. Yet she wasn't upset. "A whole shop with pies, and pie pans decorating the walls." She pointed to a wall by the door. "I can even picture a cabinet there holding cookbooks."

The banker strode forward. There was a hint of excitement on his face too.

Noah extended his hand to the woman. "Ma'am, I'd love to help you. I even have three teens—uh, employees—who can help me."

Her eyebrows lifted, and she looked skeptical.

"And you'd do it in exchange for the items you can salvage around this place?"

Noah paused before answering, studying the woman's face. Then he glanced around. There were some great items to be certain, but there was something else too.

His heart had warmed when he'd seen her standing in this room. She was petite in stature, and her dark brown hair was tucked under her kapp, but the way she held herself was different from most Amish women. She stood with her shoulders back, wearing confidence like a cloak. A gentle confidence that made her beautiful. An underdog shouldn't have confidence like that, and he wondered if she could explain it to him. *Oh, Lord, let me have a chance.*

"Yes, ma'am," he said with a firm set of his chin. "My crew will do the work in exchange for the items we can salvage. Unless, of course, there's a way we can use the items around here. I'll make sure to put your needs first."

She turned from Noah to the banker. "Jason, did you hear that? Surely you don't have any concerns now."

"Noah Yoder. Wasn't that what you said your name was?" Remembrance flickered in the man's eyes. Then his gaze narrowed on Noah, as if he was just realizing who he was.

Noah sighed. Had his reputation marred this man's opinion too?

"Yes, sir. I'm from Arcola, Illinois." He placed his hat back on his head. "And I'm willing to answer any questions you have about me." The hope that buoyed his heart a moment before disappeared, and suddenly the room seemed stuffy.

"I'm not sure that's needed yet." The man's voice softened, and he turned to the woman. "It's a nice idea, Lovina, but let's not put the buggy before the horse. Let's worry about your funding first, shall we? We know where Mr. Yoder lives. Once the money's secure and the deal is settled we can talk to him then."

The woman nodded. Noah wanted to state his case and clear his name, but instead he remained silent. He'd tried to prove himself again and again in this community. Why did he think things would change now? Maybe he should just find one more job that would be enough to provide them with fares back to Arcola, and let that be that.

Finally, Noah offered the man a slight smile. "Yes, of course." He didn't have the heart to look at the woman, to see the accusations in her gaze too. "Well, like you said, you know where I live."

He strode out across the creaky floor. The muggy heat hit his face as soon as he opened the door, but it didn't compare to the burden that weighed down on his shoulders. He took long strides toward the backyard of his uncle's place. The teens' laughter carried out through the door, causing his stomach to tighten down in knots.

Noah paused at the door, balling his fists and placing them against the wood. Maybe God should have called another follower to try to help these guys...someone with better credentials. Obviously, he wasn't going to get anywhere. Not with his past trailing behind him, carrying with it a wake of loss and broken dreams.

- -

Florida Key Lime Pie

½ cup fresh lime juice
1 (14 oz.) can sweetened condensed milk
1½ – 2 cups whipped topping
1 baked pastry pie crust
additional whipped topping

Beat lime juice and milk together. Fold in whipped topping and pour into pie shell. Top with additional whipped topping. Refrigerate before serving.

Six

ꙮ

Lovina waited until Jason had strode around the corner, toward the bank, to approach Noah Yoder's front door. She'd met Roy Yoder at church a few months ago, and he'd mentioned back then that his nephew was coming to town. The older man had a twinkle in his eyes at the time, which often meant he was planning to do some matchmaking. And matchmaking was the last thing she needed. Not when her dream of opening a pie shop was at stake. Because of that she'd steered clear of Mr. Yoder.

Once, when she'd heard Dat mentioning that Roy's nephew Noah was coming to put in a bid to fix the roof, she'd made sure she was out of the house. Dat had ended up hiring someone else to do the work on the roof, and now Lovina wondered why. Noah seemed kind and helpful. He seemed eager to work. And he was also different from most of the young men Lovina knew. Thinking of that made her smile, and she shuffled her feet on the doormat, getting up the nerve to knock.

Noah Yoder had seen a vision for her bakery. Her heartbeat

quickened even now just thinking about it. Jason had been her greatest advocate for the bakery up until now, but he hadn't caught her vision for the warehouse. After Noah left, she and Jason had talked. He was still willing to help her get a loan, but Jason was also worried that she'd bite off more than she could chew.

As they parted, she and Jason had agreed to meet again once she had a chance to talk to her father about cosigning the loan. That worried her. That's why she had to talk to Noah before talking to Dat. What Jason didn't realize was that her dat was a dreamer too. But she needed Noah's help to capture the dream in a way Dat could understand. Even now she pictured Dat's notebooks and sketches lying around their old farmhouse. He was always thinking up something he could do around their property. Dat hadn't been one to sit still for long, until his illness made him do so.

They'd had the most beautiful farm in Walnut Creek. There'd been a pond with a bridge and a tall white windmill that pumped well water through pipes in the cellar to keep it cool. Dat had built a small roadside stand on their property where Hope sold produce from the garden, where Joy sold quilted aprons, and where of course Lovina had sold pies. Lovina smiled wistfully thinking of it now.

Faith, the artist of the group, had drawn Amish scenes. And Grace, who was always the businesswoman, had worked with a local print shop to make postcards.

Of course supply and demand became a problem at times, especially when Faith was working at whatever local restaurant had the most handsome Amish bachelors as customers. Or Grace wasn't putting in her share of work because she was at the library reading business books hidden behind cookbooks.

At least Hope was committed to providing the best produce available, and Joy had more than enough quilted items to contribute. Then again, if Mem had her way, the garden or the sewing machine—or the kitchen in Lovina's case—would take up far less of her daughters' attention. Then again, Faith's interest in every handsome bachelor who crossed her path hadn't helped her much, had it?

Yet while their mother's dreams of each of them getting married and starting a family hadn't happened, their father's dreams had become their own—each in their own way. He always listened to their dreams and even shared some of his own. Still, a pie shop was bigger than anything she'd yet to try for. And Lovina knew that she'd need Noah's help for her father to see that her dreams could be accomplished.

She lifted her hand and knocked three times. A knock on the other side of the door startled her, and she jumped back. Then laughter erupted. It sounded like teen boys messing around. Lovina took another step back and the door swung open. Three young men stood there with wide smiles. They were the teens she'd seen fishing at Phillippi Creek earlier, goofing off. She'd seen them around town too, and they always reminded her of active pups who'd just figured out how to get out of the barn and romp around the farm, getting into all types of mischief.

One of the young men swung his head, moving his long bangs out of his face, and he lifted his eyebrows. "We were wondering how long it was going to take you to knock." He turned to the smallest of the three teens, who still had his Amish haircut. "And Mose here didn't think you were going to knock at all."

"I—I was thinking." Heat rose to her cheeks and she wondered if this was the work crew Noah had talked about. At the thought, some of the excitement that buoyed in her heart faded.

The third boy, whose hair stood straight up, nodded. "I do that sometimes too." He smirked.

"All right, boys, mind your manners now." A voice sounded from behind them, and like Moses walking through the Red Sea, Noah approached and the young men parted.

"Sorry about that." Noah ran his hand through his hair. "All of them haven't had an older sister around in a while to tease. I think they decided you'd fit the bill."

She liked Noah's easy manner. Liked the way he smiled at her. Liked that he didn't seem surprised to see her there—he seemed excited even.

A sweet, buttery aroma filled her nostrils. She sniffed the air, wondering if that was caramel popcorn she smelled. Her stomach rumbled, and she realized she hadn't eaten anything since that slice of toast and the strawberries at breakfast, and now it was past lunch.

"Um, I just wanted to thank you for doing what you did." She tried to ignore the teens, the delicious smell, and instead just focus on Noah.

"You want to thank me for intruding on your, uh, meeting? I should have waited."

Lovina crossed her arms over her chest. "No, I want to thank you for getting excited about the pie shop." She opened her mouth to say more. To talk about her ideas for the warehouse, but then she changed her mind. She decided to focus on the most important part. She needed Noah's help.

"I was wondering if we could talk. I could tell you had some ideas for the warehouse." She decided to just be honest, and continued. "I'm going to need my dat's financial help, and it's hard to explain my ideas…"

Noah rubbed his jaw and his smile grew. "Would it be easier if I drew up some plans? You'd tell me what your thoughts were, of course."

Oh heavens, why did Mr. Yoder have to look at her like that? His eyes were warm and kind. The soft smile on his lips made her heart leap within. Instead she squared her shoulders and told herself to concentrate on the task at hand. Noah was offering a great gift—his faith in her and help. He wasn't asking her out on a date, and she needed to remind her heart of that, no matter how it was dancing in her chest.

"Plans? You can do that?" She clasped her hands together and tucked them under her chin. "That would be wonderful." Wonderful didn't quite sum it up, but how could she ever explain how much this meant?

The teens seemed bored by the conversation, and they wandered back into the living room where a gaming system was hooked up to a television. She tried not to smile seeing that. What happens in Pinecraft, stays in Pinecraft, she'd always heard.

"Do you have some time—this afternoon maybe—for me to ask you a few questions?" Noah asked. One of the teens on the couch turned, as if suddenly interested again. Lovina couldn't help but smile.

Even though they pretended to be playing their video games the teens were listening to their every word as they munched on something from large bowls. It had to be caramel popcorn. Homemade. Had one of their mems given them the recipe or had a local friend made it for them?

"Ja, I can do that." She turned her attention back to Noah, trying to ignore the aroma of her favorite snack—besides pie, of course.

She couldn't think of anything else that she needed to do that afternoon. She wouldn't be able to concentrate on anything else anyway. She'd given up the idea of baking pies hours ago. Of course she'd want to meet with Noah.

Outside, the air was already heating up. She thought about inviting Noah to her parents' house, but she didn't want her parents to overhear. And she wanted to think through her plans before sharing them.

But from the attention she and Noah were still getting from the teens, they'd never be able to talk freely here either.

Noah must have read her thoughts. "How about we meet at Big Olaf's to talk? A warm day like this is always a good day for ice cream."

"I love Big Olaf's." The words came out too hurried, and heat rose to Lovina's cheeks. "I have a few things to do around home yet." She didn't really have much to do, but she needed some space to regroup and clear her head. Noah's gaze had a way of pulling her in.

"In an hour then? I have to get these guys working on a deconstruction project." His eyebrows lifted in hopeful anticipation, and warm eyes peered down on her. A moan sounded from the guys behind him at the mention of work, but that only caused Noah's smile to brighten even more.

His face was tan and handsome. His eyes were a light bluish green, like the color of the ocean at dawn. He smiled, and she quickly looked away. He no doubt was used to getting attention from Amish women—Englischers too.

"Yes, that will work. See you then."

Lovina hurried down the sidewalk and hurriedly walked down the road to her house. She crossed her arms over her chest, chiding herself for just lying to Noah. Why had she told him she had something to do at home? It was the way he looked at her, for starters. It was almost as if he could peer into her soul. And that smile. She blew out a big breath just thinking about it. Surely someone like Noah Yoder already had a girl he was courting.

"Lovina!" He called her name, and she turned. Instead of standing in the doorway Noah was walking toward her, pushing her bike. "You forgot something!"

She placed a hand on her cheeks, knowing for certain she'd lost her mind. She turned completely around and then watched in surprise as Noah jumped onto her bike and pedaled toward her.

The sight of the tall, muscular man riding the light blue bicycle with the white basket in front tickled her funny bone. Laughter poured from her lips, and Noah sat straighter, taking on a serious look, as if he was offended by her laughter.

He pulled up beside her and climbed off. He nodded toward the seat. "There, I warmed it up for you."

"Oh my heavens, I would have given anything for a photographer to have snapped a shot of that. It would have made the cover of an Amish calendar for certain."

"Anything to see you smile again," Noah said, and then his smile fell. "I'm sorry Lovina, that wasn't a very businesslike thing to say."

"No, but it was a friendly thing to say." Lovina took the handle bars from him, and then sat on the seat, resting her toes on the asphalt. "Thank you so much for reminding me that I rode today. Like my mother always says, I have my head in the clouds most of the time."

"Or in the pie shop," he said with all seriousness.

"Yes, that is exactly right."

"See you in an hour then!" He turned and headed back to his house, and as she rode away she wondered what she could find to do at home so she wouldn't be lying to him. Maybe if Grace was around she could also get her opinion about Noah's offer. She was the one with the most business sense. Even as a young girl Grace had organized the local children to deliver farm-fresh eggs to neighbors on the way to school—with their parents' blessing. The neighbors had fresh eggs every morning, and Grace's friends had a little bit of spending money, which was usually unheard of in Amish homes.

"Lovina!"

Noah's voice called out to her. She stopped pedaling and paused her bike, looking back over her shoulder. Noah rode toward her on a bike of his own. She paused and waited for him, and he rode up and stopped next to her.

He took a deep breath, winded from trying to catch up. "Whew, I just wanted to tell you that if you have any pictures of what you'd like, make sure to bring them."

"You chased me down to tell me that?" She searched his handsome face, wondering why she'd been dodging him all these months. Glad that she no longer was. Glad he was chasing her down.

He nodded. "Ja."

"Danke," she returned. "I will." Then she rode off, feeling his eyes upon her as she did, and not minding one bit.

Lovina thought of her notebook she kept hidden away. In the four years she'd been clipping photos from magazines and gluing them into the notebook she'd never shared it with a soul—not even her sisters. It felt intimate, in a way, thinking of sharing the notebook with Noah. Would he think her ideas too fancy? Would he really be able to bring her ideas to life...or was there some catch?

From the look on his face a moment before it didn't seem that he had any self-interest at all, that he was just wanting to help her. Of course she knew he'd make money from the things in her warehouse, maybe more than she could guess, but even then it didn't seem as if that was his first intention. Noah didn't seem the type of person to be weighed down by the worries of money. Besides, it delighted her that her warehouse could benefit them both.

A bird called from overhead, and Lovina chuckled to herself. Listen to her. She was already calling it *her* warehouse. She was far from making that happen. But for some reason the fact that Noah believed in her dream made Lovina believe it herself.

And as she parked her bicycle in the carport Lovina made a decision. She would share her notebook with Noah. She would offer that piece of her heart. In a strange way she trusted him to protect it.

The warm breeze blew, and she felt a gentle peace inside that she hadn't felt in a while. Could this be why she'd felt such urgency this morning? Was it in God's plan for her to find the warehouse and meet Noah?

Lovina's stomach rumbled again, but her heart felt full as she entered her family's house. For some reason she felt that it was.

Caramel Corn

2 cups brown sugar
½ cup light corn syrup
1 cup butter
1 teaspoon baking soda
¼ teaspoon cream of tartar
½ teaspoon salt
1 teaspoon vanilla
6 quarts popped corn
1 cup peanuts, lightly roasted (optional)

Mix brown sugar, syrup, and butter in a heavy saucepan. Boil 4 minutes without stirring. Remove from heat and add baking soda, cream of tartar, salt, and vanilla. Immediately pour over popped corn and mix lightly but thoroughly. Add peanuts if desired. Place on large cookie sheets and bake at 250° for 1 hour, stirring every 15 minutes. Cool slightly and separate.

Seven

Enjoy today. It won't come back.

AMISH PROVERB

⌒

M em was standing next to the oven, watching the timer tick down as Lovina entered. The aroma of banana sour cream bread baking in the oven gave the kitchen a homey smell. Twenty-three-year-old Faith was sitting at the kitchen table sketching. Nineteen-year-old Grace was sitting next to her, reading the business section of the *Sarasota Herald-Tribune*. Both glanced up briefly as Lovina entered and then returned to their tasks. The tip of Faith's tongue poked out from her lips as she sketched a scene that had captured her mind. Grace's brow furrowed as she read. Lovina had seen that look before and knew her baby sister was plotting to turn Amish businesses into the next "big thing."

Lovina sniffed the air. "Banana sour cream bread?" She smiled at her mother. "One of Dat's favorites. Is it a special occasion?"

"Well, I hope so. I made some for your dat, of course, but I made extra to share." The timer buzzed, and Mem used a toothpick to check on the bread in the oven. Seeing it was done, she removed it from the oven with her pot-holdered hand, placing the loaf pan on the trivet on the kitchen counter. Three loaves were lined up. The first loaf had cooled off enough to be sliced. Half of it was gone. Lovina noticed the slightest crumbs at the corner of Mem's lips as she moved to her kitchen chair.

"Share?" Lovina asked. "Will Dat let you?" she chuckled.

"Ja. I already told him. When I was outside, putting a letter to Regina in the mailbox, Howard's Vera came strolling by. She had a full grocery bag as if she was expecting company. I asked her about it, and she says that her brother-in-law, Thomas Chupp, has come to town. He has brought his dat and mem down to look at a house they hope to buy. You know how things are here. Places around here sell almost as soon as the sign is put in the yard. I thought my banana sour cream bread would be a nice welcome."

"Ah, that's *gut*. Is Thomas's wife here too?" Lovina asked. "Maybe she'd be interested in Joy's sewing circle. Joy was just saying last night she wanted to plan a frolic to finish the quilt for the Haiti auction."

Mem lifted an envelope—a letter from Regina—from the table and fanned her face. Sweat beaded at her hairline. "Speaking of the Haiti auction, I need to remember to get my crocheting out." Mem fanned harder. "It's hard to think about knitting gloves and scarves when it's so humid and hot outside, but if I don't get busy I'll have nothing to offer."

Faith shuffled in her chair, and Lovina thought she was going to say something, but she must have changed her mind.

Mem stopped fanning and looked at something on the back of the envelope and sighed. "I talked to Vera yesterday at the park, and she didn't mention Thomas having a wife."

"Thomas doesn't have a wife," Faith interjected, her words sounding more forceful than usual. Three heads turned her direction. She paused her sketching and glanced up. Her eyes widened as if saying, *Why is everyone staring at me?*

Mem lifted an eyebrow. "You know Thomas Chupp?"

Pink tinged Faith's cheeks and she shrugged. "I don't know him, but I met him. We had a nice talk…"

Her voice trailed off, and she lifted up her sketchbook and studied the landscape of a creek winding through a meadow as if it was the most fascinating thing ever. Lovina wasn't fooled.

No one said a word. Instead they waited for Faith to elaborate. It was a tactic Mem often used and one the sisters had picked up on. When one wished to hear more about a subject it was better to wait silently for the person to continue. People often felt uncomfortable about the silence and spilled the beans in short order.

"Okay, fine." Faith tapped her pencil on the table, glancing up at them. "He was at Yoder's last night when I was working. He'd gotten there early—he was meeting a cousin for dinner—and I was on break. I sat down for five minutes—nothing more—and we talked. He mostly asked questions. He was curious about our family. He asked about our move to Pinecraft. He asked if I taught school." Faith chuckled and her eyes brightened. She blew out a soft sigh at the memory.

"He said I looked like a schoolteacher." Faith paused and then turned her attention back to her notebook. She picked up the green colored pencil and returned to her sketching. "Thomas said I reminded him of his favorite teacher, that's all." She shrugged. "I told him that Lovina was the teacher of the family, and then my break was over—"

"Was Lovina *ever* the teacher of the family!" Grace chimed in, folding her newspaper and setting it down. "I had a busier school day during summer afternoons than those who went to school. When I finally was old enough to go, I can still remember Miss Patricia's face when I started reading on the first day."

Lovina smiled at the memory. Hope was often in the garden, Joy behind the sewing machine, and Faith off pestering the teen boys hired to help with the farm or sketching "the scenery," but Grace had been young enough to enjoy the full attention of her older sister.

"Ja, Lovina always was a talented teacher," Mem commented, turning to her. "Maybe you should ask if there is a position open at the school here in Pinecraft." Mem clasped her hands together. "Wouldn't that be lovely?"

Lovina nodded, but she had no intention of following through with Mem's suggestion. Teaching had been a good job—even one that she'd done well. But it wasn't her passion. Yet what would Mem say when she discovered the truth? Lovina touched her fingertips to her own forehead, feeling moisture there too. The cool rain of the morning was just a memory. Summer's heat had returned. The kitchen windows were still cracked open, and Mem had yet to turn on the air conditioning. Maybe her parents felt more justified in using the luxury only after they'd finished baking.

Lovina went to the refrigerator and pulled out a block of cheese. The sound of Faith's colored pencils on the paper brought a gentle peace to the room outwardly, but inwardly Lovina was a jumble of nerves. How would Mem respond to the idea of one of her daughters being a business owner?

Lovina didn't feel much like eating. Butterflies danced in her stomach—partly from the excitement of finding the warehouse, but also over the excitement of meeting Noah. She told herself it was because he believed in her dream, but when she couldn't get his smiling greenish blue eyes off her mind she knew it had to be more.

Lovina touched a warm hand to her cheek, wondering if all the emotions stirring inside showed outwardly. If so, her sisters gave it no mind. As she sketched, Faith hummed a tune she'd no doubt heard at the grocery store. Lovina knew the words had something to do with "everlasting love," which was just what Faith always dreamed of. Grace flipped another page in the newspaper, absorbed.

Lovina eyed her sisters, suddenly perturbed by how they were so caught up in their own hobbies. She wanted to run to them, to hug them and to tell them that her life had changed today—and that it would most likely continue to change for the better in the days to come. She knew they'd be happy for her. They'd want to know every detail. If she confessed, they'd follow her to Big Olaf's and spy on her, trying to get a peek at Noah. But she couldn't tell them, not yet. She couldn't jump ahead of herself. She had to do things right.

This was her only chance. If she couldn't convince Dat and Mem that her dream was a good investment then none of it would matter. A pain shot through her chest at the thought of it not working out, as if it had been a few years, not a few hours, since she'd walked into the warehouse.

Lovina made a simple cheese sandwich and poured a glass of lemonade for herself and one for Mem. Mem seemed distracted as she continued to fan herself with the envelope. Lovina sat down beside her, and Mem tucked the envelope into her Bible, pushing it in deep.

Had there been bad news from back home? Lovina didn't want to ask. She knew it all would come out when Mem was ready. Mem never was one to hold in her thoughts or opinions for long.

Lovina ate half of her sandwich, enjoying the peace, and then turned to Mem. "Would you like me to drop off the banana sour cream bread? I'm meeting a friend at Big Olaf's in a bit. I can swing by on the way."

Faith's head jerked up.

Lovina turned to her. "Did you want to go?"

Faith lowered her head, returning to her sketch. "Well, I—"

"No need for Faith to do it," Mem butted in, straightening in her chair. "You'll be out anyway." Mem reached for her knitting basket on the floor against the wall. "Besides, I'm sure our potential new neighbors would like to be greeted by such a smiling face." Mem pulled out a skein of navy blue yarn. "I don't know what's different about you, Lovina, but you haven't stopped smiling since you walked in that door."

Lovina touched her fingertips to her lips. "Mmm. Well then, I'll drop the bread off on the way to ice cream."

"Thomas will appreciate that, I'm sure." Mem nodded with enthusiasm. And when Mem didn't ask Lovina who she was meeting for ice cream, Lovina knew her mother's thoughts were someplace else. Maybe on the letter from Regina? She'd been preoccupied with that envelope since Lovina had walked in the door.

Lovina just hoped Mem wasn't missing her dear friends in Ohio too awful bad. While all of them had left behind people they cared for, Lovina and her four sisters had carried their hobbies with them, discovering them anew in his balmy place. Mem, on the other hand, left most of her identity behind. She'd been the organizer of frolics and the first one to be called on when young mothers didn't know what to do about a fever, tummy ache, or blister. She'd helped with weddings and had always pitched in to provide food for singings. Mem's busy, bustling days had slowed, and the more she sat and thought the more she fretted about her daughters' lack of love interests. The walls of their house were thin, and Lovina had heard more than one conversation as Mem and Dat talked into the night. Mem always worried. Dat always trying to calm her fears.

Lovina finished her sandwich and dabbed the corners of her mouth with a napkin. Mem rose and removed the banana sour cream bread from the loaf pan, wrapping it in wax paper.

"Oh, and did I mention that Thomas Chupp has a lovely farm?" Mem commented, returning the wax paper and closing the cupboard. "It's his parents who are hoping to live here year-round. As the youngest, he'll be returning to Pennsylvania to run the farm. Remember how much we enjoyed Somerset on that visit? You said you wouldn't mind living there…"

Snickers emerged in chorus from Grace's lips, but Faith sat in stoney silence. Lovina directed a glare first to one, then to the other, but they refused to make eye contact. Grace because of the humor of it, and Faith…was she jealous? Lovina looked at the wind-up wall clock in the kitchen, making a mental note to talk to Faith later about Thomas Chupp.

Lovina spun around and caught the mischievous look in Mem's eyes. How had she missed it before? Mem wasn't sad or forlorn, she was trying to be subtle. Mem was trying to set her up!

Lovina cleared her throat. "Oh, I see now the reason for me being the one to make the delivery."

Mem shrugged and took another sip from her lemonade. "Well, you were the one who offered."

"That's because you set it all up. You made it sound so innocent…" Frustration tinged the corners of her words, but then she blew out a breath and calmed down. Lovina reminded herself that Mem did all she did out of love. Out of a desire to see her daughters happy and provided for.

"Are you saying you won't help me now?" Mem's gaze met hers. Her eyes grew round with worry.

"I'm not saying that. I'll go, but I'm not going to be offering up my heart as I pass over this banana sour cream bread."

"You can't fault a mother for trying."

Lovina reached over and squeezed Mem's hand. It was cool from the condensation on the glass. "I know. I have no doubt that you and Dat care. And that's why I was hoping to talk to you…soon."

Mem looked up then, curiosity clear in her gaze. "Is it about a young man?"

"Partly." Lovina said, calmly. She was telling the truth since Noah was involved, but even as she said it she knew her answer was misleading.

"You can talk to me anytime you want," Mem said. "I'm listening."

"But Dat, well, I assume he's napping, and I'd really like to talk to you both."

Lovina glanced at her sisters. Both sat as quiet as church mice, listening to every word intently. "And more than that, I'd like to do it without an audience."

"I already know what it's about." Grace smirked. "Faith and I saw you just before you got home. You were on your bicycle talking to a very handsome bachelor."

"You saw me? Why didn't you say something?"

Faith tapped a green colored pencil on her chin. "We were waiting for you to bring it up. So who is he? I don't think we've met him before." A smile filled her face, and she returned to her sketch. "I would know. I'd never forget that face."

So much for her interest in Thomas Chupp.

"I want to talk to Dat and Mem first." Lovina rose and threw away her napkin. "Don't worry," she said, tossing the words back over her shoulder. "If things work out like I hope they will, then I'll be able to fill you in with all the details soon."

Lovina looked back to her mem before she rounded the corner

to her bedroom. Mem's jaw dropped, and excitement flashed in her eyes.

"When would you like to talk?" Mem asked.

Lovina paused her steps. She shrugged as if it was no big thing. As if her heart wasn't hammering in her chest. "I'd like to take you and Dat out to dinner. Maybe at Yoder's?"

"Ja." Mem nodded. "I'm sure we can make it work. I'll talk to your dat and let you know the time."

"*Gut.* I'd like that."

Lovina went to her room and moved to her hope chest. She lifted the creaky lid and rested it against the wall. At twenty-five, she'd had plenty of time to fill her chest with items she'd need after marriage, and it was overflowing. Yet out of all of the things she'd sewn or collected over the years, nothing meant as much to Lovina as her notebook. She moved her embroidered pillow-cases to the side and lifted the notebook from its nest of blankets. Then she took a cloth book bag, tucked the notebook inside, and put the bag's straps over her shoulder. She hadn't shared it with her sisters or Mem yet, but she would when the time was right. Something warmed inside—even warmer than the Florida sun beaming through the windows.

All eyes were on her as she returned to the kitchen and picked up the loaf of banana sour cream bread. It was still warm through the wax paper. "I'd better go deliver this. Time to be neighborly and all."

"Especially to single and eligible bachelors who are in need of a friend," Grace called out.

"A friend? Yes, that's what she's thinking…just being a friend," Faith added, a hint of sarcasm in her voice. Yet Lovina didn't have time to worry about that now. For even as Lovina stepped out the door into the muggy heat of the midday, she wasn't thinking of Thomas but of another bachelor. Noah was also new in Pine-craft, and he most likely needed a friend too.

She placed the book bag and bread into her bike's front basket and then got on, riding down the street. A new thought hit her.

Mem, more than anyone, knew every new person in town. She knew nearly every visitor too. Why hadn't she baked a special treat on Noah's arrival? Tension tightened Lovina's shoulders as she rode. Noah had also been to the house. He'd visited to give Dat a bid on the roof. Yet Mem hadn't said a thing. She hadn't invited Noah to dinner. She hadn't made him banana sour cream bread. She hadn't even mentioned his visit at dinner. A handsome bachelor had been to their home, and not one word had been mentioned about it.

Suddenly all the good feelings about Noah Yoder dissipated like the small puddles on the roadway, evaporating in the sun.

There had to be something wrong with Noah Yoder. Something big. Otherwise all of them would have gotten an earful about the handsome bachelor.

Worries bubbled up inside of Lovina, and she slowed her pedaling.

Who was Noah Yoder, and just what did Mem know?

Lovina glanced at her notebook tucked inside the bag on her handle bars. Was Noah Yoder worthy to be trusted with her dreams?

Banana Sour Cream Bread

3¼ cups sugar, divided

3 teaspoons cinnamon, divided

¾ cup butter

3 eggs

6 ripe bananas

16 ounces sour cream

2 teaspoons vanilla

½ teaspoon salt

3 teaspoons baking soda

4½ cups flour

1 cup chopped nuts

Preheat oven to 325°. Grease four small or two large loaf pans. In a small bowl, combine ¼ cup sugar and 1 teaspoon cinnamon. Use cinnamon-sugar mixture to dust pans. In large bowl, cream butter, three cups of sugar, eggs, bananas, sour cream, vanilla, and remaining 2 teaspoons cinnamon. Mix in salt, baking soda, and flour. Stir in nuts. Bake 1 hour, covering loaves with foil for the last 15 minutes of baking time.

Eight

Each new day can be a door to joys
we've never known before.

AMISH PROVERB

⁓

Noah walked in the back door of his uncle's cottage to find the three teenage boys sitting at the kitchen table. Each with a large bowl of cereal in front of them, shoveling it into their mouths. When he'd left they'd been eating caramel popcorn—one of the few things his uncle Roy could make—and playing video games. He'd told them this morning to be dressed and ready for work by noon. To his amazement they were.

Their faces were eager as they looked to him, and each of them wore their Amish clothes. In the house the teens wore jeans or basketball shorts and T-shirts. But on the drive down to Pinecraft their driver had given them advice. They'd get more work around Pinecraft if they dressed Amish. No matter if they were all in their rumspringa years.

So before they went out each day they put on the handmade trousers and shirts that their mems had made with care. Not that it helped. It had been two months and they still hadn't gotten work.

Noah had been fooling himself thinking that his reputation

wouldn't reach them there. Most Amish read *The Budget*. Most knew of Ray Yoder's wayward nephew and all the trouble and damage he'd caused. There'd also been plenty of news about the trouble these boys had caused. They'd all traveled far from home, but obviously not far enough.

"Are we still going to tear down that shed today?" Mose asked, setting his spoon on the table. His eyes flashed excitement, and Noah knew he was thankful they were going to make some more money. That's what Noah had promised, after all—that they'd build their carpentry skills and put some money in their pockets. But sifting through materials at remodeling projects and cleaning out old buildings hadn't provided that.

Noah shook his head. "I stopped by to check on that, and Mr. Hosteler would like to wait a week. There's a family in town looking to see if they want to buy the place. Mr. Hosteler figured that an old shed still standing would be less of a problem than his backyard filled with the noise and mess."

Mose scoffed. "Or most likely that he didn't want the likes of us hanging around there—giving the place a bad vibe." He ran his hand through his hair and then balled his fist.

"Now, don't jump to the wrong conclusions." Noah tried to stay upbeat. He shrugged like it really didn't matter, but he'd also had a problem with how the guy handled the situation.

Noah pulled up a chair and sat facing them. His stomach growled, and he knew he should eat lunch, but he didn't feel like cooking and it looked as if all the cereal was gone. Being a bachelor left him wanting for some good home cooking.

He debated whether to tell the guys more about the warehouse, and from the forlorn looks on their faces decided it was a good idea.

"I have a lead, and I hope it pans out. There's someone who

wants to turn the warehouse behind us into a bakery. I'm meeting with her—this person—in just a little bit to sketch some ideas."

"Yeah, we were here, remember? We answered the door. She's pretty. And kind of young."

"Too young for me? I'm not going to date her if that's what you're thinking."

"Too young to wrap herself up with a money hole like that," Gerald butted in, pointing out the back kitchen window.

"Have you learned nothing I've taught you over the last few weeks?" Noah opened the cupboard and scanned the sparse contents. He didn't feel like Ramen noodles again. He closed the cupboard, deciding ice cream would make the perfect lunch. "People often overlook treasure, thinking it's trash."

No one argued then. They'd all been there, hauling away items from the dumpsters. They'd all been amazed what people threw away. An old iron railing had been his best find and had provided enough income to keep these guys fed for a few weeks, which was saying something, considering the amount of groceries they went through.

Gerald rose and gathered up all the dishes, taking them to the sink. "So if you're off wooing that girl, does that mean we can go back fishing?"

"Yeah!" Atlee chimed in. "We saw a huge fish that someone pulled out last week. It was nearly as tall as him."

"Sure, but just watch out," Noah warned. "It's brackish water and I heard that sometimes sharks make their way up the river."

Excitement brightened their faces, which was the opposite of what Noah wanted to see. He considered telling the guys again to be careful, but he knew it would do no good. Teen boys were teen boys. At that age he would have been the first to be figuring out how to draw a shark into the area.

Mose, Gerald, and Atlee headed into their room to get their fishing poles, and he smiled at their banter. Noah had been praying that God would make a way for them to stay. He'd been praying for someone to give these guys a second chance. And he was pleasantly surprised to discover that God had sent someone pretty to do that task.

"Lovina." He let her name play on his lips. It was as pretty a name as any he'd heard.

From the hesitant way that banker was acting it sounded like her ability to get the warehouse would be a long shot, but Noah was determined to help her any way he could. It would help these teens find work. It would help his cash flow, selling items to Sarasota Salvage. More than that, he'd get to spend more time with that pretty Amish lady.

Joy mixed with anxiety over the thought. He'd like to get to know her, it was true. The problem was, he worried about her getting to know him. That's when things usually fell apart.

The boys joked about sharks as they made their way out, waving a goodbye. It was funny how that worked—how easy it was to be attracted to danger. Would building a friendship with Lovina take him into murky waters? He had a feeling it would.

He needed to keep his mind on business and not her pretty smile. Noah wasn't worried so much about his heart. It had been broken before. But if he got too close to Lovina she'd discover the truth about him—about them—and that would hinder all he was working for.

A pretty face and a warm smile from a young, bright woman was the same lure to a bachelor as a shark was to daring teens. He knew this. He did. But even as he combed back his hair, preparing to meet Lovina, Noah felt the draw all the same.

⌒

Lovina held the bread pan in one hand and knocked on the door with the other. She'd been inside Vera Chupp's house a few times. They shared a love of baking and had worked together to make a nice meal and dessert for the bishop's family on his birthday. She tried to remember if Vera had talked about her nephew Thomas before, but nothing stood out in her mind. Like most Amish families Vera had dozens of nephews and nieces. It wasn't uncommon to have rooms full of guests during season, and Lovina hoped that Thomas didn't mind Pinecraft being more quiet this time of year.

The sun's rays warmed her kapp, and she heard the sound of footsteps approaching. With a squeak the door opened. Lovina expected to see Vera standing there. Instead there was a young man. He wore a bright smile, and his teeth were the whitest she'd ever seen. He opened the screen door, and she noticed his Amish clothes were fine. They were handmade, but whoever had made them had been skilled at the sewing machine.

"Hello." He tilted his head and studied her, as if pleasantly surprised.

"Hello. I'm Lovina, and my mem sent me…I mean, what I've come for is to give you this—I mean it's for your family. My mem heard that Vera had family in town. She—we're—trying to be neighborly…" She held the bread out to him as an offering. As proof she wasn't rambling for no reason.

He sniffed the air and his smile brightened, if that was even possible. "That is so kind. Won't you come in?"

Lovina knew she shouldn't. She had less than five minutes to make it to Big Olaf's, but something about the expectant look in the man's dark eyes made it hard to say no.

"Ja, just for a moment. Is your aunt here?"

"No, she and Mem just went for coffee at Sherry's house. They read her stories in *The Budget*, and Mem went to her house and introduced herself yesterday. Mem is always one to make quick friends."

I see where you get it from, she wanted to add.

Lovina stepped inside. The air conditioning was running on high and a chill traveled down her spine. The simple living room was exactly like she remembered it, except for a guitar leaning in one corner of the room. She eyed the instrument but didn't say anything. Up north playing musical instruments was discouraged, but in Pinecraft people often gathered to listen to music or to sing together, accompanied by guitars.

Thomas moved in the direction of the kitchen. "Would you like some lemonade?"

She was going to decline, but with eager steps he'd already reached the kitchen. He set the loaf of banana sour cream bread on the counter, and then he opened the refrigerator, taking out the lemonade. She watched as he took two glasses from the open cupboard and realized it was strangely quiet.

Lovina glanced around, wondering if anyone else was in the house, unsure of what to do.

"My dat just went to lie down," Thomas said, as if reading her thoughts. "He isn't feeling too good. He's been sickly lately, which is the reason my parents are considering moving to Pinecraft."

"Ja, my dat too. It's the reason we're here."

Thomas approached with a glass of lemonade.

"I'm so sorry." Compassion filled the man's gaze. "I hope your dat is well. I'm Thomas, by the way. Thomas Chupp."

"Ja, my Mem told me. And I'm Lovina. Lovina Miller."

"Aha!" He pointed a finger into the air. "You're the Pineapple Pie lady."

"Excuse me?"

"My Aunt Vera told me she was invited to a sewing frolic at her friend's birthday and she was served Pineapple Pie, and it was the best pie she'd ever eaten. She said it was made by a young lady named Love, and that it was a delightful name."

Lovina blushed and took a sip of lemonade. "Oh, that's just a family nickname. When my sister Hope couldn't say Lovina, she called me Love. Mem and Dat thought it was sweet, having daughters Love and Hope. That hadn't been the plan. But when they had another daughter they named her Faith—after one of my mom's sisters who passed—and then they had to keep going."

"And there are more of you?" He looked at her with large brown eyes full of amusement.

"Five girls in all. Me, Hope, Faith, Joy, and—"

"Let me guess, Peace!" Thomas's grin added brightness to the small cottage.

Laughter spilled out. "No, Grace. Although if Mem and Dat had more kids Peace, Gentleness, and Longsuffering were options." She winked.

Laughter bubbled up, and the sound of it made her laugh too. Then she covered her mouth with her hand. "I'm so sorry. I hope I didn't wake your dat."

Thomas shook his head. "No. He always takes his hearing aids out before he lies down. He's a bit older. I'm the youngest son of his second wife, who is quite a bit younger than him. His first wife died of cancer years ago."

Lovina nodded, feeling the gleefulness of a moment before slip away. "I'm so sorry."

"Ja, horrible thing, but I do think Pinecraft would be a good move for my parents."

The clock on the wall chimed, and Lovina startled. "Oh no, I'm so sorry. I have to go." She handed the glass back to him and moved to the door. "I have to meet a friend." She smiled. "It was nice meeting you. I hope you enjoy your stay!"

He followed her out onto the porch, still holding two glasses of lemonade in his hands.

"I'll see you again," she said as she climbed onto her bicycle.

"I look forward to it."

The way Thomas said those words made Lovina really feel that he would. And as she pedaled away on her bicycle, she didn't know what to think. Two handsome bachelors in one day.

Of course just because she'd met two friendly, handsome men didn't mean anything would come from it. In fact, she was sure nothing would. Instead she needed to set her mind on what she could accomplish.

She'd never fared well with men. She'd never known what to say or do. She'd always felt as if every kind word offered her was given out of duty rather than interest.

But she did know how to make pie.

The sun bore down upon the top of her kapp as she rode toward Big Olaf's ice cream shop. Nervousness fought with excitement inside her. Would Noah Yoder really be able to help her?

And what about her parents? Would they think it was a good idea?

Mostly, would teaming up with Noah Yoder help or hurt her plans? After remembering how Mem had made no mention of his presence to any of her daughters, Lovina worried that the very help she needed might be the thing to keep her from achieving her dreams.

Pineapple Pie

1 large (20 ounce) can crushed pineapple with juice

2 small boxes vanilla instant pudding

1 (16 ounce) container sour cream

graham cracker pie crust

nondairy whipped topping for garnish

maraschino cherry halves for garnish

Stir pineapple and pudding together. Fold in sour cream and spread in crust. Top with nondairy whipped topping and cherry halves.

Nine

When faith is most difficult, that is
when it is most necessary.

AMISH PROVERB

∽℘

Lovina parked her bike in the rack next to the picnic tables in front of Big Olaf's Creamery. The building, she'd heard, used to be the old post office. Now the ice cream shop was up front and Village Pizza was in back. During the season, and on some cooler days during the summer—when people were out—Mike had his pretzel stand near the rear of the building.

The clerk behind the counter greeted Lovina as she entered Big Olaf's. Noah was sitting at a black garden table in the back of the ice cream shop, and she thought he seemed much too large for the small chair.

The doorbell chimed, stating that a customer had arrived, and Noah looked up. His eyes met hers and a smile lit his face. He stood up as she approached. There was a sketchbook on the table, and she placed her notebook next to it. She was about to ask him if he wanted something to drink or some ice cream when the motion of her notebook caused his pencil to roll off the table to the floor.

"Here, let me get that." She bent down to retrieve it the same time he did. He moved more quickly, and as his head came back up again it hit her forehead.

"Oh!" the force nearly knocked Lovina off her feet. She staggered backward, but thankfully Noah's strong arms reached for her. He caught her up, pulling her toward him so she couldn't topple over.

Lovina's hands rested against his chest, and she felt the warmth of his skin seeping through his cotton shirt. He smelled of soap and the ocean breeze. His nearness made her even dizzier than the knock to her head.

His breath was warm on her cheek.

"Are you okay?"

"Ja, but I think…I think you're poking my arm."

She glanced down and noticed the pencil in his hand poking into her forearm.

He jerked back, and the motion made her sway slightly again. He reached for her with the hand not holding the pencil, but she waved him away. "No, it's okay. I'm fine. Really." She touched her kapp and straightened it. "I suppose everyone needs some sense knocked into them now and again."

"Please, let me get some ice for that." He pointed to the place where her hairline met her forehead, and she assumed there was going to be a bump.

"I don't need ice, but I wouldn't mind ice cream." She settled into the chair as if nothing big had happened. Then she reached for the small wallet in her pocket.

Noah waved a hand her direction. "No, let me get it. What's your favorite flavor?"

"Pralines and cream, please."

"Oh, you're that type of girl." He rubbed the top of his head, but she pretended not to notice. "It's my grandma's favorite ice cream too. She says it reminds her of simple home pleasures— nothing too fancy."

"Ja, I suppose I am like that…not too fancy." *Simple, plain, unlike my beautiful sisters*, she added to herself.

He walked to the ice cream counter, and she couldn't help but lean forward and take a look at the sketch in his book. There wasn't much to it. It looked as if he'd made a rough draft of the warehouse layout, including the offices. He'd marked the front half as *pie shop* and the back half as *storage*. He'd separated the two by the word *kitchen*.

Lovina's stomach tumbled as she read that word, and uneasiness came over her. Even if she could get the building…and even if Noah was willing to do the work in exchange for the items inside…and even if they could put some of those items for use in the shop, there would still be the expense for all the lighting, the tables, and the workstations. And then there was the cost of the kitchen. Lovina bit her lip and pushed the sketchbook back from her.

Why am I doing this? Why am I wasting our time?

She felt her kapp and straightened it, wondering what to do and what to say as Noah approached. He handed her a large, double scoop ice cream cone, and laughter burst from her lips.

"That's for me?" She shook her head. "I'll never be able to eat it all."

He looked at her in disbelief. "It's ice cream."

"Ja, but it's a lot of ice cream."

"Here, hold this for a second." He handed her his cone, which looked to be one scoop of mint chip and one of cookies and cream, and then walked off with hers.

She turned and watched as Noah handed the cone back to

the man behind the counter, saying something. A moment later the man handed back a much smaller cone and a small cup, filled with the ice cream he'd taken off the top. Noah returned and sat, handing her the cone in exchange for his. "That's much better," she said. "But what are you going to do with the extra?"

Noah shrugged and looked at her as if he wondered if she really needed an answer. "I'm going to eat it."

"Oh, I see."

"It's ice cream, Lovina. I'm not sure you could ever get full eating ice cream."

Lovina nodded in a way that told him she didn't agree.

She watched him take a big bite out of the top of his ice cream, and then he pressed a hand to his forehead as if he'd just gotten an ice cream headache. Then laughter burst from his lips. She looked up, surprised, and noticed the twinkle of humor in his blue eyes.

"What's so funny?"

"Well, for a second I realized I was trying to figure out which hurt worse, the ice cream headache or the bump on my head. If someone was ever wanting to make a horrible first impression this would be it." He rubbed the top of his head and grimaced. "I think I'm going to have a bump up here for a while."

"And I think I'm going to have a red spot." She touched the tender spot on her forehead. "I know it's there. You don't have to try to convince me it's not. I can see that you keep looking at it."

"Please forgive me." His voice was warm. "I didn't see you going for my pencil...but you can say that's one way for me to bowl you over with my presentation."

"Did you come here thinking you had to impress me?" She lifted one eyebrow. "Because I had a feeling I was coming here to convince you that my pie shop was a worthy endeavor."

"I'm not sure I need much convincing. I need a job, mostly because I need to prove to this community that the young men I'm trying to help can put in a good day's work. But…" He flipped through some of his pages. "If I came feeling I had to impress, the answer is yes." He flipped two more pages and then pushed the sketchbook closer to her.

Peering down at the page he'd opened to, Lovina's eyes widened. She'd expected the drawing to be similar to the one she'd first seen—the one that looked more like the blueprints that her father had used when erecting his barn. But that was only the beginning. On the next page he'd brought the image to life. In fact, it was as if Noah had been able to look into her head and sketch her dream. It was as if he'd been peeking into her notebook, even though she knew that was impossible.

Lovina tried to lick her cone the best she could, but her eyes were fixed on the sketched image before her.

It was a drawing of a shop with a long counter that greeted the customers as they entered the door. Where the pie counter ended, the tables began. What looked to be a white picket wooden fence separated the customer tables from a large work area.

"I love this. I can't believe you drew this. When did you have time?"

He shrugged. "It's nothing much. You were a little late so I just tried to picture the type of place I could see you in. This is it."

Tears sprang to Lovina's eyes, and her throat tightened hot and thick. She tried to speak but no words came. A small squeak found its way out—the beginning of a cry.

Noah took one last bite of his cone, wiped his hands on a napkin, and leaned forward. "Lovina, are you okay?"

She nodded, still unable to talk. She looked to the picture again, and her lower lip trembled.

"Did I do something…" he hesitated. "Something to make you sad?"

"I'm so sorry," she finally managed to say. "I've been wanting this, well, as long as I can remember. My parents, they listened, and my sisters…they mostly thought it was silly." She waved a hand in front of her face as if wishing herself to calm. "And then for two years I worked as a teacher and I saved every penny. We moved here, and I talked to Jason at the bank, and he's the first one who really believed I could do it. But he didn't really like the warehouse, even though I feel— deep down—that it's right. And this morning, well, I felt God telling me to look, and then I did, and then I met you…" The words blubbered out, and she was sure that Noah Yoder must think she was the silliest woman he had met in his whole life. "And then you bring this, and…oh, Noah, how could you have known?"

He shrugged and offered her a small white paper napkin to wipe her eyes. She dabbed at them and then dared to look at him.

Tenderness mixed with confusion. "It's just a drawing," he said.

"But you understand what I'm trying to accomplish. Other people have listened, but they didn't see the vision like you do."

Noah reached across and placed his hand on hers. "I was just hoping you'd like it. I didn't expect a waterfall."

She chuckled and shook her head. She pulled her hand away, grabbing another napkin to dot her eyes. Thankfully, she wasn't trying to impress him. Her eyes always got red and puffy when she cried, and she was sure she looked a mess.

"I'm glad you like what I sketched, but it's only a start. I'd like to go through your notebook to get more ideas, but I have a question first."

Lovina took in a deep breath. "Ja?"

His face wore a serious look. "Do you mind if I order more ice cream?"

"More?" Her mouth gaped open. She knew he'd finished off his ice cream cone, but somewhere in the midst of her blubbering he'd finished off the cup of ice cream too.

Noah looked down sheepishly. "I didn't have time for lunch."

"Well, you don't need more ice cream. What you need is…" She held up one finger. "Hold on. I'll be back in two minutes." She left Big Olaf's and walked around the side of the building to Mike's pretzel stand.

Two Old Order Amish men stood in line, talking to Mike. They wore stiff, black hats and each of them had a pretzel in hand. Mike did most of his business in the winter months when the roads were filled with Amish men and women walking and riding on bicycles, but thankfully he braved the heat a few days a week in the summer and fall, serving anyone who happened by.

Mike glanced up at Lovina as she approached. He used to be in the masonry business, but when things slowed, he took up pretzel making. The two older men parted to let her through, and Lovina smiled and stepped up. "One pretzel, please."

Mike handed it to her. "How's your dat's health?" he asked.

"*Gut.*" She handed him two dollar bills, smiling. "He went on a walk today, which shows an improvement." She pointed her thumb behind her. "But I have a friend waiting."

Mike tucked the money in his money box. "Waiting for the best pretzel he ever had?"

Lovina nodded and then paused. She cocked her head and looked to Mike. "How did you know my friend was a *he?*"

Mike chuckled. "I can see it in your eyes. That sparkle and such."

Nods came from the two Old Order gentlemen on either side.
The pretzel smelled delicious. "Ja, well, I suppose he will like
it very much."

She returned to the ice cream shop and approached the table.
Noah sniffed and then reached out a hand, accepting the gift.

"That looks delicious, thank you. I've seen that stand, but I've
yet to try one."

"Mike told me to tell you he's sure this will be the best you've
ever had."

Noah cocked an eyebrow. "Has he heard of Auntie Anne's? My
driver says they're so popular they're all over the nation, even in
airports. A business started by an Amish couple."

"Ja, I actually know about them. My sister Grace is fascinated
by small businesses that make it big. Dat says he used to ask her
business advice when she was five, and she was always right. She's
talked to Mike a few times about trying to expand his business,
and he's been thinking about it. Personally I have been begging
Mike for his recipe for a few months. He won't give in, but another
friend, Fannie, gave me a recipe that makes one almost as good."

"Do you do that often?" Noah asked.

"Do what?"

"Share recipes? Talk about food with your friends?" he asked,
taking a bite of the pretzel.

"Ja. Food is what binds us together in so many ways."

He tilted his head as if he was trying to understand.

"What are you thinking?" She pressed her lips together, wondering how she was able to talk to Noah so easily. Had it just been
today that they'd met?

"You want to know what I'm thinking about," he finally said.
"Well, the truth is that my motives were to find work and to help
the teens, but as we're talking…" His voice trailed off.

"What?" she asked, leaning closer.

"I believe in what you're doing. I really do. You're on to something, Lovina. I mean, people can make good food that others enjoy, but you want your pie shop to do more than that. You want to build a community. Maybe you can even have customers share their pie recipes too."

She turned to the back of her notebook and jotted down the idea. "Oh! And I can choose one to serve as a special every month. I love that idea."

As they talked Noah continued to add more to the sketch. Looking it over, he pulled colored pencils from a plastic bag. "I bought these, but I can't take them home." Noah shook his head. "If I did, there would be no end to the teasing I'd receive from the guys." She smiled, thinking of the teens asking Noah to color a picture for them. She'd seen the way they played around with each other earlier that day, and such antics were unfamiliar to her. She had male cousins, yes, but for the most part at family gatherings they stayed in the barn and the womenfolk stayed inside.

"I can't imagine how a little package of colored pencils could cause any problems. I've never really seen that…I mean, being raised with only sisters."

"You'll see." Noah wagged his finger in the air. "Wait until we start working on your pie shop. Then you'll get a dose of what it's about."

They talked about the colors Lovina liked—the white of the cottages around Pinecraft and the light colors—teal, apricot, and pink—of the plain dresses that the young Amish women wore in these parts. They talked about what would need to happen first in the remodel.

"So when will you know?"

"I'm going out to dinner with Dat and Mem tonight. If it's a no I'll know by tomorrow."

"And if it's a yes?" Noah asked.

"Well, that could take more time. If Dat agrees to cosign for me I have to talk to Jason at the bank. He can figure out the loan and do all the paperwork."

"I'll be praying about that."

"Danke." It warmed her heart to hear that. While all Amish men were supposed to be men of prayer, hearing someone state it so plainly wasn't common.

The bell jingled behind them, and Lovina heard a voice call out.

"Lovina!"

The smile on Noah's face faded as footsteps neared.

Lovina turned, and her eyes widened as she saw Thomas Chupp standing there.

Soft Pretzels

1½ cups warm water
2 tablespoons yeast
5 cups flour (approximate)—
    can use up to 2½ cups whole-wheat flour
¼ cup brown sugar
1 teaspoon salt
1½ cups hot water
2 tablespoons baking soda
melted butter
cinnamon sugar (optional)
coarse salt (optional)

Dissolve the yeast in water. Add the flour, brown sugar, and salt. Knead like bread dough. Let rise 15 to 20 minutes. Roll and shape into pretzels. Dip into 1½ cups hot water that has 2 tablespoons baking soda dissolved in it. Lay on absorbent paper towel to dry. Transfer to greased cookie sheets to bake. Bake 7 minutes in pre-heated 450° oven. After baking, dip into melted butter. We like to roll them in cinnamon sugar or sprinkle them with salt. These are fun to make when you have several helping hands. Makes 10 pretzels.

Ten

If you live an honest and upright life, there is no need to "talk the talk." Your life speaks for itself.

AMISH PROVERB

Thomas Chupp strode in to Big Olaf's, walking directly to their table and pausing next to Lovina's chair.

She glanced up, surprised and a little intimidated by the way Thomas looked down at her. He was handsome and he knew it. It was clear that Thomas was used to having command of a room. It made her slightly uncomfortable, like something an Englisch man would do.

"I'm so sorry to interrupt. I just wanted to thank you for stopping by earlier. My Aunt Vera told me where you lived and Faith said you were here." He grinned. "It was nice seeing her again. She told you that I met her last night, but I had no idea you were related…" His smile brightened. "I hope I'm not interrupting anything." He looked from her to Noah and then back again, but in her opinion Thomas didn't seem sorry at all.

"Well—" she started, but he quickly cut off her words.

"You know that I'm new in town, and my aunt insists I must go to Siesta Key Beach. And since you're the only person under the age of sixty I know in Pinecraft, I was wondering if you'd join me? I thought we could go tonight."

"Tonight? No." She shook her head. "I'm sorry. I already have plans."

Thomas looked to Noah and frowned slightly, as if believing he had something to do with those plans. Noah did in a way, but Lovina didn't want to try to explain.

"But what about Faith—"

"I see." He cut off her words again. "Well, what about tomorrow night then?" Thomas's eyes widened hopefully.

"I don't know. I have some important things I'm working on." She thought about mentioning Faith again, but she needed to talk to her sister first. Lovina always hated when Mem tried to set her up, and Lovina guessed that Faith didn't appreciate it either.

"Ja, but your sister told me you haven't been to the beach in over a month. How could you let that happen, especially when you live so close?" Thomas focused on her, refusing to let her look away.

"My interests lie in other areas."

Thomas's smiling eyes locked on hers. "I won't take no for an answer."

Lovina looked to Noah as if wanting him to jump in and save her, but his gaze was turned downward. He was busy sketching something—something she wanted to see. Thomas hovered over, and she knew he wasn't going to leave until she gave him an answer. Not any answer, but the one he wanted to hear.

"Ja, well, maybe in the morning before it gets too hot. But just for an hour or so."

"Wunderbar. I'll hire a driver. I'll get some lunch items packed too. See you at ten o'clock tomorrow." And just like that, Thomas walked out without a parting glance.

He was there and gone quickly, and she almost wondered if she'd imagined it. But from the wall now firmly erected between her and Noah, she knew she hadn't.

Lovina brushed a strand of hair from her cheek. She didn't know what to say.

"The pretzel is *gut.*" Noah held it up. And then he took his final bite. "And if you don't mind, I'd love to look in your notebook. To get an idea of things you like."

Noah spoke to her in a kind, gentle tone, but there was a coolness to their interaction that hadn't been there before.

"Ja, of course." Her heart sunk. The playfulness of their meeting was gone just like that. And Lovina wondered if she should have done something differently. But really, what could she have done? It wasn't as if Thomas had given her any chance to decline. And why should she have? Someone who was new to town had invited her to the beach. That was all. It was nothing to be ashamed of. And Noah wanted to work for her, nothing more.

Mem will be pleased. . . pleased about the date, that is. Lovina was still worried about Mem's opinion of Noah. But she supposed time would tell concerning that too.

She opened up her notebook and flipped through a few pages, trying to get Thomas's intense, brown-eyed gaze out of her mind and trying to decide what to show Noah first.

"I do like this cupboard." She pointed to a large cupboard on one of the pages. There was nothing fancy about its design. It was wooden and had four shelves, but the shelves were filled with colorful dishes. Mostly old Pyrex bowls, mugs, and plates in colors of teal, sea foam green, yellow, and white.

Noah ran his finger over the page. "I love how they used those reclaimed letters on the top shelf to spell out EAT," he commented, yet with little emotion.

"Ja," she smiled, "but in my shop it would spell out PIE." She chuckled.

"That only makes sense." A bit of his smile returned. "I've seen a lot of those salvaged letters around from old signs. I wonder if you might find some old theater letters around your warehouse. I wouldn't be surprised."

"I like how you call it *my* warehouse."

Noah shrugged. "I know it's not a certain thing yet, but I'll continue to do what I can to help."

He sketched the shelf next, and it reminded Lovina of the way her sister had sketched earlier. With such concentration. It amazed her how people were able to take what was in their thoughts and put it on paper. That was something she had no talent in whatsoever.

Lovina continued to point out items, and Noah drew them. Another hour passed, and when they were through Lovina was holding three sheets of paper in her hands.

She spread them on the table before her. She had what she needed for tonight's meeting with her parents. If her father wouldn't say yes now, she knew he never would.

"Thank you." She looked across the table at Noah, knowing her simple words could never convey her heart. "I'll let you know when I hear something."

"Thanks for considering me too." He rose and tucked his sketchbook under his arm, but he left the colored pencils on the table.

She pointed to pencils on the table. "You really aren't going to take those?"

"No, but you're welcome to take them." A smile showed a slight dimple in his cheek. "Consider them a souvenir of our meeting."

"I'll give them to my sister. But let me pay for them. I know you just bought them today."

He nodded with a grin. "Yes, I'll accept payment. But not in money."

"What then?" She rose, standing next to him, peering up into his face.

"The first piece of pie from your pie shop."

Her heart jumped at those words, and she couldn't help but smile. "That sounds like a deal, Mr. Yoder." She extended her hand, and he took it. His hand was rough—a working man's hand—and she liked that about him. "That's a deal I can work with."

⌒

Lovina couldn't help but notice her sisters watching from the window when she returned home and parked her bike. She couldn't erase her smile, and she wished she could tell them everything—all about the warehouse, about Noah and his sketches—which she now had tucked inside her notebook.

She couldn't do that, mostly because they'd never be able to keep it from their parents. Lovina wanted to be the one to tell Dat and Mem about the money she'd saved, the bank loan that Jason was working on, and her remodeling plans. She had the sketches that would capture her father's creative nature. She also planned to downplay Noah Yoder's involvement. She wasn't sure what Noah had done to get on Mem's bad side, but the fact that Mem hadn't mentioned him once to any of her daughters proved that he wasn't in her good graces.

Lovina strode into her house determined to hide her smile, but the four grinning faces looking up at her from around the kitchen table made it impossible.

"Okay, tell us all about it." Grace was the first to jump in.

Lovina's cheeks warmed at the thought of Noah Yoder. Of the way that he listened to her. The way he'd captured her dream in a simple sketch. And how he'd placed his hand on hers before they'd parted. "Tell you about what?" She fiddled with the sleeve of her dress.

"Oh, please! You act like we don't know," Hope huffed. Her sisters were sitting around the table, enjoying a glass of Southern Breeze Punch, as was often the custom in the hot afternoons. "Even if we didn't have any idea what was happening between you and that handsome bachelor we could read it all over your face."

Lovina looked away from their intent stare and went to retrieve a glass from the kitchen cupboard. She turned on the water from the tap and filled the glass, taking a long drink.

"He came by here, Lovina," Faith said, yet her words didn't have the same playful tone as Grace's. "You can't hide it from us."

"He came by here?" She spun around then, trying to figure out how that was possible. She'd met Noah at Big Olaf's, and then they'd parted ways and she'd come right back home. There was no way he could make it here before she did and then leave again.

She studied Faith's face, wondering if they were playing a joke—just to try to get her to say more than she should. They used to do that when they were little, four sisters teaming up against one to weave a fanciful tale. She'd fallen for it many times, until Dat had overheard them once and reminded them that weaving tales like that was no different from lying. But if they were lying now they were getting better at it, for all of them were looking at her as if she was the one who lost her mind.

"You seem confused." Faith narrowed her gaze on Lovina. "Did Thomas Chupp show up at Big Olaf's or not?"

"Oh, Thomas!" It was all starting to make sense now. He *had* told her he'd come to the house.

Faith narrowed her gaze. "Who did you think we were talking about? Unless you thought we were talking about that other bachelor you met today. I never did hear what his name is. Boy, did you get Mem all excited when you mentioned him—and mentioned that you wanted to talk to her and Dat tonight." Faith studied her face as if trying to get an answer to something. The only problem was that Lovina didn't know what the question was.

"I think Mem might faint straight away when we tell her that Thomas Chupp stopped by looking for you." Grace chuckled. "Maybe there is hope for the rest of us yet!"

"Have any of you ever had a conversation with a bachelor? Ever? Just because you talk to someone doesn't mean you're going to spend your life with him." Lovina sighed. "Both Dat and Mem went on dates with others before they were married." She wagged her finger at her sisters. "I think the four of you are trying to make a big deal out of nothing."

Joy grinned. She was working on some handstitching on a small potholder, most likely for a gift. "Are you looking for Dat and Mem? Mem walked down to take some salve to Abby Troyer. One of her twins touched the hot barbecue grill, and Mem offered to do some doctoring. Dat offered to walk with her, which means he's improving. This is his second walk in the same day."

Then her sisters started talking at once, all of them having thoughts on their parents, the bachelors, and what Lovina was hiding. They talked about her as if she wasn't in the room.

Overwhelmed with the commotion, Lovina stuck two fingers in her mouth and gave a big whistle. Even though her mother said it wasn't ladylike, she'd used it for years to call in the cows and dogs on the farm, and occasionally to rein in her sisters.

The voices in the room stilled and Lovina took a deep breath. She was going to have to tell them something. She quickly weighed what information would appease their curiosity but also give her space and freedom to meet with Dat and Mem tonight.

Lovina held up her hands, palms out. "All right, I will tell you about Thomas Chupp. I took him—his family—Mem's loaf of banana sour cream bread, and he was very kind. And then, when I was at Big Olaf's he showed up. He asked me to go to the beach with him tomorrow, because at least two of my sisters told him I hadn't been there in over a month."

Joy and Grace gave each other knowing looks. Lovina noted disapproval on Faith's face.

Hope drummed her fingers anxiously on the tabletop. Hope never was one to involve herself in such conversation. Her mind was most likely someplace else, like flipping through a mental seed catalog. But Faith's eyes were focused on her. "So are you going?"

"Ja, I told him I would." Lovina pointed at her sisters one by one. "But you can't tell Mem and Dat. I want to take them out tonight to discuss a few things."

"To talk to them about Thomas Chupp? Already?" Grace shook her head, her blue eyes full of humor. "I don't think one date warrants a conversation with your parents."

"Maybe it's about the other bachelor," Faith said. "The one she was talking to this morning." Her voice held a tinge of hope.

"*Ne*, I think it's something more than that." Hope took a sip of punch with her straw. "I think it has something to do with a pie shop. Maybe Lovina found the perfect location to set up her shop today?"

The excitement in the faces around her fell, their disappointment clear. It was obvious they were far more interested in hearing about romantic pursuits than business ventures. All except for

Grace, who tilted up her chin. "Just remember not to expect it to turn a profit for a year, maybe two," Grace commented.

"Ja," Lovina said. "I'll keep that in mind."

With the cloth bag slung over her shoulder and her notebook tucked inside, Lovina made her way to her bedroom. The blankets on her bed were still smooth and neat, as they'd been this morning when she'd left. Hope's were still rumpled, just as they'd been all day. Just as they always were. Lovina had decided long ago not to get too burdened down by the actions of her sisters. They had their unique gifts and talents, and she had hers.

She sat on her bed and pulled out Noah's sketches. Lovina sighed. If she was going to invest herself in anything, this would be it. And she couldn't think of anyone she'd enjoy partnering in this project with more than Noah Yoder. Lovina gingerly pressed his sketches to her chest and closed her eyes. Now she just needed Dat to say yes.

She had to trust it could happen. She had to trust that the peace she'd felt earlier that day was for a reason. She had to know that it was God who'd placed that dream in her heart all those years ago. And pursuing it was even more important than turning the head of a handsome bachelor. Yes, she had to know that, truly believe it.

Southern Breeze Punch

1 envelope blue raspberry Kool-Aid
1 (6 ounce) can frozen lemonade concentrate
1 cup sugar
7 cups water
2 liters ginger ale
1 (46 ounce) can pineapple juice

Mix all ingredients. Fill each glass with ice cubes and pour punch mixture over them to fill glass. Stir briskly and allow a few minutes for the cubes to thaw into the punch. This is a very refreshing drink and not too sweet. Keep some ice cubes in the freezer so you can quickly mix up a refreshing drink to serve your guest.

Eleven

When fear knocks on the door, send faith to answer!

AMISH PROVERB

❧

The dining room of Yoder's Restaurant hummed with conversation. Lovina sat against the back wall with her parents. Every table in her vision was filled with customers, Englischers mostly. Lovina knew that once it was the season and the Amish and Mennonites from up north began arriving on buses, that wouldn't necessarily be the case.

She'd invited her parents out to dinner so they could talk…alone. She'd brought her satchel, and inside were the sketches from Noah. It was hard to believe that it had been just this morning when she'd first seen a For Sale sign in the warehouse. It was hard to believe that it had just been today that she'd first met Noah. Her heart warmed just thinking about him. But she couldn't dwell on that. Not now.

Even before finding the warehouse, she and Jason had spent many hours talking about the possibility and the details of her getting a loan. The bank would loan her money for a building for a pie shop on two conditions. First, that she'd use the money she'd saved as a down payment. That savings represented two years of work as a schoolteacher in Walnut Creek. And second, that her father would agree to co-sign her loan. With his remaining property in Walnut Creek and his savings tucked in the bank from the sale of their Ohio home, Dat's assets were protection for the bank in case her dream fell short.

They ordered their favorite meals. Smoked ham with Amish noodles and three-bean salad for Mem. Meatloaf for Dat with mashed potatoes and buttered corn. And roast turkey breast and stuffing with a baked sweet potato and green beans for Lovina. As they ate, Mem and Dat spoke about friends back in Walnut Creek who were getting married. They also discussed Mem's ideas for a screened-in back porch. Lovina waited until their waitress, Sallie, brought hand-dipped ice cream with fresh strawberries for dessert before she dared to bring up the warehouse.

Dat was intently scooping a small bite with both ice cream and a strawberry when Lovina cleared her throat. Her parents paused and looked at her—two spoons in the air, halfway to their mouths.

"Dat, Mem, I need to talk to you about something."

She lifted her satchel from the seat next to her and then pushed back her water glass and dish of ice cream to make room on the table. She laid the three sketches on the checkered table cloth as Mem and Dat finished off their last bites. She was just about to tell them about the day's discovery when someone walked up in the familiar green apron. Lovina assumed it was their waitress, but when she looked up it was Faith who stood there with a coffeepot in one hand. The look in her middle sister's eyes was mischievous, to say the least.

"Lovina!" Faith picked up the sketch that displayed the entry area of the pie shop. "This is amazing. Who drew this? Where is this place?"

"Faith…I didn't know you were working tonight." She reached up and motioned for her dark-haired sister to hand the drawing back to her.

Faith shrugged. "Anna-Beth's son has a fever. She called to ask if I could cover for her tonight." Faith refilled Dat's cup with coffee and eyed the paper again. "This place looks wunderbar. You'll have to take me to it someday. Where is it?"

Mem reached for the sketch, and Lovina handed it over.

"Is this restaurant someplace around Sarasota?" Mem asked. "It does look inviting."

Lovina stared up at Faith and furrowed her brow, hoping she'd get the hint to leave. "Actually, Mem, this place is just down the street, right across from the Tourist Church."

Faith didn't get the hint, and she stood still, coffeepot in hand, waiting for Lovina to continue.

Mem pushed her glasses farther up the bridge of her nose to get a better look at the sketch. "I don't remember this place. Surely it isn't where you said. I'd know about it for certain."

"It—it doesn't look like this now, but it can." Lovina turned her gaze to her father. "Do you know the old warehouse near the back of Roy Yoder's place? It's for sale, and I'd like to buy it. It would be the perfect place for a pie shop. I know I've wanted to have one for such a long time, but Dat, this is the perfect time. This is the perfect place!"

She raised her hands, palms out toward Dat. "Don't say anything yet. I've thought everything through, and I know it's been an unreachable dream for so long, but I really think this can happen now."

Lovina went on to explain about the cost of the building and how she'd already worked on all the paperwork with Jason Schlabach over at Everence Credit Union.

"Ja, Lovina. I know this has been your dream for a long time… but there is a big difference between buying a building and opening a pie shop."

"Faith!" One of the other, older waitresses called out to her. "Your table is ready to order, dear."

Faith took a step back reluctantly. "I best go." The concern on Faith's face was clear. And both of her parents wore the same looks of concern and reluctance in their expressions.

Lovina was thankful when Faith turned and strode over to the table, smiling at her customers waiting to order. Lovina was going to have a hard enough time trying to convince her mem and dat. She didn't need Faith butting in with her opinions too.

"There is going to be a huge cost for the remodel and all the supplies. There are advertising costs and…"

"Advertising?" Lovina couldn't help but chuckle. "It'll be in clear view of the parking lot at the Tourist Church, where all the buses stop. There's a crowd there numerous times a day during season. More than that, you know how word always spreads in Amish communities. The Englischers have to pay to get the word out about their products, but I'd wager that news spreads far quicker at Amish sewing frolics and church socials."

Mem sat next to Dat, as quiet as a church mouse, but she didn't need to speak for Lovina to know her thoughts on the matter. Mem's round face was all pinched up as if she'd just eaten a lemon.

"Dat, that's not even the most amazing part," Lovina continued, ignoring her mem's focused gaze. "The warehouse is filled to the top with all types of old things. It looks like a lot of junk to me, but there is someone who is willing to do all the remodeling of the building in exchange for those things. He sells them to Sarasota Salvage and—"

"Who is this?" Dat asked. "Who is willing to do such a thing?" He clicked his tongue and pushed his ice cream bowl to the side. "And you have to know that a job like that is impossible for one man alone."

"He won't work alone. He has a crew."

Mem's eyes widened in disbelief. "A crew...a whole crew of men who are going to remodel a warehouse and turn it into a pie shop in exchange for some junk?"

Mem's eyelids fluttered closed in disbelief, but Dat's gaze was fixed on Lovina. He tilted his head and wore a knowing look.

"Tell me about this, Lovina. It seems you've given it a lot of thought. This man you spoke of, was he the one who did these sketches?"

"Ja, Dat. It's Noah Yoder. He's a carpenter and..."

"Noah Yoder? Roy Yoder's nephew? I think not." Mem's voice rose, causing the patrons at the next table to pause their conversation and turn. "Lovina, surely this is some type of joke. Do you know anything about this so-called crew? What are their names? What are their ages? Do they have experience?"

"I—I'm not sure. I don't know."

"Of course you don't." Mem lowered her voice. "Do you ever pay attention to this world around us? Are pies all you think about?"

Lovina turned to her father, hoping for an explanation.

Dat rested his arms on the table and leaned forward. "I've met Noah Yoder, and I know the three teens who are living with him, working with him. Stories have followed those young men down from Illinois." Her father's voice was gentle but firm. "It seems a few years ago Noah got himself in trouble too. He was in an accident, as a driver of a car..."

"A car, of all things," Mem interrupted.

"A few years ago?" Lovina's eyebrows furrowed. "He was in his rumspringa no doubt. Dat, please. If you discounted every young man who got in trouble during his rumspringa years there'd be no more marriages in Pinecraft! Or in any Amish community!"

"It's more than that." Mem pushed her ice cream back from her. "It's this whole thing, Lovina. Do you really want to go down this path? Opening up a business is a lot of work. All that money and all that time. Is this really what you want to do with your life? Have you ever considered having a family?"

Had she ever considered having a family? What young Amish woman hadn't? But it was easier to dream about a pie shop than about a husband. She could build a pie shop with her two hands, but gaining someone's love and favor seemed daunting, impossible almost.

Lovina let her eyes flutter closed, reminding herself that the best response was a kind one. She opened her eyes, picked up her spoon, and slowly stirred the melting ice cream. How could she explain that although Mem had other dreams for her, Lovina was content to live the life God had called her to? Not every Amish woman married. Would Mem ever understand that Lovina had no expectation of that?

She lifted up the drafting sketch of the warehouse and looked at it. She was about to explain their ideas for remodeling only half of the warehouse to start when Faith hurried to the table, moved Lovina's satchel off the chair, and sat.

"All right, things have slowed down. I don't think I'm intruding, am I?" Faith picked up Lovina's spoon and took a bite of her nearly melted ice cream.

Lovina glanced at her sister, wondering what to say next, wondering if she should just give up the idea when Faith reached across the table and placed her hand on Mem's.

"Do you know what I like about the idea of this pie shop? It'll be the perfect gathering spot for the young people of Pinecraft. Mem, just think about it. A pie shop will be the new talk of town. It'll be a destination spot—the first place people go when they get off the bus." The words bubbled out of Faith. She was in a much better mood than she had been this afternoon.

Mem jutted out her chin. "There are other places. There is the park…"

"The park is always so crowded," Faith continued. She looked around. "Both Yoder's and Der Dutchman are always busy too. A pie shop like this will not only be the first place visitors go, but think of the bachelors. Don't you think they'll be eager to watch the bakers working in the open kitchen?"

Lovina glanced from Mem to Faith to Mem again. She never, in a million years, would have thought Faith would have jumped on board about this. And she'd never have guessed how quickly Mem's look could soften. Even Dat's gaze was focused on his wife, as if curious about her response. The assets were in Dat's name, yes, but maybe Mem was the one who held a grip on the purse strings.

"How did you remember that I wanted an open kitchen?" Lovina asked. "That I wanted to have a counter out front where customers could watch the bakers roll the pie crusts?"

Faith looked at Lovina with dark eyes that were so similar to her own—at least that was what everyone told her. "I listen too, ja? I know this has been on your heart for a while, Lovina. And sometimes, when I think about it, I even pray that God would make your way clear." Faith's voice was soft, but there was something unsettling about her words. Why was this pie shop suddenly so important to her sister?

"But a pie shop." Mem sighed. "That is so much work. Especially for a single young woman."

"And we're all going to remain single too if something's not done about it." Faith took another bite of ice cream. "It's not like back in Walnut Creek, Mem. We don't have singings and such. How else are we going to find husbands? Where are we going to meet bachelors? Nowhere. There is nowhere to go."

Mem's forehead wrinkled even more, and Lovina knew she was thinking hard.

"I was worried about that when we moved to Pinecraft," Mem mumbled to herself more than them. "There aren't many bachelors to choose from."

"Ja, and a pie shop like this will be a *gut* place for young people to gather. But if you don't agree..." Faith trailed off.

Lovina tried to act as if her heart weren't about to burst. She reached over, gripping Faith's hand tightly, and held her breath. This had been her dream for so long, and then there was Noah. She swallowed hard just thinking about him. She wanted to spend more time with him. The idea excited her.

Mem glanced over at Dat. "The girls are right. There aren't very many ways to meet bachelors in these parts. At least a place like this would get them out of the house and they'd have better opportunities."

Dat tilted his head in surprise. "Are you saying we should do it, Anna?"

Faith smiled and rose, as if sensing her job was done.

Mem shrugged. "It's your money, do with it as you will." Which Lovina knew was as much approval as Mem would give, lest something happen later to prove it hadn't been a good idea after all.

Then Mem sat straighter in her chair, as if just remembering something. "But I do not like the fact that Noah Yoder will be the one helping with the remodel."

"There is no harm in Noah," Dat interjected. "I told you before that I've had a few conversations with him, and he seems an upstanding young man."

Faith straightened her apron and then leaned down, as if offering up one last secret. She narrowed her gaze on Lovina. "Ja, and why should Lovina be worried about him when she has a date with Thomas Chupp tomorrow? He's taking her to the beach." Then, without another word, she hurried over to the nearest table, checking on their meal.

"To the beach?" Mem clapped her hands together. "I haven't met him yet, but Vera says he's quite handsome, and that he inherited his father's farm up in Pennsylvania. Why did you wait so long to tell me?"

Lovina forced a smile. *Maybe because I care far more about the pie shop*, she wanted to say. Instead, she fingered the edge of the sketch and looked up shyly. "Well, maybe because I wanted to save that news for last."

"That does it, John..." Mem turned to her father. "That does make the decision for us, doesn't it?"

Lovina understood Mem's train of thought. Mem was saying that opening a pie shop was unnecessary since Lovina already held the interest of a bachelor and wouldn't have time to run a business while going on dates and possibly getting married.

She didn't dare look at her mem, lest the wrong words— unkind words—slip from her mouth. Instead, she focused on Dat and felt tears rimming her eyes. She would take no for an answer, and she would learn to live with it if she had to, but more than anything she wanted to know that it was his opinion, his decision.

Dat let out a sigh, suddenly looking very old and very weary. "I wish I could say yes to cosigning your bank loan, but I'm afraid

I can't give you the answer you want. I've watched you over the years. I know how hard you've worked. You've always cared for others, and you've never given up your dream. But I've never felt comfortable in owing anyone. Not another man. Not a bank."

Lovina's throat tightened. She took the sketches, refolded them, and put them back inside her satchel. "I—I understand, Dat."

Emotions fought within her. Sadness and disappointment made their way to the top. But she wasn't going to argue. Dat had her mother and sisters to think of. She was just one of his daughters. He couldn't support her if it meant risking the welfare of the others.

Dat reached his hand across the table, and she looked up, surprised. "Your hand, Lovina."

She removed her hand from her lap and placed it on the table before him. He grasped it and gave it a warm squeeze. Heat rose to her cheeks. He'd never acted like this before—not in public. Showing affection like this didn't happen often. It wasn't the Amish way. Yet Lovina had seen a difference in him in recent months. The move to Pinecraft had changed her father. Or maybe it was his sickness. He seemed more tender with all those around him. But even a tender father had to put his foot down at times. Especially with matters such as this.

"Lovina." He spoke her name, and it was just a whisper. Hardly distinguishable in the crowded restaurant. "Lovina, I will not cosign a loan for you. Instead, I will give you what you need. Let me talk with Jason at the bank and with Noah Yoder and see what they think."

Lovina's eyes widened and her jaw dropped open. She wanted to say something, but what could she say? She didn't dare glance over at Mem either, sure that the expression on her face would ruin the moment. Instead, Lovina decided to focus on her father's face and soak up all the tenderness there.

"Thank you," she managed to whisper.

He smiled. "I just want you to know that I'm not doing this so you and your sisters can draw in bachelors. I'm doing this because of who you are—who God created you to be. God put this in your heart for a reason, and it seems He's finally revealed the way for it to happen."

The tears came then, unbidden, and Lovina couldn't hold them in. A tear slipped down her cheek, and she quickly wiped it away.

The tables around her were still filled with people, eating and talking. Waitresses still hurried by, caring for their customers and delivering orders. The wonderful aromas of fried chicken, coffee, and even the sweet strawberries from their dessert filled the air, but that wasn't on Lovina's thoughts either. The only thing she could think about was that others not only acknowledged her dream, but they wanted to help fulfill it. First Jason and Noah, then Faith, and finally Dat. She'd never been given a more perfect gift.

"There's one more thing," Dat said as their waitress approached with the bill. "I've been wanting to do this for a while. I've felt it was in God's plan—your opening a pie shop."

Lovina placed a hand over her chest, feeling her heartbeat quicken. Such knowledge was almost too hard to comprehend. "But Dat, why did you wait? Why didn't you say something sooner?"

Dat's smile grew, and he placed his hand on Mem's as if welcoming her into their conversation. "I was just waiting for you to ask, dear daughter. I wanted you to want this enough to risk your heart to ask. To trust me and trust my care for you."

Potato Soup

1 can cream of chicken soup
16 ounces heavy whipping cream
1 (32 ounce) carton chicken broth
10-15 potatoes (cut in small pieces)
1 (8 ounce) container sour cream
12 slices bacon, fried crisp and broken into pieces, or 1 3-ounce jar
    of bacon bits
seasoned salt

Heat soup, cream, and chicken broth on medium heat. Add potatoes to this mixture and cook until done (keep on medium heat).
When potatoes are tender, turn heat to low, and add sour cream,
bacon, and seasoned salt to taste. Makes 15 servings

Twelve

If you hear a bad report about someone, halve it, and
quarter it, and then say nothing about the rest.

AMISH PROVERB

Tuesday dawned with a warm wind blowing from the east. After eating a breakfast of dippy eggs, bacon, and toast, Noah stepped out the back door and eyed the warehouse, wondering how Lovina's conversation with her parents had gone the night before. Wondering if his sketches had made any difference. Wondering what her dat had to say about the idea. And what John Miller had to say about him.

Noah had talked with Lovina's dat a few times, and the older man had been kind enough to his face. But when he met Lovina's mem, Noah had no doubt that news of who he was and what he'd done had proceeded him. John Miller had mentioned he had five daughters, and Anna Miller had changed the conversation before Noah could ask anything about them.

Noah glanced at his watch. He hadn't worn one up north on his dat's farm. Things on the farm got done as they'd got done. His dat had been the timekeeper of the family, making sure everything was set up in time for their weekly auctions. But now that he was in Pinecraft and he depended on drivers to get him and the guys to their jobs, a watch was a necessity.

He opened the door and strode back into the house, happy to see the guys were pulling on their boots. "Ready to head out?"

As if on cue, an old truck pulled up to his uncle Roy's house. They exited the front door as a group. Noah climbed in the front seat next to the driver, Daniel. Mose, Gerald, and Atlee climbed into the back.

"I got a call from one of my contractor friends late last night," Noah said. "There's an old house in the West of Trail neighborhood he told me about." Noah gave him the address, and Daniel nodded.

"Someone doing a remodel?" Daniel asked. His eyes lit up, and Noah knew why. The West of Trail neighborhood was comprised of an eclectic mix of Bay Front mansions and older 40s and 50s style ranches. Many of the homes in this highly desirable neighborhood had been torn down and rebuilt, but others had been substantially remodeled, which meant they were often throwing out anything that didn't fit in with their modern designs. Noah had been able to get some wonderful pieces that he'd resold to Sarasota Architectural Salvage. On days like that Daniel seemed just as excited about the haul as Noah. To Noah, stepping into an old house, barn, or attic felt like a kid stepping into a candy store.

So far the three teens had been a fine help in sifting through construction garbage, hauling large architectural pieces, and cleaning things up to sell, but he knew their restless spirits wouldn't be content with that for long. He wished he'd heard something from Lovina already—good news especially. The teens seemed extra sluggish today. Maybe it was the heat, or maybe it was the knowledge that no one around Pinecraft wanted to give them a chance.

In the last two months since moving to Pinecraft not a day had passed that Noah Yoder hadn't wondered if he'd made the right choice. He'd had plenty of work in Illinois. Had God really sent him to Florida? Or had he just imagined he could be used in this way?

His whole life Noah had been drawn to broken things and enjoyed fixing them up and giving them new life. Maybe it was because he'd been broken for a while—drawn to the ways of the world. Yet a godly man—his father's friend—took the time to help him, to teach him a trade. To guide him in paying restitution and showing him that life could be different.

But could he do the same?

They pulled up to the large bay view cottage, and Noah imagined the description on the realtor's website—"charm and character throughout." The large, rambling house was half-hidden by mature trees. The long white porch looked freshly painted, but the shingled siding could use some work.

They climbed from the truck to get a better view of the place. The ocean breeze was refreshing, even in the heat of the day. He imagined what it would be like to sit on the lawn behind the house on a cool evening. Of course, what realtors considered "charming" new buyers often saw as just old. He'd seen more than one house like this being completely gutted and updated. It was sad to him.

"Rick is coming in tomorrow, and they're stripping it down to the framing," Noah said. "He said we can have anything we can haul away. They're bringing a large dumpster tomorrow for everything else."

Daniel gave a low whistle. "It's just a shame. I think it's pretty just as it is."

They walked up the steps and the teens took off first, which surprised Noah.

"There're some great columns in here," Atlee called out.

"Hey, Noah, you need to check out this paneling in the dining room. It's vintage for sure," Gerald said.

"Yes, the paneling can go with us," Noah called to him. "Rick already mentioned that."

The older driver walked with them, keeping pace. Daniel liked to go along with them. He'd sit and watch the work, and he always had some type of story to share about things he'd done or people he'd met.

"It makes no sense." Daniel shook his head. "People buy old houses and then they gut them out and make them new." He chuckled. "But then folks who buy new houses buy all the old stuff and make them look old."

Noah had seen the same thing. That was why Sarasota Salvage was doing so well. People liked adding old pieces like sinks, faucets, mantels, and columns, into their new homes. Those things made them comfortable. They gave people a sense of being connected with history, even in modern times.

"One man's trash is another man's treasure." If Noah had heard that one time growing up he'd heard it a thousand.

"You should see my grandpa's place up in Arcola," Mose commented. "It's an auction yard and you can find anything you need there."

"And lots of things you don't need," Noah said with a smirk.

He walked over and eyed a large hall mirror. He ran his hand down the molding. He knew with a little work and a lot of patience he'd be able to remove it from the wall. And it was exactly the type of thing his friends at the salvage store liked.

"I grew up with all those things. I loved it when a new customer showed up and needed help unloading," Noah told the group. "I tried to be the first to haul and sort things—just so I could see what was there. Most Amish boys don't get to be around much stuff, but my friends and I used to play in the old cars. I test drove a small motorcycle when I was only seven. I took apart broken electronics that my dad was throwing away just to see how they worked."

"Not much of an Amish upbringing with all those worldly things," Mose teased.

It was heating up outside, and that made it even hotter inside. Noah took a handkerchief from his pocket and wiped his brow. As if reading his thoughts, Atlee walked to the front windows and opened them, letting in a breeze.

"Sorting through all that junk was good for me, though. It gave me a better understanding of the outside world. Of course, that also made it too easy to walk away from the Plain life."

Mose nodded and moved to head upstairs. Noah knew he'd heard the story many times. Mose had been heading down the wrong path that Noah had been on for a good while. A path that brought only pain, loss, and heartache along the way.

Noah had stepped in and tried to be a good influence on his nephew. The thing was, it was hard trying to save someone who didn't want to be saved.

At least Mose had agreed to come to Florida and encouraged his friends to do the same. That was why Noah was hoping to get a big project like the warehouse. He wanted something—one project—that they could invest themselves in. He wanted them to see that they could make a difference. He wanted them to have their hands in the transformation, and maybe through that they'd allow God to work in them too.

He walked through the house, and Gerald walked by his side, most eager to see what was in the next room.

"When we start unloading the rooms, let's start upstairs,"

Noah said. "We'll load up the truck with big things, and then Mose and Atlee can help unload while we work on getting the stuff downstairs."

"Where are Mose and Atlee?" Gerald asked, peering over the railing and looking downstairs.

A sinking feeling hit the pit of Noah's gut. Then he heard it— the sound of an outside water faucet turning on. The creak and groan of water moving through old pipes rumbled through the walls. Noah moved to the back window and peered out. The other teens were splashing each other to cool off. At least they weren't causing any trouble.

Noah took a small notebook out of his back pocket and pulled a pencil from the pocket in his shirt. He ripped out a piece of paper and handed both to Gerald.

"Why don't you make a list of everything worth taking upstairs? I'll start with the downstairs."

Gerald's face brightened. "You're gonna trust me with that?" he asked.

Noah saw the hopeful look in his eyes—the look that told him Gerald appreciated being trusted. "If I don't trust you, you'll never learn."

Noah went downstairs and walked through the house, making a note of anything someone might be interested in. He smiled as he considered how excited he was to find original bathroom fixtures. Very rarely did people leave behind light fixtures, because they knew those had worth. They just had no idea how the little things that were often overlooked could add up.

When Noah got to the kitchen he paused. The kitchen was both long and wide, and in the center was a counter long enough for four or five women to work side by side. Through the windows in the back of the house, Noah could see a lawn and a few tall trees. Beyond that was a private beach. The sound of ocean waves could be heard, bringing life to this place. Yet it wasn't the view that got him excited.

He pulled his cell phone from his pocket and gave Rick a call, pushing the number with his thumb. Back in Illinois, many people had cell phones that they used for business. They kept them hidden most of the time unless they needed to make a business call. But no one seemed to think twice about phones down here.

On the other end of the line Rick answered the call. "Hello?"

"Hey, do you know that long counter in the kitchen? Is that going too?"

"Yup. You know how designers are these days—everything is open concept. Not only are the center cabinets and counter going, but the wall between the kitchen and dining room too. That way guests can also see the waves roll in while they're dining."

"How much would you charge to deliver that counter to my uncle's place? It's too big to fit in my truck."

"Is that in Pinecraft?" Rick asked.

"Yes."

"Well, that's not too far off my trek home. Tell you what. If you can get your guys to load it and unload it, I can deliver it for free."

"That sounds like a deal to me. Will you be by later?"

"Yup, before you leave tonight. I'm guessing it'll take you that long to strip the place."

"Sounds like a plan, Rick."

"See you then."

"See you then," Noah responded, looking around. They had a big day ahead of them, and Noah hoped the hours would go quickly. He also hoped that Lovina's dat hadn't said no—otherwise he'd have to explain to his uncle why they had a long cabinet and countertop combination in his yard.

Noah was just wondering if he should get in touch with Lovina when he heard Mose call up the stairs.

"Hey, Gerald, come here. I want to show you something."

Next came the creak of the floorboards overhead and the sound of Gerald's booted feet coming down the stairs. Then came a large bang, and a man's shout filled the air. Noah jumped, his heart pounding. Without question he immediately knew that Gerald had been the victim of yet another prank.

Laughter echoed from the family room area, and Noah rushed that direction. Gerald was sprawled on the floor at the bottom of the stairs. Atlee and Mose were doubled over with laughter in the entryway. Noah rushed over. Thankfully the look on Gerald's face was one of confusion more than pain.

"I can't believe you fell for that," Mose gasped. "It's the oldest trick in the book."

"Hey." Noah rushed forward, checking to make sure Gerald was all right. "Are both of you responsible for this, or do I only need to whip up on one of you?"

The teens looked at each other, and then Atlee piped up. "We both did it, but it was nothing big. We only loosened the board on the bottom step so he wouldn't fall far."

More laughter bubbled out of Mose. "Man, you should have seen the look on your face!"

Gerald picked himself up off the floor. "Yeah, well, I'd have to say it's not nearly as ugly as your face is all the time."

"Hey!" Mose lunged forward. Even though Gerald was two inches taller, Noah guessed that if they did really fight Mose would win. Blond, thin, with a baby face, Mose looked innocent, but there was an inner pit bull in him that begged to be set loose.

"Hey now, hey now." Noah stepped between them, stretching out his hands. "This is not the place for that. Neither the fighting or the pranks. This is someone else's house."

"Yeah, and we're doing all this work to line someone else's pockets," Mose muttered under his breath. He ran his fingers through his hair and leaned against the wall.

"Is that what you think?" Noah took off his hat and tossed it to the floor. "That I brought you down here so I could make you work like mules? And that I'm getting rich on this? Do you know how much it cost to get you three down here? Do you know how much it costs to keep you fed?" Noah lowered his voice, but Mose's disrespectful words played over in his mind.

Noah bent over, picked up his hat, dusted it off, and placed it on his head. "Listen, I know this hasn't turned out like any of us thought, but I'm doing my best. And if you'd rather I just pay your tickets back to Illinois so you can sit in the county jail, let me know. Because that's where you'd be right now if you weren't here." Noah halted his words and the roar of the ocean waves out back seemed even louder than before.

They stood there quiet, each one in his own thoughts, and then Atlee approached the staircase. He pulled the hammer from his hammer loop. "Gerald, can you run to Daniel's truck and get some nails from the tool chest in back? Then we can fix this step—make it better than before."

Gerald turned and headed to the truck without another word. Mose kneeled down and straightened the boards. Even though they didn't say it, Noah knew that was their way of making amends. They were offering an apology by fixing what they'd messed up.

"I made this list of the items we can salvage downstairs, if you want to get started." Noah handed his notebook to Mose. "I'm going to go check out the back sunroom and back deck. Rick mentioned last night there were some old metal yard pieces they wanted to get rid of too."

Noah strode to the back of the house, the blood still pumping through his veins. He went straight to the back deck, sat at the top step, and placed his face in his hands, sending up a silent prayer for wisdom.

"Seems like you've decided to skip all the fun parts of parenting and go straight to the teen years," a voice said.

Noah glanced up and noticed Daniel sitting on an old lawn chair on the back porch.

"I'm not their dad."

Daniel pushed his glasses farther up his nose, peering down. "No, but from what you told me, according to the courts it's close enough."

"I just wish they'd take ownership of their lives. Wish they'd realize that not everything is a game."

"Yeah, well. If most us could figure that out sooner we'd all be better off." Daniel threaded his fingers together and then placed them behind his head, leaning back against the wall. He sighed. "Sometimes we try to save people only to have things get worse for a while. And oftentimes I think God allows things to happen so they'll see—we'll see—that His hand is doing the saving, not ours."

Noah focused on Daniel more closely, searching the man's eyes. In the two months since Daniel had been driving for him they'd talked about many things, but God wasn't one of them. Yet from the kindness and peaceful attitude Daniel displayed Noah had guessed the man's relationship with God was strong.

"Do you think I'm getting in God's way by trying to help them out? Is that what you're saying?" Noah asked.

"I don't think you're getting in the way of God. Just the opposite. God asks us to reach out and help those who need help, need grace. How are folks supposed to know about God's love if we don't show 'em what it's like?" Daniel put his hand back on his lap, resting elbows on knees. "But I also think God often has different plans to reach people than we have. Sometimes they need to face hard times—really hard times—before they're ready to turn to Him." Daniel shrugged. "Of course you can't blame us for trying. We do our best. You're doing your best, Noah. But just don't be surprised if things get worse before they get better."

Noah stood, knowing he needed to get back to work. Knowing he needed to check on the guys to make sure they were doing what they should. "I wish I could see the future—see what it's going to take to bring them around." He crossed his arms over his chest.

"The good news is that God knows. He's already beat you to it." Daniel smirked. "And it's not like it's fair odds either, since God has that all-knowing, all-seeing thing going on."

Noah thought a moment more about Daniel's words, and while he liked the idea that Lovina's pie shop would play into God's plans, there were no guarantees. In his opinion that would make things easy, but maybe Daniel was right. Maybe the harder stuff, not the easy stuff, would be what finally broke through to the guys. He just hated to think what that would look like.

Daniel rose from the chair and mumbled something about having a box of glazed donuts in the truck, and hoping that would sweeten up the guys' attitudes. Noah nodded, but he didn't move. And instead he watched the sea green waves rolling out and crashing back in.

"If you have better plans, I'm open to them," he said in a low voice, as if speaking to the waves. But instead he was speaking to the Wave-Maker. The One who designed the whole universe and all the systems in it. "I'll try not to get in the way."

Noah hadn't really talked out loud to God before, not like this, but in a way it just seemed right. God had them in Pinecraft for a reason. And when the time was right, God would show what that reason was.

He also hated to see the guys hurt, but Noah knew that pain was how he'd learned some of the most important lessons in his life. He wouldn't pray for hard stuff to come in their lives, but he was starting to reason that if hard stuff did come, it would be for God's greater plan.

Noah rose and moved back into the house, hearing the creaking sound of century-old wood being removed with a crow bar. He walked in the kitchen, placing two hands on the long counter, and then he closed his eyes and pictured the warehouse space.

His own good plan would be Lovina's dat agreeing to the purchase of the warehouse. Maybe, soon, they'd be working there, but until then he had to stay focused. It wasn't time to turn his attention to the warehouse, not yet…or to the pretty Amish woman who hoped to make it hers.

Dippy Eggs

Break eggs one at a time into the same heated skillet you fried bacon in. Do not stir or turn eggs. Spoon bacon grease over eggs as they cook for about 3 to 4 minutes.

Glazed Donuts

2 cups mashed potatoes
½ cup butter
½ cup margarine
1 cup sugar
1 quart whole milk, scalded
3 packages dry yeast
¾ cup lukewarm water
3 cups flour
2 eggs, beaten
1 tablespoon salt

Combine mashed potatoes, butter, margarine, and sugar. Add scalded milk. Dissolve yeast in lukewarm water. When yeast has begun to work, add to mashed potato mixture. Add half the flour and let set until it sponges. Add eggs and salt, then add remainder of flour and mix well. Let set until double in bulk. Roll out and cut out donuts. Let set again until double in bulk. Fry in hot shortening at 375° until golden brown.

Thirteen

The grand essentials of happiness in this
life are something to do, something to
love, and something to hope for.

AMISH PROVERB

Lovina's heart pounded as she rode her bike away from the center of Pinecraft. The pounding wasn't from exertion. Her legs were used to the exertion. Excitement urged her on.

She'd visited the bank no less than a dozen times in the last two months, but this time she had a greater purpose than all the times before. She had to get to the bank, and she had to talk to Jason. Then she had to get home before her outing with Thomas Chupp, even though that was the last thing she wanted to spend her time on today. There was so much to think about. There were so many plans to make!

Two minutes later Lovina parked her bicycle in front of the bank and hurried in. "Is Jason Schlabach in?"

The man behind the desk shook his head. "I'm sorry. He had a meeting across town. But I'll tell him you stopped by."

Lovina's heart fell. Her hands dropped to her side. "That's all right. I can stop by later." She turned to leave the building. She knew she could talk to Jason another time, but she wished she could do it now.

"Lovina!" the man called after her and she turned.

"Your father called this morning. I believe Jason has plans to meet him after lunch."

She felt like jumping up and down with excitement, but instead she simply nodded. "Danke. Thank you. That's wonderful."

On the way back home she rode slowly by the warehouse. She also eyed Roy Yoder's house, hoping to see Noah. She thought about stopping to tell him her father's decision, but she decided now wasn't the right time. There was an order to everything, her grandmother always told her. And when one got out of turn, one usually ended up at the end of the line.

No, she'd wait for Dat to meet with Jason. Only then would she talk to Noah. The last thing she wanted to do was jump out of place.

By the time she got back to her house Thomas was waiting. He sat in the back seat of a blue car. A driver she didn't recognize sat behind the wheel. Lovina parked her bike and hurried to the car. Thomas exited, walked around, and opened the door for her.

"I'm so sorry I kept you waiting." She looked up to him as she slid into the seat. Instead of seeing anger on his face, she noticed a warm smile.

"Don't think anything of it, please. I was early. I was just so eager to start our day."

They chatted in the backseat on the way to the beach. Lovina shared what it was like growing up with four sisters, and Thomas talked about growing up with twin older brothers and all the pranks they'd play on neighbors and teachers.

By the time they reached the beach Lovina felt comfortable

with Thomas, but that didn't make things easier. The driver pulled over to let them out, stating he'd be back in four hours.

Four hours? Lovina held in a sigh. It was going to be a very long day.

Lovina walked across the parking lot with Thomas by her side, but her mind was far from this place. Trying to carry on pleasant conversation with him was the last thing on her mind.

The large beach was packed with people, even though it was September. People came this time of year to avoid the winter crowds, which she always found humorous.

As soon as they walked from the parking lot to the beach, they entered an area with pine trees, picnic tables, and playground equipment. Lovina noticed eyes upon them as they walked—she in her Amish dress and kapp and he in his homemade clothes.

She was used to that. Her whole life it had been the same. Back in Walnut Creek busloads of Englischers would come to get away from their fast-paced lives and spend time with the Plain people. Here in Sarasota, she and her sisters couldn't go to the beach without people staring.

Lovina smiled even now thinking of the surprised looks on the Englischers' faces when her younger sisters took off their dresses to reveal modest swimming suits underneath. They even gawked when Faith and Hope played a game of volleyball with other Amish youth or asked if they could join in with Englischers—as if all Amish did was sit and quilt or cook, never having any fun.

As they walked along, looking for the perfect spot on the beach, Thomas chatted about his family's drive down to Sarasota and their flat tire in the middle of nowhere.

"Our driver was old, and he couldn't change it himself." Thomas chuckled. "But my uncle and I figured it out, which surprised him. I don't think he realized that buggies have wheels too."

She laughed at that, and when they found a sandy spot away from the crowds, she took off her flip-flops and let her toes wiggle into the sand. White sandy beach stretched as far as she could see. Noticing her bare feet, Thomas paused, took off his sturdy black shoes and socks, and rolled up his pants.

Lovina glanced at the sky. The sun was rising higher, and she wondered what time Dat and Jason were meeting. Dat had told her last night that since the building was "For Sale by Owner" and she was paying with cash and offering a good price, he guessed the deal could move very quickly. But how long did "quickly" mean?

The sand was warm under her feet, and Lovina chided herself, telling herself to enjoy the present. Thomas spread a blanket for her and she settled in, noticing how the sun shined on his dark hair. He smiled at her and she smiled back, but although he was handsome, she didn't have the same feelings as when Noah was by her side.

There you go, she chided herself. *You have the attention of Noah Yoder for one day and then think you have the right to be choosy.*

She knew she shouldn't get her heart set on either of the two men. Lovina had a feeling that Thomas's invitation was only a chance for him to have something to do, a distraction from a quiet village. And as for Noah Yoder, one always had to be extra nice to a person who might offer you a job, right?

"I wish you could be here in season," she said as Thomas settled down beside her. "The village smells so good. All the orange trees are ripe with fruit, the temperatures are cooler, and there are people everywhere."

Thomas shielded his eyes and scanned the waves hitting the shore. "My dat's been before, and he's told me about the shuffleboard and volleyball games."

"And there is music and singing on Birky Street in the evenings. They line up chairs and near fill the streets."

"It sounds like I'll have to visit again in a few months." He scooted next to her, closer than she thought he ought. "Which won't be a problem since Dat and Mem put an offer on the house. It looks like they'll be staying. Will you be around?"

Instead of looking at Thomas she looked to the water, focusing on the seagulls that floated over the waves looking for their lunch. "Ja, I hope to be here for a while. I can't imagine returning to Ohio without Mem and Dat." She thought about telling him about the warehouse and the pie shop. She considered telling him that Dat had finally agreed to her dream, but something felt wrong about that. Thomas might be interested, but Noah would be thrilled. She smiled even now considering how much fun he was going to have entering the warehouse and looking through all the items left behind.

"So you've decided to make Pinecraft home?" Disappointment was clear in Thomas's voice. He leaned forward and picked up a handful of sand, letting it fall through his fingers.

"I mean, if there were other reasons to go back I'd consider it." She looked at him, attempting to focus on this moment, on Thomas, the best she could. "I like it up north too. It's not that I didn't enjoy living there. It's just that everyone who's important to me is here. If there were a reason to return. If I were to marry and…well, that could change things." The words were out before Lovina knew why, and wondered if she'd been too forward. "Ja, I've learned one never knows what tomorrow will bring, that's all."

Heat rose to her cheeks. Had she really just implied to this man—one she hardly knew—that if she met someone special she'd return up north? Lovina pressed her lips together, reminding herself that it really didn't matter. Thomas would go back north soon himself, and that would be the end of that. And by tomorrow, hopefully, she'd know more details about the warehouse. Then it wouldn't matter if she never won a bachelor's heart. At least she'd have something meaningful to pour her time into.

"Have you ever been to Somerset, Pennsylvania?" Thomas asked.

"No, but I've read about it in *The Budget*."

"Oh, I'm sure *The Budget* can't fully describe it. That's where our farm—my farm—is. It's a small community. We actually have a meetinghouse, like here in Pinecraft. There are rolling hills and winding dirt roads. No matter the season the drive is always pretty." Thomas's eyes brightened as he spoke of the place, and she wondered if that was the look she got in her eyes when she talked about her pie shop.

"It sounds like a lovely place."

"It is, especially in the summer. Nothing like this hot muggy air. My sister is a schoolteacher, but she will only be working one more year."

A seagull swooped down, but noticing they had nothing interesting on their blanket, it flew away.

"So she's getting married?"

Thomas nodded. "Ja, although it's not published yet." Then, noticing the seagulls, he pulled out a paper bag with lunch. "Some for us and some for the birds." He smiled and handed her a sandwich, muffin, and bottle of water. She thanked him and took a drink.

Lovina tilted her head and eyed him. Instead of looking at her, as he'd been doing all day, he was tossing pieces of bread crust to the sea gulls. His mood changed, and she wondered why. He'd been so eager to talk before, and now he was hesitant.

She took a big bite from her sandwich and eyed the muffin. Her guess was that his Aunt Vera had made them. Her blueberry streusel muffins were always requested at special gatherings. Lovina knew that having her family in town was good enough reason to bake.

"I hear that you taught school for two years," he said, trying to sound casual.

Her sandwich was halfway to her mouth when he spoke. A rush of emotion ran over her, and suddenly her stomach turned, feeling sick. Is that what this was all about? Was he interested in her because their community needed a *schoolteacher?*

Thomas glanced at her and frowned. "Are you all right? Your face…it just turned very red. It's not too much sun, is it?"

"Sun?" She glanced overhead and then shook her head. "It might be. I don't know. It is warm out here." She took another bite of her sandwich, but what had tasted delicious before now tasted like cardboard in her mouth.

"So did you teach school?" Thomas asked again.

"Oh, ja, in a one-room schoolhouse where we lived in Walnut Creek."

Thomas dug his bare toes into the sand. "Did you like it?"

Lovina shrugged. "It was fine. Nothing I'd want to do again. Unless I had to." She thought again about telling him about the warehouse, about her pie shop and her plans to remodel, but where the words had spilled out with Noah yesterday, today they balled up in the center of her throat.

"Teaching school takes a special person," he added. Then he finished off his sandwich and turned to her. Uncertainty still filled his face. "Are you sure you don't need to cool off? We can walk to the edge of the water."

"Ja, I'd like that."

They walked to the water and walked side by side for a while. Once, when a wave came in fast, splashing upon her legs, Lovina rushed out of the way and found herself crashing into Thomas. He caught her, keeping her from tumbling to the ground. He held her arms longer than she expected him to.

He helped her steady herself. "You all right?"

She nodded. "Ja."

His gaze moved from her eyes to her lips and for a moment she wondered if he was going to kiss her. Her heartbeat quickened, but she smiled awkwardly and pulled away. Then, as they continued down the beach, they walked closer than before and every now and then their fingers brushed each other's.

Lovina sighed as she took in the scent of the ocean, the roar of the waves, and the feeling of the sun on her skin. She couldn't think of a more romantic setting or a more beautiful day. It was a moment she never expected to experience, not really. So why was there a sense of anxiousness in her gut?

She should be relishing the moment, but more than anything she wanted to leave. She wanted to go back and peer in the windows of the old, dirty warehouse. She wanted to see the look on Noah Yoder's face when she told him they were going to have a project to work on together. A big one.

Because no matter how romantic Thomas was trying to make this day, Lovina's mind was on another place and another person.

But it's only business, she scolded herself as they walked. *Just because Noah can see my vision for a pie shop doesn't mean we have a future together.*

Just as endless as the sand on this seashore were God's plans for her—plans for her future. But no matter what Lovina's heart told her, there was no guarantee how many of those plans included Noah Yoder.

Her heart sunk a little at that thought and a piece of seaweed snagged on her toes. She kicked it off and then continued on. And beside her Thomas Chupp kept pace.

Blueberry Streusel Muffins

½ cup sugar
½ cup butter, softened
1 egg, beaten
2⅓ cups flour
4 teaspoons baking powder
½ teaspoon salt
1 cup milk
1 teaspoon vanilla
1½ cups blueberries, fresh or frozen

Streusel
½ cup sugar
½ cup flour
½ teaspoon cinnamon
¼ cup butter

Preheat oven to 350°. Cream sugar and butter. Add egg and mix well. Combine flour, baking powder, and salt. Add to creamed mixture, alternating with milk. Stir in vanilla. Gently fold in blueberries. Fill 12 paper-lined muffin cups. For streusel, combine sugar, flour, and cinnamon in a small bowl. Cut in butter until crumbly. Sprinkle over muffins and bake 25-30 minutes.

Fourteen

A happy memory never wears out.

AMISH PROVERB

‿◦

In all their years of marriage Anna had only seen John use the cell phone a handful of times—mostly when he had to make calls concerning their house sale in Ohio. The cell phone was for emergencies only, and that was why it was so shocking when he made two calls before nine o'clock in the morning. One to Jason Schlabach at the bank and the second to Roy Yoder. John had set up a meeting with Jason, but he'd spent more time on the phone with Roy. Anna didn't like it one bit—any of it. But John hadn't asked for her opinion.

Anna poured herself a cup of coffee, adding two scoops of sugar and plenty of cream. The aroma of tomato soup simmering on the stove filled the kitchen. She'd picked up some tomatoes at the store a few days ago and knew she had to use them before they went bad. Tomato soup sounded like a *gut* lunch, but at moments like these she missed her garden back home. She also missed the days when John would discuss major decisions with her. What had gotten into him? Why had he agreed so readily to Lovina's plan without discussing it with her? He'd barely said a thing last night when they'd gotten home. He'd turned in early and risen early too. And then he'd called Roy, discussing with the man more details than he'd even discussed with her.

She took a sip of the coffee and it burned her tongue. If she hadn't been such a dutiful wife she would have said something to her husband. The held-in words burned her tongue too, but in a different way.

Even though she could only hear one side of the conversation earlier she'd learned that Roy's nephew Noah was working outside the village that day. She also paid close attention to her husband's small talk, knowing that he had a deeper purpose for his questions. John wasn't one to talk just for the sake of talking, and it was clear he was trying to find out as much as he could about Noah Yoder and the teenage boys who worked with him.

By the time John hung up Anna could tell he was satisfied, but that made her feel only slightly better. She'd tossed and turned all night, worried about so many things. If Lovina dedicated her life to this pie shop, she'd never settle down and get married. And what type of example would that be for her younger sisters? And what if Lovina did set it up and then realized it was too much work, or she wanted to get married instead? What would that do for their investment?

Anna sighed heavily and wished she could visit Regina. Life seemed easier when her best friend was just down the road. Maybe because she didn't have to carry her burdens all on her own.

One consolation was that the purchase of the building wasn't done yet. No official offer had been made to the seller. No papers had been signed. They hadn't gone so far that they couldn't back down.

Her other consolation was that Lovina was on a date with Thomas Chupp at this very moment. Would it be wrong to pray that a spark of romance would start today and that Lovina would come home having second thoughts about the pie shop?

Anna said a short, silent prayer for that very thing and then opened her box of stationary. Even if she couldn't chat with Regina over coffee, Anna knew she could pour out her heart to her friend. Regina knew her better than anyone. Regina would listen to the heart behind her words and not judge. Anna needed someone who could carry this burden with her, even if her friend was so far away.

Dear, dear Regina,

I promised myself when I sat down to write this letter that I wasn't going to allow myself to ask if you've heard any news of a vacation. I wasn't going to ask if you were coming down our way anytime soon. I was instead going to tell you about the weather and the visitors who've come to town first, but then I remembered that it was you I was writing to and you'd expect nothing less from me.

Please, dear friend, let me know as soon as you are able if you'll be visiting Pinecraft for the season. I'm praying Abe will be excited about the idea. I want nothing more than to see your smiling face. I always look forward to letters from you, but far better is talking face-to-face.

Fall should be on the way, but you'd never know it from the weather. It's just hot here. Hot and humid. But by the time the first Pioneer Trails bus drives into town the weather will be perfect. I'm counting down the days until we don't have to turn the air conditioning on first thing in the morning. And I'm counting down the days until I see old friends climbing down off the bus.

This afternoon there was a notice on our door stating that the Offender Work Program is coming up to clean up the park. I'm glad I don't live as close to the park as some. I never liked the idea of becoming too friendly or too trusting with those who've had run-ins with the law. You know John. He's always been quick to forgive and forget. But you just can't be too cautious, I'm thinking.

Last night when John and I were walking by Phillippi Creek there were two men launching an airboat. I chuckled to myself, trying to picture such a thing back in Walnut Creek. A boat like that is sure to stir up the gators. (I suppose you won't find them in Walnut Creek either.)

Thank you for asking about John. He seems to be doing better. For so long he's been so weak—hardly able to catch a breath—but the weather here is helping. We went on two walks yesterday and he's been dreaming again. That's always a good sign.

I'm still discouraged by the lack of young men. I fear the health we've provided for John will cost the girls greatly. I suppose the Lord knows the ways that are best. I'm trying to trust Him, but at times I fear my daughters are becoming too independent and too focused on things beyond caring for a home.

My only happy news concerning young men is a recent occurrence. As I write this my Lovina is at the beach with Thomas Chupp from Somerset, Pennsylvania. His Aunt Vera is a neighbor of ours down the road a bit. Yesterday Lovina took over some banana sour cream bread, and she must have made some impression because not an hour later he was at our house trying to find her, seeking out a date. I've yet to see him, but both Grace and Faith say he is quite handsome. I hope Lovina feels the same.

If you come we'll have to go to the beach. Even though it is close I have been only a few times. It seems unnatural to just sit and watch the waves roll in and out when there's always work to be done at home or a neighbor to tend to. I suppose it's easier for the younger ones to let themselves relax and such. Our generation was never raised that way.

Not that I have to worry much about my girls being idle. Each seems caught up in her own pursuits. Lovina has it on her mind that *she wants to open a pie shop. I don't think she really knows how much work that will be. It's different from baking pies in one's own kitchen. Doesn't the Bible talk about counting the cost before you start a project? I want to remind Lovina about that.*

There is a young man who's stepped up to help her, but I'm hoping his true colors come out before things get too far. I don't want to see my daughter taken advantage of. I just keep thinking on what my mother always used to say: "Patience is a virtue that carries a lot of wait." I'm trusting that if I wait all will be revealed. One can't put on a show for too long, can they?

But even more important is another saying that Mem would often repeat. "A happy memory never wears out." Even though many miles separate us there are many happy memories that I can replay during moments of loneliness. Hope you're able to do the same... when you're not entertaining family! Days like today, with Lovina finally on a date, I can once again hope that more family members will be my future too.

Your dearest friend,
Anna

⁓

Lovina rode her bike slowly past Roy Yoder's house. She'd spent most of the day at the beach with Thomas, and then the driver he'd hired had taken her home. Mem had greeted them at the front gate, and she'd invited Thomas to stay for dinner. Regrettably he'd declined, saying he'd promised his Mem he'd take her to Der Dutchman. Mem must have been planning to invite him for she'd cooked up a large meal—much more than they typically ate for supper on weekdays.

Lovina ate as quickly as she could, helped clean the kitchen, and then headed out on her bicycle. No one questioned where she was going. Everyone knew that the only thing she had on her mind was the warehouse. Everyone except Mem, who neatly turned every thread of conversation back to the Chupp family and what a beautiful place Pennsylvania was.

Yet when Lovina left Dat had given her a knowing look and a message for Noah. One she was all too happy to deliver.

Even though it was nearly seven o'clock in the evening the sun was still high in the sky. Lovina parked her bicycle by the front gate and was preparing to knock on the front door when she heard voices around the back. She walked around the side of the house, noticing how meticulously Roy Yoder tended his flowers. In the back she saw Noah and the teens. It looked as if they'd just finished grilling hot dogs, and the whole back yard smelled like a campfire. The most interesting feature, though, was the large counter that nearly filled the backyard space.

It looked as if it was an antique piece, maybe from a nice, older home. It was just the sort of thing she'd want for her shop. Lovina paused and sucked in a breath. Had he...found that for her? She froze in her spot, not knowing what to say or do. It was Mose who saw her first, and he chuckled.

"Well, Noah, remember your idea for surprising Lovina with her new counter? You can throw that idea out the door."

Noah looked up, his gaze met hers. He had a hot dog in a bun in one hand and a bit of ketchup was tucked in the corner of his lip. He smiled and then quickly wiped at it.

He put the hot dog back on his paper plate and set it on the overturned milk crate he was using for a table. Yet the whole time his eyes stayed fixed on hers as if truly seeing her for the first time.

"Did someone say *surprise*?" she managed to say.

He stood and walked toward her. "You came too soon."

Lovina pointed her thumb over her shoulder, pointing out the way she'd just come. "I can leave if you need me to. I mean if you don't want to hear the big news..." She pretended to turn as if she was going to leave.

"No! Wait." He took a step toward her. "I do want to know. I do want you to stay. I was just hoping I'd have my surprise cleaned up first."

Lovina pointed to the long countertop. "Is that for me? Is that what I think it is?"

Noah nodded. He approached and lifted his hands in front of her, making a forward and backward L with his hands, as if framing a shot for her. "Can you picture this counter with four bakers lined up behind it as you enter the pie shop? They call out their greetings as you enter, and you stand mesmerized as you watch them so effortlessly rolling out the pie crusts and fluting the edges."

Emotion swelled in Lovina, and she blinked back tears.

Noah paused and the sparkle in his eyes faded. "Unless." He gulped. "Unless you've come to tell me your dad said no."

She covered her mouth with her hands, and her shoulders trembled as she tried to hold in her tears. Mose, Gerald, and Atlee looked at each other and then at Noah. Worry was clear on their faces.

Lovina lowered her hand. "No, that's not it. That's not why I'm crying. He actually said yes." More tears came and she wished she could hold them in. She took a step closer to the counter.

Gerald scratched his head, causing his dark hair to stick up even more. "Well, if he said yes why are you crying?"

"I'm crying because I've been dreaming about this for so long."

"So it's a yes?" Noah asked, wanting to make sure he'd heard her right.

She nodded.

"A yes that you can buy the property, or a yes with us helping with the remodel?"

Lovina nodded again and then mouthed the word. "Both."

Noah jumped and punched his fist in the air. "Yes!" He looked to the teens, who were still busy eating their dinner. They'd moved past their hot dogs and were now digging into chocolate whoopie pies—probably ones they'd picked up from Yoder's.

Noah crossed his arms over his chest. "Boys, it looks like we have the job."

"*The* job?" Atlee asked.

"Yes, the perfect job for us…right out our back door."

Lovina brushed at her tears and then discretely wiped her moist hands on her skirt. Taking a deep breath, she stepped forward. She pictured the counter covered with flour and rolling pins. She ran her hand down its surface and then turned to Noah. She patted her temple. "Everything—all my dreams—have been up here for so long. And now I feel like I'm seeing them come to life."

"And it's just a start, Lovina." His gaze followed the paved driveway that ran along the side of his uncle Roy's fence, following it to the parking lot and then to the warehouse beyond. "I have so many more ideas. I can't wait to get started."

She continued to run her hand down the counter, noticing the nicks and worn spots.

"It's a perfect counter. Just looking at it I can picture meals cooked. I can see the worn spots where crusts have been rolled out." Her hand paused on one spot where the Formica was no longer cream but white. "Wherever did you find it?"

"We were pulling some stuff from an old house that was going to be remodeled. I saw this, and I knew it was for you."

She dared to look up into his face, knowing she'd have a hard time not feeling her heart cinching one notch closer to his. Lovina had spent the day on a beautiful beach with a handsome bachelor. Thomas had said all the right things and had done all the right things, and yet there had been nothing truly memorable about their time together. Yet standing here with Noah, with her hands on this old, worn countertop and the smell of hot dogs in the air, Lovina's heart swelled. This was the most romantic moment of her life.

Noah knew her. Noah believed in her dream. And he not only believed…he was backing her up. Lovina looked at the warehouse again, picturing it open and ready for business. Not only because she believed it could happen, but because the man working alongside her would make certain of it.

Chocolate Whoopie Pies

Pies

1½ cups shortening

3 cups sugar

3 egg yolks, beaten

3 teaspoons vanilla

1½ cups buttermilk (or sour milk)

3 teaspoons baking soda

2 teaspoons salt

1½ cups hot water

1½ cups unsweetened cocoa powder

6 cups flour

Filling

1½ cups shortening (not butter flavored)

5 tablespoons milk

3 cups powdered sugar

1 tablespoon vanilla

3 egg whites, beaten stiff

For pies, preheat oven to 350°. Cream together shortening and sugar. Add egg yolks and vanilla. Stir in buttermilk. Add baking soda, salt, hot water, cocoa, and flour. Beat well. Drop by tablespoons onto greased cookie sheet and bake 12 minutes.

For filling, cream shortening and milk. Add powdered sugar and vanilla; mix well. Beat in egg whites until filling is fluffy.

To assemble pies, spread a heaping spoonful of filling on flat side of half of the cookies. Top with remaining cookies. Makes approximately 40 whoopie pies.

Fifteen

If at first you succeed, try not to look astonished.

AMISH PROVERB

⁓

When Jason Schlabach had told Lovina that things could move quickly with the purchase of the warehouse, she hadn't quite understood what he'd meant. It had been less than two weeks since she'd first seen the warehouse. It had been only a week and a half since they'd made their first offer. And now Jason held the escrow papers in his hand.

Lovina had been up early and dressed. She'd read her Bible and had cleaned the kitchen. When she still had time before their meeting, she decided to walk to the bank instead of riding her bike.

At the park she'd taken in the sight of Mrs. Beiler sitting on an overturned five-gallon bucket, fishing. At the school, she'd paused and watched the children practicing for a Columbus Day program, performing on the lawn. She walked with slow steps past the bookstore and then across Kaufman Avenue to the bank.

She wasn't surprised to see Noah standing and waiting there, with her dat by his side. And even though it was expected, the sight of Noah made her heart flutter. Ever since Dat and Noah had met to discuss the warehouse and go over more details of the plan, the two men had become constant companions. Noah had come to the house, mostly because Dat hadn't been feeling well. Her sisters enjoyed talking to him, and were always offering him whatever they were cooking up. But Mem was a different story.

Mem hardly said anything worthwhile to Noah—mostly just small talk. When he showed up she usually made an excuse to visit one of their neighbors. Lovina tried to pretend it didn't bother her, but it had. For Mem not only ignored Noah, but she also refused to discuss anything about the pie shop. It was almost as if Mem believed that if they didn't talk about it, it wouldn't happen.

And while Lovina enjoyed having Noah over so often, she rarely got any of his attention. She knew that Dat and Noah mostly discussed construction, but there were many days she felt left out. Was Noah becoming the son Dat had never had? She liked the thought of that, but what would happen after the pie shop was open? Would Noah stick around—if not for her, then for Dat?

She reached the bank door and Noah opened it for her. She walked in and the two men followed.

Jason was waiting in the lobby. "Lovina, gentlemen. I have everything ready on my desk."

Lovina settled into one of the chairs across from Jason and her dat sat in the other.

"Should I leave while you sign your paperwork?" Noah asked. He glanced between her and her father, as if suddenly worried he'd overstepped his bounds.

Dat stroked his beard. "Not at all, son. If it wasn't for you we wouldn't be able to do this at all." Dat turned to Jason. "Do you think we can get a chair for my friend?"

"We already have one coming." Jason stepped aside as another man brought in a chair for Noah.

"Okay, friends." Jason sat. "I have three stacks of paperwork. One for each of you." Jason turned to her. "If you don't mind, Lovina, I'll do Noah and your dat's paperwork first, because it's less complicated than yours."

"Noah's paperwork? Dat's?" her brow furrowed. "I don't understand." She looked from Jason to her father. And then back to Jason again. "Last time we talked the sale was going to be in my name. Dat simply was going to provide the funding and…" She let her voice trail off. She didn't even know what to say about Noah.

Dat looked at her. "I've been thinking about it, and that's a great burden of responsibility for you to carry. I've decided to change things." Dat cleared this throat. "The amount for the building will be covered, but I'm going to give you money for the remodel too. Noah is going to be a signer on that portion of the paperwork, so he can have access to the money and buy supplies as needed. For example, we'll need to make sure the kitchen is up to code…and I don't want you to have to worry about that."

Lovina's mouth dropped open, and tears filled her eyes. "Dat, no. I can't accept all that."

He placed his hand on hers, halting her words. "You can, because it's my choice what to do with my money. Mem and I still have enough to live on. I wouldn't do anything that would hinder that. Besides, it'll make things easier for Noah. He won't have to bother you for every little thing he needs to buy. That'll leave you time to focus on the baking part, and in hiring the right help. There is a lot of setup that needs to be done, a lot of figuring to make your dreams come to life. I want you to focus on that."

Thankfulness flowed from her heart, and she wondered what

she'd ever done to deserve it. She didn't feel worthy to receive such a gift, and for a moment she felt like insisting that her father not be so generous. But then, as she looked into his eyes, a peace settled in her heart. He was doing this—giving so much—because he loved her. Dat was offering it not because she'd been good or she'd worked to deserve it. Instead, simply because she was his child. Tears rimmed the corners of her eyes at that thought.

She nodded, wiping her eyes, and then she glanced at Noah. He had a worried look on his face, as if concerned that she was angry that she wasn't going to be in control of every aspect. She offered a slight smile, hoping to ease his worries.

They signed a few papers, and then Lovina listened as Jason explained. "In addition to the financial papers there is also liability paperwork." Jason passed a paper across the desk to Dat. "John, by signing this you're saying that you understand there is no insurance if anything happens to the property during construction or after. Even though we are a Mennonite bank, the state requires liability insurance for all bank loans."

Dat scanned the paperwork as Jason continued.

"These papers state that you alone will cover all the cost if there is any type of damage, injury, or problems during the construction and renovation."

Lovina's gut tightened as she heard those words.

"Dat?" She searched his eyes again, understanding the cost.

He smiled at her. "Lovina. All you have to say is thank you. And you have to sign these papers too. It's not that it's costing you nothing. All your money will be invested in this. Two years' worth of income from teaching school, and everything else you've managed to save up from pie sales here and there."

"I know, Dat. I know what I'm giving, but I'm...well, I'm

overwhelmed by what you're giving too." Lovina's fingers folded together. "And…does Mem know?"

"Your mem has never asked about finances. She has always trusted my judgment. I'm not hiding anything from her, but I feel no need to explain everything either. I told her I will make sure you're taken care of, and she was grateful for that."

Lovina nodded, but she didn't know if *grateful* was the right word. Mem seemed out of sorts lately. This pie shop wasn't Mem's dream for her, she knew.

Jason continued to explain the papers set in front of them, and with each stroke of her father's pen a heavy sensation came over Lovina. Yes, there was joy and excitement that her dream would soon be coming true, but there was a heavy burden too. She had to make this work now. There was no choice. All the money she'd saved was at stake, yes, but now her dream would forever affect her parents too.

When Jason moved to Noah's paperwork, the tears were hard to hold back. He was giving so much with no guarantee he'd make any money at all. What if the items in the warehouse weren't worth as much as he thought? They'd be working for so little. Noah too was giving to her at great cost to himself.

Lovina's fingers trembled on her lip, and she wiped away a tear. She knew how Noah cared for those boys, and they were dependent on her now as well.

As she sat there it was as if the weight of everything hit. The community, her neighbors, and her future employees. Why, they'd all be looking at her, counting on her.

It took everything in Lovina not to stand and bolt out the door. She even thought about Thomas Chupp's mention of a schoolteacher position that would be opening up. He'd made his intentions toward her clear. Would it be too bad to let her heart journey that direction? She could follow him back to Pennsylvania. She could teach school and spend more time with him. She could get to know those in the community. She could start over with a new life—a life that was expected of every Amish woman. And she was sure he'd be a fine husband. Just like her dat had always been. Wasn't that *gut* enough?

Lovina had almost convinced herself to go down the path to Pennsylvania—and Thomas—when Jason turned his attention to her. "All right, Lovina. Your turn to sign."

She opened her mouth to tell him she couldn't do it. There was too much at stake. She was too worried to hurt those she cared for.

Then she saw Noah from the corner of her eye. He was handing her the pen. She reached for it and noticed something in his eyes. Trust...and protection. He was going to stand by her. Noah Yoder wasn't going to make her do this alone. Seeing the care in his gaze reminded her that God wasn't going to leave her alone either. Hadn't He first placed this dream on her heart?

"Come, daughter. You can sign the papers quicker than that. My stomach is telling me it's lunchtime." Dat sniffed the air. "I know I must be imagining it, but I am certain I can smell Yoder's chicken stuffing casserole and fried chicken from here."

She took the pen and turned to Jason. "Okay." She breathed out slowly. "Okay."

She'd carried the dream for so long, and now she had these men who would help her to see it through.

She sniffed the air too, but she didn't smell chicken casserole. Instead, Lovina smelled the scent of rain from the open window. And something else too...the beautiful aroma of God's goodness. And of good things to come.

Yoder's Restaurant Chicken Stuffing Casserole

1 large potato, cubed
2 carrots, diced
8 ounces crumbled cornbread
½ cup butter, melted
3 cups cooked chicken
1 can cream of celery soup
1 cup chicken broth

Preheat oven to 350°. Simmer potatoes and carrots in salted water until nearly done. In medium bowl, toss cornbread and butter. Spread half in a buttered 13x9-inch pan. Top with chicken. Combine soup, broth, and vegetables and spread evenly over chicken. Add remaining cornbread on top. Bake uncovered 45-60 minutes.

Sixteen

Children are living messages we send
to a world we will not see.

AMISH PROVERB

～⑤

After enjoying lunch at Yoder's, Lovina was eager to get to the warehouse. She'd been in it only one other time with Jason, but Dat hadn't seen the inside. Noah, too, hadn't been inside since that first day when he'd walked in and offered his services.

Lovina held her breath as they walked up to the building. But the closer they got the more her dat's steps slowed. She looked at the warehouse from Dat's eyes, and Lovina's heart fell.

The sun was bright overhead, spotlighting the building. The two times she'd been inside the soft light from the early morning and the mist of rain had hidden some of the building's shortfalls.

The large gray structure had a metal roof, but the siding needed a coat of paint. Peeling paint around the window frames gave it a shaggy appearance.

Jason waited by the door with the key. He had chosen to eat lunch at home with his family. He approached Dat with a smile and shook his hand. Dat greeted him, but he didn't make small talk. Instead, he pointed to the door. "Go ahead and open it up. I'd like to take a look inside."

Jason swung open the door, stepping inside. The odors of oil and dust greeted Lovina as she entered.

Once she got inside Jason held the key out to her. "This is yours now, Lovina."

Dat walked ahead of all of them. He eyed the ceiling. He looked at the walls. He didn't seem as interested in all the stuff that filled the warehouse.

Lovina took a few steps to follow him. Jason reached out and touched her arm. Lovina stopped, understanding. Dat had just invested a lot of money in this place, and she needed to give him time to sort his thoughts.

Then Jason turned to Noah. "Was this some type of a shop before?"

Lovina crossed her arms over her chest, wishing she could read Dat's thoughts. Worried he felt he'd made a mistake investing so heavily in her. Doubts wiggled in to her mind too. What if they couldn't get this place fixed up like she thought? What if they didn't get the response from the community that she thought they would?

"Ja. It did used to be an old shop. I asked my uncle about this place," Noah said. "The man who owns it—*used to* own it—worked on automobiles, but business wasn't good." Noah chuckled. "I wonder why, though? Maybe it wasn't that wise setting up an auto shop on the edge of an Amish village."

Noah looped his thumbs through his suspenders. "Then he was going to turn it into a theater. He put in those big windows where the automotive entrance door use to be. He got the idea for a theater after seeing the Blue Gate up in Shipshewana. He bought out the contents of an old theater a few years ago and then moved those things here. My uncle says that owner must have passed away because the man who sold it to Lovina was his younger brother."

Those words brought a heaviness that Lovina hadn't expected. "It's sad. The former owner must have had so many dreams and plans…" Seeing the changes in Dat's health had made her realize that life was fragile, and you could work your whole life for something just to have it slip away—just as he'd seen with his farm. It had made her think long and hard about what she wanted to invest herself in.

Like her grandma had always said, what you spend your days doing is what you spend your life doing. Her grandpa also told her that if people really understood that they were writing their own autobiography, maybe they'd think a little harder about the chapters they put in.

Suddenly the weight of her decision bore down on her. Lovina placed a hand over her heart, feeling the ache. From what the doctor had said, Dat was in his last chapter. In good weather and with a lot of rest, he could still have a few years with them, and they all hoped that would be the case. But by investing so much in her pie shop, Dat was in a way choosing how his story continued. And he was doing it by believing in her.

Her eyes grew moist again as she watched him walk through the warehouse with careful steps. With the signing of the papers today it was as if he was choosing her to finish *his* story. It was no longer the story of a simple Amish girl who lived with her parents, spent time with her sisters, served those in her church, and baked, but rather a business owner who had dreams of shaping the community she was a part of in an important way.

Dat returned from his examination of the place, walking up to her side. He gave a low whistle and looked around. "Lovina, do you really think you can get this open by season? That's less than three months away. It seems like it'll take that much time just to clear out all this stuff."

Noah approached, placing a reassuring hand on Dat's shoulder. "Leave that up to me, sir. I have some items in my mind for Sarasota Salvage. And there are other items that can be repurposed. And because we won't need this whole space, the first thing my guys are going to do is build a wall between the kitchen and the back area. That will be our storage area for now."

Dat nodded. "I know you'll take care of it, Noah." He walked over to a dusty cabinet and leaned against it. He looked tired and overwhelmed. One of his legs trembled, and Lovina found a chair and brought it to him. Dat sat heavily as if unable to hold up his weight any longer.

The emotions of the day continued to build upon her. Worries of Dat's health mixed with excitement over her new property and the burden of responsibility about this place. "I'm going to see if Larry has his solar-powered buggy going. See if he can give you a ride home." She resisted the urge to brush the hair back from his forehead.

"I'm sure I can make it home. It'll just take me a while." He stood, but he still wasn't steady.

"No." She squeezed his arm. "You've done too much already today. You've been pushing yourself."

Noah hurried over. "John, let me help you." He took her dat's arm, and Lovina made a motion as if to follow.

Dat shook his head. "Lovina, you stay here. Look around. You have a lot of plans to make without having to worry about me."

She stayed rooted in place as she watched Noah lead Dat out. When the door closed Lovina looked around, wondering what in the world she'd gotten herself into. She had no idea where to even start.

Jason must have seen the panic of her face, for he approached. "Don't let yourself get so caught up in your worries, Lovina, that you miss the joy in this process."

"Excuse me?"

Jason continued to look at the door where Dat just exited. Then, with a heavy sigh, he turned to her. "Well, the way I see it, hope is what got you into this mess." He chuckled and winked. "And I mean mess literally." Then he placed his hand on the back of the chair where her dat had just been sitting. "And I have no doubt you're going to see this place turned into a pie shop. But you have two ways to do it. You can do it with the same joy that was on your face when you first saw this place. Or you can do it with fear and dread."

She nodded, understanding what he was saying. "And what if I can't do it?" She looked down at her feet and the dust that now clung to her tennis shoes.

"You have to succeed. Your dat's counting on you." Jason stroked his chin. "It reminds me of something my own mem used to say. 'Children are living messages we send to a world we will not see.'"

She lifted her eyebrows. "Well, no pressure or anything."

"Don't see it as pressure, Lovina. Whether your dat's time on earth is one year or twenty more, his message will go on through you and your sisters. The way I see it, it's already one of hope—otherwise we wouldn't be standing here. So just continue on in the messages he's been writing from the day you were born. It'll be the most natural thing for you to do."

Lovina nodded, crossed her arms, and looked around. She forced herself to think back to that first day she'd seen this place a few weeks ago. That morning she'd felt eagerness in a way that she couldn't explain. As she set out on her bicycle she could tell God had something for her. That morning she felt so certain that God's Spirit had been guiding her. And if that was the case, then Jason was right. She just had to keep stepping forward.

As if sensing she needed time to think things through alone, Jason walked toward the door. "I'm going to head back to the bank. My oldest daughter had some grape jelly bars cooling and she promised to bring some by work when they cool."

"Sounds delicious," Lovina said with a smile, remembering being a little girl and baking for her dat. Remembering how excited he'd been about her attempts, no matter how well they turned out. Even the time she'd accidentally added three table-spoons of baking soda instead of a teaspoon. Dat had eaten a whole piece of cake before she realized her error. "I think I'll make some for my dat tonight too. I bet he'd like that."

Jason cast her a small wave and then left the building. And as she stood there alone, looking around at all the work they had to do before her dream was even close to becoming realized, some-thing else her grandma used to say came to mind.

After beginning by the means of the Spirit, are you now trying to finish by means of the flesh?

Lovina was sure it was from somewhere in the Bible, and she didn't need to know where for the truth of its message to sink deep. If she trusted that God had led her here that first day, she had to trust He was with her still. God had led her to this big, dirty warehouse for a reason. Maybe it was like Jason said: This was how Dat's message of caring for others would continue.

She swallowed hard, accepting the weight of responsibility, and then she squared her shoulders. She fingered the key in her hand. God had brought her too far to leave her now. And if He brought her here, He'd no doubt see her through.

And then she smiled, realizing God didn't expect her to do it alone. He'd brought her Noah. And even if their growing friendship was for this project alone, she was thankful that out of all the people in Pinecraft, God had brought him.

Grape Jelly Bars

2 cups quick oats
2½ cups flour
1 cup oil
1 egg, beaten
1 teaspoon vanilla
1½ cups sugar
½ cup brown sugar
½ teaspoon salt
1 teaspoon baking powder
2 cups grape jelly

Preheat oven to 350°. Mix all ingredients except jelly and press half of mixture into a 13x9-inch pan. Spread jelly on top and top with rest of crumbs. Bake 30 minutes. Makes 18 bars.

Seventeen

The best things in life are not things.

AMISH PROVERB

❦

Three young men trailed after Noah as he entered the warehouse early Monday morning. Noah wasn't surprised to see that Lovina was already waiting for him, even though it was barely seven o'clock. Her eyes were wide and bright with expectation.

"Lovina, you're here bright and early. Please tell me you got some rest last night. We have a lot of work ahead and you'll need your energy."

Her eyes sparkled, and if she'd missed even a few minutes of beauty sleep it wasn't evident. Her dark hair was brushed neatly under her kapp. Her dress today was light blue, and it brought color to the drab space. At least it was drab for now. Noah put his hands on his hips and looked around. Over the next few days a lot of those big items would be gone, and the windows would be replaced, starting today.

On cue, Noah heard the rumbling outside and he walked to the door. Lovina's footsteps followed. A large truck pulled up with huge window panels strapped to the side.

Lovina gasped. "Are those windows for here?"

"Ja. This place could use some sunlight, don't you think?"

As Noah strode out to talk to the delivery driver, another truck pulled up. *Sarasota Salvage* was displayed on the side. The owner, Jill, had been excited on Saturday when he'd stopped by and told her about some of the items. They'd worked together enough over the last month that she bought a few of the best items sight unseen, trusting he was giving her a good deal. She'd paid him by check on Friday, and Noah smiled, realizing it had come at a perfect time. He'd made it to the bank in time to cash it, pay his Uncle Roy's rent, and stock the fridge and cupboards. The guys had eaten well all weekend, and he'd even given each of them some spending money. He hoped that initial investment would motivate them for the work to come, but now he was starting to worry. Maybe he should have waited until they had one good day under their belts to receive any sort of reward.

As Noah walked toward the truck he eyed his uncle's house, hoping Mose, Gerald, and Atlee weren't going to blow this. They'd talked about the plan last night. Even this morning he'd reminded them of what they needed to do.

The driver from the window company jumped from his truck, shaking Noah's hand.

Noah was about to excuse himself to go rouse out the guys when the back door opened and they walked out. They were wearing their Amish clothes, and Mose held a clipboard in his hand. As Noah watched, Mose approached the Salvage truck and shook the driver's hand. Noah couldn't hear their conversation, but he guessed by their smiles that it was going well.

Noah turned back to the window guy, eager to get started. "Thank you for bringing these out. I appreciate it."

They walked to the side of the truck. Noah couldn't wait until the windows were put in. It would take the four of them all day, he guessed.

"Listen, do you have any plans for those old windows?" the driver asked.

Noah shrugged. "I have a construction dumpster coming later today. I was just going to throw them in."

"I'm headed to the recycler after this. I can stay to help you remove them and then haul them off if you'd like."

"I'd like that, but I don't have any extra money—"

The man held up his hand. "You don't need to pay me. I hear you're turning this place into a pie shop. I'd be happy for a few pies when it's open. My mom passed away a few years ago, and I've missed her homemade pies."

"What was your favorite?" Lovina's voice called from behind Noah, and she approached with a large smile. The man got a wistful look on his face. "I loved her coconut cream. It was high and fluffy, but not too sweet."

She pulled out her notebook and flipped to the back. "Ten coconut cream pies for…what is your name?"

"Mike. Mike Jefferson. But I really don't need ten pies."

Lovina chuckled. "Don't worry. You don't have to eat them all at once. You can come for one pie at a time. Or by the slice."

"That's really nice of you. Unexpected."

"And your staying around is nice and unexpected too." She reached out her hand. "I'm Lovina. Lovina Miller. Welcome to Me, Myself, and Pie!"

Mike chuckled. "That's a cute name for a business. Our window warehouse is just a few miles up the road. I'll have to tell the guys about this place once it opens."

"Thank you. I'd appreciate that."

From that moment the morning never slowed. Gerald, Mose,

and Atlee helped load up the items, and Sarasota Salvage made an appointment for the next day to come pick up more items. The windows were removed and a flood of light flowed in.

Noah's eyes warmed when he watched Lovina standing in the open window. Her arms were crossed over her chest, and she wore a satisfied smile on her lips. He followed her gaze to the parking lot of the Tourist Church. Was she picturing the buses arriving, and the groups of Amish and Mennonites spilling out and eyeing the shop? Noah guessed she was.

She spent most of the morning cleaning—sweeping, collecting garbage, and using a long duster to rid the corners of cobwebs. After they'd been there a few hours two of Lovina's sisters showed up. Lovina introduced him to Hope and Grace. Both of them had light hair and rounder faces. Both displayed their excitement with squeals and gasps as they looked around the place.

They stopped beside a pile of framed movie posters. Hope hunkered down, squatting in front of the posters to get a better look. "I can't wait for Faith to get off work at Yoder's. She's going to go crazy about this artwork." Hope was taller than Lovina, and she had a no-nonsense air about her. While Lovina seemed to be the type of person who would love to gather people in a group and feed them and listen to their stories, Hope seemed like someone who'd roll up her sleeves and get to work in the garden or out in the barn. Even though she wore flip-flops Noah could easily picture her in heavy work boots tromping around a large pasture or garden.

"Yes, the posters are nice. My friends at Sarasota Salvage are going to love them too," Noah said. "Which reminds me." He turned to Lovina. "I need you to go through this place and pick out anything you think will work for the shop, or anything you want to keep."

"Oh no. All these items are yours." Lovina peered up at him, her eyes growing serious. "We made an agreement. You would do all the remodeling work in exchange for the items in this warehouse."

There was a smudge of dirt on her cheek, and Noah wanted nothing more than to reach down and wipe it with his thumb. Did she realize how beautiful she was? Didn't she understand that her passion about this place was one of the reasons that made her so?

His chest warmed with attraction for her, and he cleared his throat, trying to keep it at bay. "I told you I'd do it in exchange for items in this warehouse. I didn't mean every item. There are some things that I think will be wonderful in the pie shop."

"Oh, like what?" Grace asked. She was the youngest of the sisters, and her joyful exuberance was hard to miss.

Noah motioned for them to follow, and he took them to one corner that held all different types of chairs. There were a number of items that he knew could work for the pie shop, but there was one that stood out from the rest. He pointed to the small bench that was part seat and part drawers.

Grace brushed it off with a rag in her hand. "What is this?"

Noah chuckled. "I'm not surprised you haven't seen one of these before. It's an old telephone seat. Probably from the 1960s. Back then the phones had cords—not like our cellphones—and people used this to sit on while they talked. It was also a way to display their phones."

Hope peered at him curiously. "And this is something we can use for the pie shop?"

"Ja." He pointed to the front door. "I thought it would be good for the waiting area."

"Waiting area? Will we really need that?" Lovina asked.

He smiled at her. "Where is that faith you are known for, Lovina? When there is a crowd waiting for a table or to pick up a to-go pie, they'll need someplace to sit."

She glanced from the telephone bench then to the door, and then to the bench again. She kneeled before it. "Oh, and we can put menus in these drawers. People can read the descriptions of the pies while they wait."

He smiled and snapped his fingers. "Now you're talking."

Then he turned to her sisters. "Would you two be able to go through these chairs and things and see what grouping you think might work?"

Both of them nodded excitedly.

"Can we take some of them up there and move things around, seeing what looks good?" Grace asked. "Maybe I'll even take some photos on my phone and upload them to our Facebook page."

Noah's jaw dropped. "Facebook page?" He hadn't been on Facebook before himself, but Jill from Sarasota Salvage had shown him some of the things he'd found for her displayed on her page.

"Well, Lovina may bake the best pies you've ever tasted…" Grace tapped the side of her head. "But I have some business sense that I think will help her. Social media is a wonderful way to get people to find out about you. I'm working on a logo now, and Joy is working on some aprons—" Grace paused and her eyes widened. She bit her lip and looked to Lovina. "I…I wasn't supposed to say anything."

A smile filled Lovina's face, and she shrugged. "What? I have no idea what you're talking about." She winked at her sister. Then her gaze turned to Noah, and he was once again swept up in the dark brown of her eyes.

"So is it all right?" she asked. "If they move those things up there?"

"Ja, but just so you know they won't be able to stay there. Over the next week we're going to put up a wall, splitting this large area in two. This half we're on will be a bakery, and the back half will be storage for now. The kitchen will go up in the middle…" He pointed to the area, showing them where that would be. "And then we're going to clear everything out of this side. Most of the big stuff will be gone, and we'll store what's left in the storage area. I want to be smart about going through these things. I want to do some research about the value of some of these items."

"You seem to know a lot about old stuff," Grace commented, looking intrigued. She wrinkled her nose. "How old are you?"

He laughed. "I'm twenty-seven, but I grew up around all types of vintage items, or 'old stuff' as you say. My dat has an auction yard up in Illinois. Dat's pretty much seen at least one of everything made since the industrial revolution, or so he likes to tell people. And my father always told me not to rush into any sale. People often lose something valuable in an effort to make a quick buck. Sometimes people don't know what they have until they lose it."

"So what's going to be the first step after everything's cleared out?" Grace asked.

Noah could tell that her mind was already moving ten steps ahead. Maybe she was already thinking about photos she could post on Facebook.

He looked to Lovina, and she seemed interested in the answer too. "See this concrete?" He tapped his foot on the floor. "It's going to be cleaned, sealed, and stained."

"Stained?" Lovina's brow furrowed and he knew she was thinking back to the white and light gray-checkered pattern he'd drawn in the sketch for her.

"Ja. I've done stained concrete before, and I've seen it done a lot in newer homes or remodels. When it's done it'll look like tile, but it'll be cheaper and more durable."

Grace looked to Noah and then to Lovina. She pointed her thumb at him. "Sister, where did you find this guy?"

"God sent him to me," Lovina said simply, and her eyelashes fluttered with her words.

Grace nodded in agreement. "I have no doubt about that. No doubt at all."

The two younger sisters picked up chairs and moved toward the front door. But they only got a few feet before Gerald and Atlee came to the rescue, taking them from the young women and insisting the chairs were too heavy.

Lovina laughed. "I was wondering how long it was going to take before those guys exerted some muscles in order to get my sisters' attention."

"Ja, me too. And it took longer than I thought." Then Noah took a step closer to her, realizing that it was the first time all day when they'd been alone—well, alone if one counted the building filled with over a half a dozen people in various stages of work. He tilted his head, studying her face. "How are you doing? I'm sure this is a lot to take in."

"I'm doing well, but I could hardly sleep last night. Part of me was so excited to get started, but another part of me worries, even when God reminds me again and again that this is all part of His plan."

"I understand. Investing all your money from two years of work is a big risk, but I'm going to do my best to make sure you succeed."

Noah extended his hand to her—palm up, wanting her to place her hand in it. Lovina looked at his hand, and for a second he wished he hadn't been so bold. His hand was the large, rough hand of a laborer. It wasn't pretty to look at, but he wanted her to know they were in this together.

She showed tenderness in her eyes, and her cheeks grew pink. His heartbeat sped up, and he guessed that hers did too.

Still, he waited. Finally she placed her hand in his. It was warm. Soft. Noah blew out a heavy breath. "You have all the right instincts about this place. You shouldn't be afraid, Lovina. I'll do my best…and I'll make sure the guys do too. I believe in your dream. I believe that God placed it inside you."

She bit her lower lip and nodded, and from the look in her eyes he knew she needed to hear those words. He had a feeling she'd need to hear them over and over again as the days went on.

He squeezed her hand, holding it a moment longer, and then something over his shoulder caught Lovina's attention. Lovina's face blanched white, and she quickly pulled her hand away.

Startled, Noah turned slowly, and that's when he saw her. Lovina's mem stood in the doorway, and her eyes were on them. He couldn't see her expression from this far away, but he could tell by her arm-crossed stance that she wasn't happy.

Lovina stepped back. "My mem is here. I—I didn't know she was coming. I'd better go." She took another step back and then looked around at the warehouse, as if suddenly overwhelmed by the poor state of the place.

Noah wondered for a moment if he should follow. If he tried to explain that he was only attempting to encourage Lovina it would probably do no good. To be fully convincing he'd need to tell Anna Miller that his only concerns for her daughter were for this place—to help her remodel the warehouse into a pie shop—but deep down he knew it wasn't true.

Taking a deep breath and sending up a quick prayer for favor from Lovina's parents, Noah turned back to the new windows, knowing he had a lot of work to do to get them into place. It was already a great first step with the old ones out. Everything was brighter now that the light was able to come through.

He was thankful that Lovina couldn't look into his heart as easily. Or her mem. Because with each day that passed Noah knew he was falling in love.

Eighteen

Before we speak we should think twice
or perhaps keep on thinking.

AMISH PROVERB

⁓

Anna Miller slowly made her bed and smoothed the covers, scouring her brain to think of what she could do to get herself out of the house today. John was already up, either drinking a cup of coffee at the kitchen table or poking at Hope's potted plants in the backyard. Maybe he was outside talking with Noah Yoder about the progress on the pie shop. The young man had a habit of stopping by every morning before he headed to the warehouse, taking time to chat with John over the white picket fence up front. Most mornings Lovina would join them, her cheeks as pink as the roses blooming in front of the house.

Anna shook her head. She didn't know what she was going to do with her husband and daughter. When they set their minds on something they set after it with diligence. Then again, it was a trait she saw in all of her daughters. Just as determined as Lovina was about turning that old building into a pie shop, Hope was determined on learning how to make something grow in this southern climate. When in the world did the people in her family get so stubborn?

She could also hear Lovina humming away in the kitchen, and she wondered if her eldest daughter was going to be spending a lot of time home today. That could be a problem. It was easy to excuse herself from helping at the warehouse when Lovina was working there, but how was Anna going to face her daughter in her own kitchen?

Anna finished making the bed, and then she moved toward the small mirror above her dresser to check her kapp. Try as she might, Anna couldn't make herself comfortable with what Lovina was doing. In the weeks she'd been working on the warehouse, Lovina had all but ignored the interest of Thomas Chupp, and instead she took on the doe-eyed look of a young woman falling in love. With Noah Yoder, of all people! How hard it had been for Anna to keep her mouth shut about the whole matter.

If Anna's mother had taught her anything it had been not to say an unkind word. And Anna hadn't. She'd held her tongue, and the only way she'd been able to do that was to keep herself far from Lovina's work at the warehouse.

In the last few weeks she'd visited every sick person she could think of—even those she'd heard were just coming down with a cold. She'd taken part in a sewing frolic with the excuse of getting items ready for the Haiti auction in January. But now…what would she do if Lovina was going to spend the day at home?

Lord, give me patience and help me hold my tongue.

She shuffled out of the bedroom and the aroma of baking pie shells greeted her. Usually it was a welcome aroma, but today it simply caused a knot in the pit of her stomach.

Lovina was humming as she entered. Outside John was indeed chatting with Noah Yoder at the front fence, and Anna forced a smile.

"It's a good day for pie," Anna chirped with a cheerfulness she didn't feel.

Lovina turned to her with a twinkle in her eyes. "Every day is a good day for pie. I hope you don't mind raisin cream pie for breakfast!"

Anna poured herself a cup of coffee. She took a spoon from the drawer, adding in a bit of sugar from the dish on the counter. "Sounds good."

Lovina chuckled. "You don't sound too enthusiastic. I thought raisin cream was your favorite." Then she turned back to her mother, biting her lower lip. "Do you think enough people like raisin cream? Up north it's popular but…" Lovina wiped her hands on her apron and worry flickered on her face. Anna wanted to step forward and comfort her daughter, but something inside held her back. Instead of encouraging her, she needed to be there for Lovina if things didn't work out as her daughter hoped.

Anna smiled to herself. Yes, she liked the idea of being a soft landing after a hard fall.

Lovina let out a sigh, the joy on her face from a moment before replaced with uncertainty. "Well, I suppose I'll put raisin cream pie on the maybe list for now." She turned back to her mixing with less enthusiasm than before.

Then Lovina paused and turned back to a pile of mail on the counter, pointing. "Oh, and there's a letter for you from Regina. It was put in a neighbor's mailbox by mistake. Amish Henry brought it by this morning."

Anna sat at the table with her coffee, stirred it a few times, and then pushed the mug to the side and opened the letter. She released a breath she hadn't realized she'd been holding. If she ever needed encouragement she only needed to look as far as a letter from Regina to find it.

Dear Anna,

Greetings in the name of our Lord Jesus Christ. It's a beautiful day to be alive and to see the wonder of all God's creation around us.

It's getting mighty cold here in Walnut Creek already. Fall's come early, and I can feel it in my bones. I haven't heard if we'll be able to make it down for the season. You know how my husband likes to take his time and think things through. It's a good thing, I suppose. It's saved us in so many ways.

Things are the same in Walnut Creek. There has been a larger number of tourists than ever. It seems as if everything in the stores now has a label that says, "Amish Made." Ten years ago there was nothing special about that, but not true today. I think all those Amish romance novels are getting people's attention and bringing folks up to these parts. I thought about picking one up, but I wouldn't want to become discontent with my Amish life. I imagine those ladies in the books never spend too much time doing laundry by hand or canning boxes of fruit! Just wouldn't be that exciting in the pages of a book.

Our favorite time of the year is coming up with the Coblentz Chocolates Christmas Open House. I've never understood why they start promoting Christmas at the beginning of October, but I don't mind all the taste testing. I'll just miss doing it with you. You're the only one willing to trade your chocolates with nuts for my chocolates with crèmes.

Of course you might not be thinking of chocolates when you no doubt have been up to your eyes in pies. It seems that everywhere I go people stop me and ask what I've heard about the new pie shop going up in Pinecraft. I'd already known about it from your note, of course, but it was exciting to read in The Budget. *There are many here who remember how wonderful Lovina's pies were. Remember the cute little signs she used to place in front of her pies when she was a child? "Made by Love." Does she still go by that nickname, Anna?*

I love getting your letters, and I'm sorry it took me a few weeks to write you back. We had an abundance of produce this year that needed to be canned. It was a blessing indeed but I find myself taking longer than I used to. My hands get all knotted up. I suppose it comes with our age. (You must be chuckling at this because I'm starting to sound like my mother.)

I'll understand if I don't hear from you for a while. I know things will be quite busy in the next month, trying to get things ready for the opening of the pie shop. I can't imagine all the work. I'm sure Lovina is thankful to have you. I've never met someone so good about writing a list of tasks and marking them off one by one in a timely manner.

Marcus and Betty Yoder were visiting family in Walnut Creek yesterday, and they came to church. I had a chance to talk to them at lunch, and they told me some interesting news that I heard from a few others in Pinecraft too. I can't remember the name they told me, there was so much going on that day. Was it Nathan or Nicholas Yoder who is working on the construction of the shop? They say he is an Amish bachelor from Illinois, but I didn't get more out of them than that because we were interrupted.

I became curious, and I wondered why I hadn't heard of this. Anna, there must be a good reason why you didn't tell me such news. This young bachelor must be spending plenty of time with Lovina since they are working on such a large-scale project together. I've never known you to keep secrets from me. The only thing I can think of is that you do not approve of him. It makes me wonder why.

I would love to have an update when you have time. Until then give Lovina a big hug from her Aunt Regina. It takes a lot of bravery to follow one's dreams. And to follow one's heart.

Love, Regina

Anna folded the letter and put it into the envelope. She let out a sigh. What in the world was she going to tell Regina now? What could she say about Noah Yoder that wouldn't be seen as unkind? He was handsome enough, to be sure, but there still was something inside Anna that made her uncomfortable about him. His past, in part. No one would offer such help without an ulterior motive. And from what she'd seen he wasn't only interested in Lovina's pie shop, but also Lovina. Yet had he told Lovina the truth of what he'd done?

She glanced up from her letter. Lovina was once again humming as she mixed the ingredients for her pie. Anna's stomach rumbled, and she had to admit that raisin cream pie didn't sound bad for breakfast at all. It would fill her belly, but as long as Lovina was set on working on this pie shop with Noah Yoder, Anna doubted anything could ease her heart.

Raisin Cream Pie

2 cups raisins
4 cups water
1 cup brown sugar
1 cup sugar
2 tablespoons flour
2 tablespoons cornstarch
4 egg yolks
1 teaspoon salt
2 cups milk
1 teaspoon vanilla
1 baked pie shell
nondairy whipped topping

Combine raisins, water, and brown sugar in a saucepan. Bring to a boil; turn off heat and let soak for a few hours or overnight. Bring back to a boil and add sugar. In a large bowl, mix flour, corn-starch, egg yolks, salt, and milk. Slowly add to raisins to thicken. Add vanilla last. Pour into baked pie shell and top with nondairy whipped topping. Makes 1 10-inch, deep-dish pie.

Nineteen

The foundation of understanding is
the willingness to listen.

AMISH PROVERB

⟨⟩

As the third week of construction dawned, Lovina stepped into the warehouse with a renewed determination. She was certain they'd be able to be open by the time the first Pioneer Trails bus rolled into town at the beginning of November. A lot of the larger furniture pieces had been sold. The wall had gone up between the two sides of the warehouse, and all the smaller items had been moved into that part of the building. There was even a door on that side that made it easy for Noah to remove the items as needed.

More than once people from the community had come to look at the things Noah had back there. Word was getting out that he'd come upon some special pieces. Noah tried not to let that get in the way of his construction work, but Lovina could tell it was what he loved to do best. He loved talking to others about the age of items, their use, and their worth. Grace had started to call Noah their resident historian, but in Lovina's heart she considered him a treasure seeker. He had a knack for finding the worth in broken things. She saw that daily not only in his salvage work, but his work with Mose, Gerald, and Atlee.

In addition to putting up the walls, they'd also given the whole interior a fresh coat of paint. The buttercream was the perfect color, in her opinion.

Then, last Saturday, the guys had come in and stained the concrete. As she walked on it now, Lovina felt as if she was walking on marble tiles. Gone was the grungy look of the concrete. Gone was the smell. She stepped in the middle of the room, lifted her arms like a dancer, and made a slow circle, feeling renewed excitement.

She turned back around, and it was only then that she noticed Noah leaning against the doorframe, watching her. She froze, and then dropped her arms and patted her skirts into place.

"I didn't know you were watching," she said, her eyes lowered.

"I couldn't help myself. It's wonderful to see you appreciating our hard work."

She smiled. "It looks beautiful in here. Everything…"

Noah removed his hat and ran his fingers through his hair. "Why, thank you. I'll take that as a compliment."

He bent down to pick up a bucket that had tipped over. She could see his shoulder muscles through his homemade Amish shirt and heat rose up her neck.

"I think you could do this for a living. Those teens are learning great skills."

Noah chuckled. "They're learning, but…" He let out a heavy sigh.

"But what?" she asked.

"But boys will be boys." He shrugged. "One of them—I still haven't figured out who—managed to rig the concrete sander so the low setting was actually high. You should have seen me when I turned it on. I had a tight hold on it, thankfully, but it dragged me across the room." Noah chuckled. "I bounced off the wall over near the windows, and I only left a small dent." Noah rubbed his shoulder. "Thankfully my body sustained most of the damage."

Lovina stepped toward the window, and sure enough she saw a dent in the wall about two feet from the frame.

"Don't worry." Noah stepped up next to her. "The guys promised to fix that dent today. And touch up the paint."

She could see in his gaze that he didn't take it lightly.

"It's very close to the window." Her fingers touched her neck. "I…I'm so thankful you hit the wall instead of…" She shuddered, unwilling to finish that sentence.

Noah's face grew serious. "I know." He stroked his chin. "Don't worry. I had a serious talk with the guys. They like to do this—play pranks on each other—but I told them this isn't the place to do it. They told me they wouldn't."

Lovina's fingers touched the wood. "No one's been injured by their pranks, have they?"

She thought about sitting in Jason's office, about the bank, and about the liability papers that they'd signed. Lovina swallowed hard. The last thing she needed was for something to happen and her Dat to be responsible for the medical bills…or worse.

Noah didn't answer, and she turned to him. She searched his eyes and she could tell he was trying to figure out how to answer.

"Well, I'll tell you the truth. I know I'd expect the same from you." He sighed. "There have been minor injuries before. Once Mose thought it would be funny to heat up Gerald's wrench with a blowtorch. Can you imagine Gerald's surprise when he picked it up? That one did warrant a trip to the emergency room, but the others have been only minor."

Lovina's gut tightened at his words, and she nibbled on her lower lip as worries and concerns flooded her mind.

Noah reached forward and placed his hand on her arm. "Push away those fretful thoughts, Lovina. I talked to the guys, and I'll talk to them again. There's a time for fun and games, and there's time to be serious. I'll remind them that this job isn't a game."

There was both sternness and compassion in Noah's gaze, and relief flooded over her. Noah walked a tight rope between helping out the teens, making sure they didn't get into too much trouble, and doing a good job on this remodel.

Lovina looked around, amazed at the work that had already been done. She couldn't imagine what the cost would have been had she hired a crew to do the same work. She glanced back at him. "I know you are doing your best, Noah, and I appreciate everything you're doing. I know you'll continue to make sure the guys work hard in a *safe* way." She emphasized the word, and he nodded.

Outside they heard a car pull up, and they walked to the door side by side.

A man stepped out, and he approached them. He looked to Noah. "Are you Noah Yoder?"

"Yes."

The older man with silver hair and tanned skin looked to Lovina and then back to Noah again. "I hope I didn't interrupt your work, but Jill from Sarasota Salvage mentioned you have some old movie posters. She said I might be able to take a peek."

Noah looked to Lovina. "I was actually going to get working on a bathroom. We need to redo—"

"No, it's all right." Lovina held up a hand, interrupting his words. "I'm sure the bathroom will still be there." She pointed to the teens, who were approaching from Uncle Roy's yard. "I was going to use their help for a few minutes anyway. I need them to move some stuff around in the office area, and their muscles can be put to good use."

Noah nodded, and a slight smile touched his lips as he focused on the man. "Ja, I do have some old movie posters. They're framed but the other day I took a few out to study them. They are authentic and when I was searching for their value I discovered there are some real gems there." Noah chuckled. "Now, I'm not one to know much about movies and such, but I've heard that *Gone With the Wind* was a popular flick?"

The man's eyes brightened and the two men walked toward the back of the building. There was a lightness to Noah's step, and seeing that brought joy to Lovina's heart.

"God, only You could create a plan so perfectly to meet the desire of both our hearts," she whispered. "As long as the teens don't mess things up with their pranks." Her smile fell.

Gerald, Mose, and Atlee walked forward, and they must have noticed the concern on her face because their smiles faded. Lovina eyed them as they stood silently before her. She considered lecturing them about messing with the sander and nearly causing an accident. She considered giving them the cold shoulder so they would understand how serious their actions were. But more than anything she knew the Amish way. It was a way of forgiveness. It was a way of reconciliation. And she decided to offer both.

"I know you have to fix the wall," she said simply, "but I was hoping you'd help me move some things around the office first." And then she smiled at them, and relief flooded their faces. She turned and they followed, talking about the breakfast muffins they'd eaten for breakfast.

Lovina looked back over her shoulder as she walked. "Someone brought you muffins?"

"Ja." Atlee nodded excitedly. "It was that older lady from the quilt shop. She came by last night when we were cleaning up garbage around the property."

"She thanked us for doing such *gut* work around the place," Gerald added, brushing his longer hair back out of his eyes. "She said that she'd prayed about this place every time she passed— that God would use it 'for His good work.'" Atlee elbowed Mose. "Isn't that what she said?"

Lovina looked to Mose.

Mose was the shortest of the guys and the quietest. "Ja, that's what she said." He snorted. "She called them Morning Glory Muffins, but all I could think about was those flowers. Thankfully they didn't taste like flowers."

"That's one good reason to stay Amish," Gerald added. "Amish girls do know how to cook."

Lovina laughed at that. "Yes, they do." Although Noah had never explained, she knew that these youth were weighing whether to stay Amish or go the way of the world. And while Lovina knew that being Amish wasn't the only way to heaven—that accepting Jesus was—she hoped for the sake of the teens that they'd find God in the midst of their searching. Whether they continued on with the Amish way of life mattered little in comparison to that.

"I'll have to ask for that recipe," Lovina commented as they walked into the office area. "I always enjoy cooking up something new, especially for Dat."

She paused just inside the door and looked around. The large desk and two file cabinets filled the space. There was a large window there too, and a fan was plugged in.

Lovina fanned her face. "For some reason this room gets very hot. I was talking to the building inspector about it, and he said the air conditioning ducts weren't vented correctly to this area of the building. Instead of spending a lot of money on ducting, he suggested that I put in a window air conditioning unit. It'll buy some time until the pie shop gets up and going, gets profitable."

The teen boys listened respectfully, but she could tell they were mostly just interested in what she needed from them.

"So, what I need for you to do is…" She pointed to the desk. "Put the desk on the wall by the door." Then she pointed to the file cabinets. "And then move those cabinets to the wall with the window. One on either side."

"Got it!" Mose said. Then he smiled at her, and she could tell that he truly was sorry for the dent in the wall.

Lovina left the teens and returned to the large, open area. Her plan was to write up some ads for *The Budget* regarding bakers and other staff positions that would soon be available. She also was going to post an ad on the community bulletin board at the post office in Pinecraft. She'd already had some inquiries from year-round residents, and she'd gotten a few letters from young women who were interested in coming down and working during the season, which was when she'd need extra help.

Remembering that she'd left her notebook in the front basket of her bicycle, Lovina opened the front door and walked directly into a tall man.

"Oh, I'm so sorry." She jumped back. Looking up, she saw that it was Thomas Chupp. "I really shouldn't rush out the door like that."

"It's my fault." He took a step back and then reached a hand to her. "Are you all right?"

"Ja. I'm fine. I…" Lovina's words stopped when she noticed someone right behind Thomas. Mem stood there with a bigger smile than Lovina had seen in a long time. "Mem! I didn't know you were here too."

Her mother had only been to the warehouse once. She didn't say much about all the work Lovina was doing, which was the same in Lovina's mind as speaking against it.

"Mem, what are you doing here?"

"Oh, I was out walking—uh, coming here—and Thomas saw me and said he was on his way over. He asked if he could walk along."

Lovina nodded, guessing the real truth. Thomas had seen Mem walking, and when he asked if Mem was headed here she changed her plans and came. Still, what did it matter? They were here.

"Thomas, it's so *gut* of you to come. Would you like to see inside? I've been impressed by the progress."

"Sure." He nodded and smiled, but he only seemed partly interested in what she was doing as she showed him around. Mem walked around too, silent. Taking it all in.

"It's amazing what you've done with this place." He bent down and looked at the floor, running his fingers over the concrete. "This really is great work, and I bet you've already increased the property value. Even if you sold now I bet you could make a nice profit."

"Oh, that is true," Mem commented. "Just seeing how everything is cleaned up, well, I bet you can't even limit the possibilities of what could be done with this place. In fact, the people of Pinecraft have been talking about building a community center—a place for people to gather when the weather doesn't cooperate." Mem smiled. "As good as our weather often is here, there are some days when the park doesn't work. Wouldn't this be a wonderful place to set up tables and gather?"

Thomas nodded in agreement.

Even though the room was expansive, Lovina felt as if she couldn't breathe. Their presence—their pressure—was suffocating. The teen boys walked through the main area, trying to walk quietly and not saying a word to disrupt them. Had they overheard the conversation?

"Yes, I'm sure I could sell this place. But money matters so little in comparison to having a dream fulfilled." She smiled. "I'm eager to walk through the next steps." She glanced down the wall by the windows and pointed. "To see tables lined up there with happy customers eating pie."

"Speaking of pie." Thomas rubbed his stomach. "I didn't have much of a breakfast, and I was wondering if you'd like to go to lunch?" He smiled at her mem, and then looked back at her. "I hope you don't mind, but while all this is nice to look at, I'd love some time alone with you, Lovina. I hope you'd do me the honor."

A heaviness cloaked Lovina's shoulders, and Mem's gaze seemed to burn into her. She knew nothing would make Mem happier than for her to go to lunch with Thomas, but she had so much to do around here. She also wasn't interested in giving him any hope that there could be something between them, especially since she and Noah were growing closer by the day.

"Actually, I have a lot to do around here." She remembered something else, too. "I also told Noah and the guys that I'd pick up lunch for them."

Mem stepped forward. "I'll tell you what. I'll pick up lunch for your workers at Yoder's—my treat—and you two can go to Der Dutchman. Lovina, you've been working so hard. You need to get off your feet."

From the look on Mem's face she knew her mother wasn't going to back down. It would also be a good time to let Thomas know that she appreciated his friendship…but she couldn't imagine anything more.

"Okay, ja." She looked to Mem. "They all love the chicken and mashed…"

"No worries. I'll take care of it." Mem shooed her away.

Lovina left with the stares of the teens on her back as she

and Thomas walked to Der Dutchman. The only thing she was thankful for was that she didn't have to see Noah watching as she walked away. She didn't want to know what he thought.

The restaurant was busy, and it took a while for them to get seated. While Thomas enjoyed the lunch buffet, Lovina picked at her salad and a side of macaroni and cheese.

"I'll be returning to Somerset tomorrow, Lovina."

"You are? Already?" Lovina hoped that he couldn't notice the relief in her voice. "I know you'll be happy to be back at your farm, and just think…by the time that you return the pie shop will no doubt be up and running."

"Ja." He took a big bite of cherry pie and swallowed. "I'll be curious to see how your pie shop does, especially with two good restaurants in town that already serve pie."

Lovina winced at the statement but offered a smile. "I trust God, Thomas. I know He's put that pie shop on my mind for a reason."

"Well, that makes sense," he said in a way that told her it didn't make sense at all. "And I was wondering…do you think I can write when I'm gone?"

"Write me?" Her eyes widened.

"Ja. Who did you think?"

She twirled the cheesy noodles with her fork, refusing to meet his gaze. "Well, I suppose you can write…if you don't mind my not being able to write back. I'm going to be pretty busy running a pie shop."

Disappointment clouded his face, and then he set down his fork. "Yes, I see." He leaned closer. "Well, I suppose that I'll be able to see you when I visit…at the pie shop."

Lovina nodded, and she could tell by the emotion that flickered in his gaze that Thomas Chupp understood. The only thing was that the emotion she saw wasn't hurt or disappointment…but anger. As Lovina pushed her plate to the side she guessed that Thomas Chupp was used to getting his way. Only this time he wasn't.

Thomas finished up his meal, and then he rose to go pay the check. In his mind their date was over, and relief flooded Lovina to know he finally understood that they weren't meant to be. The only problem was, she knew Mem wouldn't understand at all.

Morning Glory Muffins

2½ cups flour

1¼ cups sugar

3 teaspoons cinnamon

2 teaspoons baking soda

½ teaspoon salt

3 eggs

¾ cup applesauce

½ cup vegetable oil

1 teaspoon vanilla

2 cups grated carrots

1 medium tart apple, peeled and grated

1 (8 ounce) can crushed pineapple

½ cup flaked coconut

½ cup raisins

½ cup chopped walnuts

Preheat oven to 350°. In a large bowl, combine the first 5 ingredients. In another bowl combine eggs, applesauce, vegetable oil, and vanilla. Stir into dry ingredients just until moistened (batter will be thick). Stir in rest of ingredients. Fill paper-lined muffin cups two-thirds full. Bake 20-24 minutes or until toothpick comes out clean. Cool 5 minutes before removing from pans. Makes 2 dozen.

Twenty

If you must doubt, doubt your doubts, not your beliefs.

AMISH PROVERB

⤳

L ovina was only too happy when she returned to the warehouse. Thomas walked her there, but he didn't stay or dawdle. She stepped inside the warehouse, and a wonderful aroma greeted her. Right inside the doorway there were boxes of food from Yoder's. Mem had brought food for Noah and the teens as promised, but it looked as if it hadn't even been touched.

Voices came from the back office area, echoing across the expansive room. She followed the voices and found the guys working in back. An old toilet sat in the hallway. Everything else had been removed too, including the sink, the railings, and the broken light fixture. A flood light had been set up, and Noah was fiddling with something in the hole where the toilet previously sat.

She stood in the hallway, wondering what she should say to them. Should she apologize for leaving? Should she offer to bring the food back to them? No. That didn't seem like a good idea. They'd need to wash up before they ate. Maybe it would be better if they ate at Roy's place?

Mose was sitting on the floor, handing his uncle tools. He

looked up at the light fixture. "You know I heard that you can actually fill a light bulb with gasoline, and then when someone flips it on the whole thing will explode." Mose chuckled.

Atlee sat up straighter. "Man, that would be one way to—"

"Don't even think of it." Noah's voice was stern. "That's stupid, and you're going to get yourselves seriously hurt. You'd better not try *anything* like that around here."

Noah returned to his work, and Lovina took a step back, not wanting them to know she'd overheard. She stepped into a shadowy area of the hall.

"You guys should be thankful that judge didn't give you a harder sentence," Noah mumbled under his breath. "Half of the school gone—burned down—because of a stupid prank."

The room was silent. They didn't say a word.

"Wrench." Noah said.

And then she heard the sound of tools being moved around in the toolbox.

She couldn't see what they were doing, but she guessed that Mose handed Noah the wrench.

"It was an accident…" Gerald started, and then let his voice trail off.

"Which is the very reason the judge let you off. Why he let you come down here." Noah sighed. "Please don't mess it up."

Lovina waited a minute longer, and then she walked up to the door, clearing her throat. "There you are. I can't believe you've gotten so far on the bathroom." She tried to offer a cheerful tone, and she focused on Noah. But he didn't pause. Didn't turn.

"Yup, it's going good," Gerald finally said, looking at her. Gerald and Atlee sat against one wall watching Noah work.

"So, did you know that lunch is waiting?" She tried to sound cheerful.

Made with Love 207

"Yes, we know," Mose said, frustrated.

"We have to wait until the new toilet is in," Gerald said. "Noah wants us to know how to do this so we can install our own toilets someday." The sarcasm was clear in his voice.

"I see."

She stood there a moment longer watching Noah work, but it was clear she wasn't wanted. "Well, I think I'm going to go work from home today. I have some advertisements to write and...other business paperwork to get done."

"Have fun," Gerald called, but other than that no one said a word. A heaviness weighed her down, and she wondered what the problem was. Noah had been so happy this morning. He'd been excited about the progress. He had a hop in his step as he'd headed back to show off those old movie posters. And now...now he wouldn't even look at her. Why? Was he starting to regret getting involved in such a big project? That thought, and a dozen other worries, filled her mind as she rode her bicycle home. It didn't help that her mem was standing at the window, as if watching for her, as she rode onto the small driveway.

Lovina sighed as she parked the bike and forced a smile as she entered the house. Mem still stood there, looking at the back door. Her eyes were wide, expectant.

"So, how did it go?" Mem moved to the kitchen table and sat. Her stationery box was there, and it looked as if she'd been working on a letter.

Lovina guessed that Mem was writing to Regina. How many conversations had Lovina overheard between the two women growing up? Over cups of coffee, they'd chatted about all their concerns for their community and the people. They always seemed to know what was going on and they had an opinion on all of it.

Lovina had no doubt that letters had been flying back and

forth about what she was up to. Had Regina been the one prodding Mem about a romantic interest for Lovina? Or did Mem come up with the idea that Thomas Chupp would make a good husband on her own?

Lovina darted her eyes away from Mem's expectant gaze, and then she hurried toward the refrigerator, pouring herself a glass of lemonade.

"How was it?" Mem asked again. She scooted up the chair, causing the chair legs to scrape on the ground.

"Well, when I last checked in Noah and his crew were working in the bathroom. They were replacing the toilet and everything else in the bathroom. I can't wait to see what it's going to look like when they finish. It'll be like a whole new bathroom!"

"That's nice, Lovina. Bathrooms are important…but I was wondering about your lunch with Thomas."

Lovina knew she wasn't going to escape her mother's questions. If she didn't answer them now she'd have to later. She picked up her glass and carried it to the table, sitting across from her mother.

"Well, the truth is that the food was good, but the conversation was barely adequate. I mean, Thomas is nice enough…for a friend."

Mem's face fell, and her smile was replaced by a frown.

"It's clear he misses Somerset. He's very proud of his farm and his life there. I'm thankful that I'm not attracted to him, since I'm setting up roots here…building a business and all."

"It's not as if the business is up and running." Mem straightened her shoulders. "Like Thomas said this morning, with the work you've already done on the building you could put it on the market and make a nice profit."

Lovina took another sip of lemonade and set her glass down. Instead of anger, she felt pity for her mother—having so many expectations. She felt sad that she'd never been the daughter Mem wanted. She also felt a bit of relief too. Relief that they were having this conversation.

"Mem, I appreciate that you have such high regard for the changes in the building, but my goal has never been to make money. The pie shop—it's something I've wanted to do for so long. And I'm thankful the opportunity has arisen. Thankful for Dat's help, and for Noah—"

"Noah Yoder," Mem interrupted, "may be a *gut* carpenter, but I sure hope you don't let your heart get wrapped up in him. He's the last person you should consider as a future husband."

"The *last* person?" Lovina sputtered. "Really, is that what you believe?"

Mem picked up the pencil from the table and began tapping the eraser on the tabletop. "You have put so much trust in him, but you never even looked into his past. Did you ever call for references? Did you ever ask *how* Noah knows so much about construction? Or why? Do you know why he ran away from Illinois? Or what he's running from?"

"Ran away?" Lovina cocked an eyebrow.

"Ja, that's what you do when you're not respected by your community. What you do when your bad reputation follows you wherever you go. You leave. You find a new community." Mem stopped the tapping and placed the pencil on the table, smoothing out the letter in front of her. "Well, that would work for most people, except those in the Amish community. The Englischers think they are so connected, being on their computers all the time, but we have our ways of protecting each other. In addition to *The Budget* I've heard about Noah Yoder from all sorts of folks. He may have fooled you, Lovina, but there are some people he can't fool. More than that, I can see the way you look at him. I would have to question if the reason you hurry out of here each morning is to go work at the pie shop…or to see him."

Lovina's jaw dropped. She couldn't believe the words she'd just heard come out of Mem's mouth. Her heart pounded in her chest, and she tried to calm herself. She focused on her words, on her attitude, determined to keep herself in check. Determined not to let her own tongue run away from her.

"Mem, I know that Noah left behind his community. I'm sure he'll tell me all his reasons when he's ready." She spoke as calmly as she could. "And just because I have friendly feelings for him doesn't mean I'm going to marry him. I have one thing on my mind, and that's opening my pie shop. I'm just thankful God chose to send someone like Noah to help me." Lovina stood. "Without him I'd be unable to open it." She picked up her glass of lemonade and her notebook. "And if you'll excuse me, I have work to do. There are business plans I need to make. On our timeframe I can't waste even a few hours trying to dig up someone's past, especially someone whom I so greatly respect."

She hurried to her room and shut the door. Leaning against the cool wood, Lovina's knees trembled. And for a moment she didn't know what made her more upset. Was it Mem's comments about Noah or the way Noah had treated her this afternoon, ignoring her? Or that deep down she knew both of Mem's statements were true—that Noah had run away from something, and that Lovina did look forward to seeing him as much as she enjoyed working on the shop, maybe more.

Lord, am I making a mistake letting my heart get wrapped up in him? You've given me a mission—a dream to fulfill—with this pie shop. Am I letting myself get distracted?

Lovina placed the glass of lemonade on her bedside table and sat on her bed. She had to admit that Noah was on her thoughts most of the day. She also could see from his gaze that he cared about her too. He didn't try hard to hide it.

But was he the right person to be holding her heart? Mem was right. She didn't know much about his past. She knew hardly anything about his family.

More than that, was this the right time to be letting her heart lead? She didn't need anything—*anything*—to distract her from her pie shop. Dat had invested a lot in her. Mem knew this too.

Lord, help me know the truth. Help me to see...

Lovina thought of that tapping pencil. Mem was usually a happy person, but there were a few things that got her troubled. Money problems and the unmarried state of her daughters. And where Lovina was concerned, both of Mem's greatest worries were on display before her.

Lovina felt emotion building in her throat as she considered things from Mem's point of view. Dat had no doubt confessed to her that all his money was wrapped up in that old warehouse.

And with Dat's illness was Mem worried about the financial future for her and her daughters? Lovina guessed she was.

More than that, Lovina was twenty-five years old and had never had a serious relationship. Mem was never one to carry a grudge for long or to look unfavorably upon her neighbors. For her to know so much about Noah Yoder from the moment he'd moved to Pinecraft, there must be some merit to her worries. Even before Lovina started working with him, Mem had encouraged Dat not to let him work on their roof—a simple project.

A chill traveled down Lovina's spine, and the room seemed to dim around her. Mem hadn't mentioned what Noah had done, but then again neither had he.

Why hadn't Noah said anything about his past...unless he was trying to hide it?

The beginning of a headache pounded at Lovina's temples. She wanted nothing more than to curl up on her bed and sleep. She suddenly felt tired and overwhelmed—so different from the way she'd felt this morning. How quickly things could change. The progress on the building continued, but inside she felt as if everything was falling apart.

Maybe Mem was right. Maybe she shouldn't allow her feelings to be wrapped up in Noah Yoder.

From this day on, Mem would be watching her like a hawk. Because even worse than not getting married, in her mother's opinion, was for her to fall in love with someone like Noah Yoder.

⌒

Anna knew from Lovina's face that things hadn't gone well with Thomas. Lovina hadn't met her eye when she'd come in the door. She'd hurried to her room instead, not even pausing to enjoy a slice of upside-down cinnamon pudding cake, one of her favorite desserts that wasn't a pie.

Anna was alone in the kitchen, but from the feeling deep inside it seemed that the nearest kind smile was a thousand miles away. She supposed Lovina was upset that she'd pushed the issue about a date with Thomas, but didn't her daughter realize that sometimes mothers do know best? It had been her own mother who'd urged her to go on a date with John. Where would she be if her mother hadn't urged her? She wouldn't have been married to such a wonderful man all these years. She wouldn't have these girls or this cottage. Yet to whom could Anna explain this? No one except Regina.

Lovina wasn't ready to listen. Not yet. John, well, he wouldn't understand. So she sat down with her stationery once again.

Dear Regina,

How thankful I am for the Lord Jesus Christ who has blessed us with adequate health, good friends, and love that endures forever. I'm also thankful for gut *friends, no matter the miles that separate us. Thank you so much for your letter.*

Things have been busy, and I haven't spent much time at the warehouse. The warehouse is the old building that Lovina is turning into a pie shop. Or at least that is the plan. I have to say that I was impressed today when I saw the improvements that have been made in such a short time. Still, there is so much to be done. So much. Lovina has help from an Amish crew. That's all I'll say about that for now.

What has kept me so busy as to not be involved in this endeavor? (I know this is the first thing that you'd ask.) First, I've been spending time with new friends. Many have been ill and it seems fresh-baked muffins or upside-down cinnamon pudding cake can brighten anyone's day. I've also been working with Joy on some quilts for the Haiti auction. Joy works with diligence, and she's found a dear friend in the elderly woman who owns the quilt shop, Elizabeth Beiler. Joy had always been close to her grandmother and perhaps this friendship is filling a hole that has been there since her passing.

You mentioned news about the pie shop in The Budget. *I was surprised that the local scribe mentioned it already. In my opinion it's like boasting about the harvest before it comes. Besides, what type of a business name is* Me, Myself and Pie? *If anything the pie shop needs a better name.*

It seems to me that too much is being focused on that pie shop and too little on common sense. Today I saw Thomas Chupp, that nice young man I wrote to you about. He's very interested in pursing Lovina, and she's treating him as if he has the plague. Too much dreaming is happening in Love's head. And there is an Amish bachelor from the work crew who has caught her fancy, I'm afraid.

From what I heard from Thomas's Aunt Vera, Lovina made it very clear to Thomas that she thinks of him as nothing more than a friend. After all these years of praying for a husband for my oldest daughter she pushes him away just like that! I'm not sure I'm going to be able to sleep tonight. My mind's too full of all the things Lovina should be worrying about but isn't. Like the fact that she just threw away her chances with Thomas, and the state of our family's finances if this endeavor does not succeed. I know that God can bring good out of anything. I just don't know why there are some folks who make Him work so hard to do so! There, I finally said it.

I still wonder if I should just sit Lovina down and tell her what I know about Noah Yoder. He is the one helping Lovina with the pie shop. Do you remember what we heard about him and that horrible accident? Was it five years ago? I can't imagine my daughter with that type of person. What do you think, Regina? Oh, I wish you were here to give me your advice.

Well, I suppose I do know one thing you would tell me. "Anna," you would say, "instead of focusing so much on your worries, be thankful for your gifts." So, yes, I will end my letter with that. John's health continues to improve and, even though I hate to admit this, I believe it's due in part to having something to dream about as much as it is the gentler climate. If anything, Lovina's pie shop has given him that.

I hope the chocolate tasting went well. I guarantee the only chocolate we'll be tasting around here is chocolate pie!

Sending all my love,
Anna

P.S. Oh, and other exciting news is that Yoder's gift shop is carrying some of Faith's sketches! The shop owner even worked to help Faith frame them. If you do come down we'll have to stop by so I can show you the display. And if I were to guess Faith was the one who showed

*the most interest in Thomas Chupp. Yet once I saw Thomas's atten-
tion turning to Lovina I tried to discourage Faith. Now I wonder if
I made the wrong choice—pushed the wrong "friendship." Oh, the
challenges of being a mother with five unmarried daughters. You'd
better eat another piece of chocolate for me!*

Upside-Down Cinnamon Pudding Cake

2¼ cups brown sugar, packed
3 tablespoons butter
2½ cups cold water
2 cups flour
½ teaspoon salt
2 teaspoons baking powder
2½ teaspoons cinnamon
2 tablespoons butter
1 cup brown sugar
1¼ cups milk

Preheat oven to 350°. Combine 2¼ cups brown sugar, 3 table-spoons butter, and water. Bring to a boil. Set aside to cool. In a large bowl, sift flour, salt, baking powder, and cinnamon together. In a separate bowl, cream 2 tablespoons butter and 1 cup brown sugar. Add to dry ingredients, mix well, and add milk. Spread into greased 13x9-inch pan. Pour cooled brown sugar mixture over the unbaked batter. Optional: Sprinkle ½ cup chopped nuts over the unbaked batter. Bake 35-40 minutes. Serve warm with ice cream or whipped cream.

Twenty-One

The trouble with experience is that you
never have it until after you need it.

AMISH PROVERB

Noah Yoder paced the swatch of concrete by the front door of the pie shop's interior, waiting for Lovina to show up. She was usually at the shop by eight in the morning, but not today. He'd walked by the Miller house this morning, but her father, John, wasn't sitting outside as he usually did. Normally Noah would have stopped to knock, but he couldn't bring himself to do it. A burden weighed on his heart. He'd been horrible to Lovina yesterday. Instead of confronting her about her lunch date with Thomas Chupp—and instead of fighting for her—he'd ignored her. His heart ached at the thought of it.

Noah paused and leaned against the front counter. He'd made it from an old bar, and Lovina had claimed it was perfect. But what good were all the things he did for her if he treated her with contempt? He'd been working hard out of his growing love for her, but had he let her know that? No, not in the slightest. He'd just expected her to guess his feelings for her. Noah ran a hand through his hair. What a fool he'd been. No wonder she'd accepted that lunch date with Thomas. Any girl would be drawn most to the one who made his intentions known.

He sat down on the phone bench that Lovina was going to use to display menus, and he leaned forward, placing his elbows on his knees. He ran a hand through his hair, remembering what it was like to be ignored. It was worse than being confronted and accused. And suddenly then he was twenty years old again, with a battered body and a battered reputation.

The memories surprised him, surfacing before he could push them down. Those in his community started ignoring him around the time of his rumspringa. Not that he'd gotten a lot of attention before. In the Amish community most families had eight, ten, or twelve kids, so keeping track of them all wasn't easy. But once Noah bought his own car and started wearing Englisch clothes, people went out of their way not to talk to him.

And after the accident, well, he understood a little of what it was like to be shunned. After that it was like he didn't even exist. He knew then that not being acknowledged was an even worse punishment than being yelled at or accused. At least when people accused you they acknowledged that you were there. And that was another reason he'd decided to take the young men to Pinecraft. Even if their misdeeds were known by the people here they wouldn't be completely ostracized—not like back at home.

He blew out a breath. This past pain wasn't worth thinking of now. Now he had to think of Lovina. Was it too much to hope that his foolishness hadn't pushed her into another man's arms? Instead of ignoring her, he needed to be pursuing her! And he was determined to start now.

Noah rose and looked to the large box he'd set just inside the doorway. It was an ordinary cardboard box, and the lid was folded so she couldn't see inside. The box still smelled like the laundry soap it once held, but that wasn't what was inside. Instead it was something special. Something for the shop...something he hoped Lovina would like.

He peeked in the top and then closed it up again, smiling. Was it a silly gift? Noah frowned. Maybe he should have gotten flowers or chocolates instead, like he'd seen other guys do. But Noah didn't have a chance for second guessing before the shuffling of bike tires on gravel caught his attention. It had to be Lovina parking her bike. Noah sucked in a deep breath and forced a smile.

The door swung open and Lovina hurried in. She stopped short when she saw him, and her brow furrowed. Normally Lovina's hair was perfectly combed back under her kapp, but today dark, wispy strands curled around her temples. Her face looked pale, and dark circles rimmed her eyes. Noah swallowed down the lump in his throat, wondering if she'd slept. Wondering if he was the cause of her disheveled look. From her sad look as she peered up at him, he knew he was.

"Lovina, I need to apologize for yesterday." The words came out in a rush, and he stepped toward her, wishing he could wrap her up in his arms. She looked so worried. So weary. Noah wasn't sure he'd ever seen her like this before. He reached out and offered her his hand, palm up. She looked at it, and then placed her hand in his. It was trembling.

For a moment he pushed aside what he was going to say. Noah squeezed her hand. "Is something wrong? Did"—he sucked in a breath—"Did something happened to your dat?"

"Oh no, nothing like that. And..." She gazed up at him. Her eyes were large, round, and so innocent. So hopeful. "I thought something *was* wrong. You, well, you didn't even speak to me yesterday afternoon. I wanted to explain. I was up all night trying to figure out how to tell you...I still don't know how, or if I should."

"Tell me what?" Noah kept his voice soft. Then he waited as her eyes searched his. He knew what she was doing. She was weighing to see if he could be trusted. If she could lay out her heart. He wanted to fill the silence with his apology, but something inside stirred, urging him to wait.

"I'm sorry I didn't take time to explain about Thomas," she finally said. "I should probably be flattered by his attention, but…" She bit her lip, trying to figure out her words. "But he's not someone I want for more than a friend, no matter what my mother thinks."

Noah wanted to pull her closer. He wanted to kiss her, but he also knew better than to do that. Now was not the time. This was not the place…or at least not yet.

Resisting the urge, he dropped her hand and crossed his arms over his chest, taking in her words. "I see."

Lovina attempted to brush stray strands of hair off her face, but as soon as she removed her hand they fluttered back to her temples and cheek. "Thomas asked me to lunch yesterday, and I wanted to use that time to explain to him that I wasn't…well, that I wasn't interested in spending more time with him."

"And he understands that now?" Noah kept his tone serious, even though his dancing heart was anything but. He forced himself to hide his smile, enjoying the way she squirmed.

"Ja." She nodded. Lovina must have noticed the humor in his gaze because one eyebrow cocked. "He understands that, but I could change my mind."

"Change your mind?" Noah scoffed. "And what has he offered you in comparison to me? Thomas Chupp took you to the beach and he took you to lunch." Noah tapped his boot on the concrete floor. "I made your concrete look pretty." Then he swept his arm toward the windows. "And look at that sunshine."

"Ja." Lovina tapped her chin. "Sunshine was the deciding factor to be certain. I'd rather spend time with a man who gives me beams of golden light." Then she hesitated, as if suddenly worried that she was reading too much into the playful conversation. "Because of our, uh, work relationship, of course."

"Is that what you think this is?" He motioned to the box. "The contractor in me does enjoy fixing up your old building…but the man inside loves being in your presence more and more each day. And he just had to buy you this."

She didn't reply, but from the look in his eyes she didn't need to. She smiled. "So, can I open it?"

He kneeled beside the box, the coolness of the concrete seeping through his homemade pants. "Of course."

Maybe he should have found a way to wrap it. Instead, he watched with excitement as Lovina opened the top of the box.

She sucked in a breath and pulled out a vintage Pyrex mixing bowl. It was turquoise blue with a simple pattern on the side. He'd seen it at an estate sale the previous night, and Noah knew he had to have it.

"It's—it's just like the one in that photo I tore out of the magazine. That wonderful cupboard I loved so much was decorated with these bowls."

"Yes, well, take it as an apology. I'm so sorry I ignored you like that. I didn't like the fact that some other Amish bachelor was trying to spend time with my girl."

"Your girl?" Lovina laughed, and the sound was music to his ears.

"If you don't mind," Noah said.

Her eyelashes fluttered and she glanced back down at the bowl. "I don't mind. Not one bit."

Noah's chest filled with warmth and heat. He thought again

about kissing her—on the cheek at least. But she kept her attention fixed on the bowl. She examined it as if she were holding a priceless diamond. Maybe to Lovina this was. Maybe the fact that he understood, supported her, was the most valuable gift she'd ever received. He hoped so.

"This is the perfect gift," she said with a heavy sigh.

His heart bounced a little in his chest, knowing that she'd soon be even more surprised. "I'm glad you think so because I have twenty-four more of them coming—to be used to decorate the shop."

Lovina gasped. "Twenty-four more?"

He nodded toward the back area of the warehouse, where he kept all the items they weren't using and the things he hadn't managed to sell yet. "I'm going to build you a cabinet, just like the one in the picture. I came upon an estate sale, and I couldn't resist. I didn't know those bowls were so collectible."

"Noah Yoder, goodness knows I'm not paying you for your work as it is, and then you go and use the little money you've earned to buy me bowls." She sighed, pretending to be exasperated, but he could tell from her expression that she was thrilled. "This is the most amazing gift. I can't wait to show my sisters and Mem. She used to have one like this, but one of us broke it years ago..."

As she placed the bowl back into the box her expression changed. She took a deep breath and blew it out slowly. "Speaking of years ago, there is something I want to—need to—ask. I mean, if we are going to consider more than a friendship..."

The lightness he'd felt in his chest moments before sunk like a lead balloon. "Yes, of course. Ask..." His words trailed off. He was going to say, "Ask anything," but from the look on her face he already knew what the question would be.

"Speaking of years ago—"

"Knock, knock!" A voice called out from the other side of the front door, and then came a gentle knock. "Anybody here?" It was a woman's voice, one Noah didn't recognize.

Lovina's lips sealed close, and she hurried to the door, opening it. An Amish man and woman stood there. From the woman's kapp Noah guessed they were from Pennsylvania.

"Can I help you?" Lovina asked. From her puzzled expression it was clear she didn't know them either.

"We're Leon and Marsha Kurth from Lancaster. We haven't met, but I feel as though we have," the man started.

"We heard about the pie shop in *The Budget*. This is our first time down south. We came a bit before the buses arrive to fix up our new place," Marsha jumped in. "We just bought it last week." She looked around and her eyes grew wide. "This place is even more beautiful and spacious than I envisioned. And please tell me you're going to have pecan pie on the menu. It's my favorite. Do you mind taking a minute to give us a tour of what's going to be where? Are you going to put the tables by those windows? Oh, look! Diners will have a perfect view of the buses coming in."

"I don't mind…" Lovina looked toward Noah, their gazes meeting. Her mixed emotions were clean on her face. She liked sharing her dream, but it meant their conversation would have to wait for another time. "I'd love to show you, and I have to introduce you to Noah Yoder, who's done all the work with the help of his nephew and a few other young men."

Leon removed his hat and scratched his head. "Noah Yoder. That name sounds familiar. Are you a scribe in *The Budget*?"

"No, sir. I'm not." Noah's gut tightened down as if being cinched by a rope. "If you'll excuse me, I need to check on the young men who are painting around back."

"Are you from Illinois?" The man's brow furrowed. "I know I know that name for some reason."

Marsha gave Leon's arm a playful tap. "Do you know how many Noah Yoders there must be?" she chuckled.

Ignoring his wife's comment, Leon stepped toward Noah. "Oh, you're going to give the outside a makeover too?"

Noah shrugged, feeling the man's gaze on him. The man was searching his mind's archives, trying to figure out where he'd heard that name. Noah could see it in his eyes.

"Just a coat of paint. It's nice meeting you both. I'll probably see you around." He hurried out before they asked any more questions, and before they could follow. He also hoped that Leon would not remember why his name sounded so familiar. Five years ago there had been numerous reports in *The Budget* about his accident. And he had no doubt many an Amish preacher had used his example in their sermons too. If ever there'd been an example of how following the ways of the world could lead to destruction, he was it.

He just hoped that he had a chance to tell Lovina before someone connected him with the accident. And—even though it seemed impossible—he dared to hope that maybe a bit of the good he was doing now with the guys would help to redeem his deeds.

As Noah strode around the back of the building to check on the progress of the painting, one of his mem's old sayings came to mind: "The trouble with experience is you never have it until after you need it." He'd make a different choice now because of that experience. He supposed he could be grateful for that. Grateful for wisdom and a second chance. Noah just hoped Lovina would understand, and that her thoughts of who he was *now* wouldn't be darkened because of who he was *then*.

Pecan Pie

One 9-inch unbaked pie crust
3 large eggs, beaten
½ cup firmly packed brown sugar
⅓ cup butter, melted
½ teaspoon salt
1 cup light corn syrup
1 teaspoon vanilla extract
½ cup chopped pecans
1 cup pecan halves
vanilla ice cream (optional)

Preheat oven to 350°. Mix eggs, sugar, butter, salt, corn syrup, and vanilla in a bowl. Stir in chopped pecans. Pour into pie crust, reserving ¼ cup of filling. Top with pecan halves. Pour reserved filling over the top of the crust. Bake 60-70 minutes. Serve with vanilla ice cream, if desired.

Twenty-Two

The dearest things of life are most near at hand.

AMISH PROVERB

⌇

Lovina looked at her warehouse, amazed at the pipes and wires running through the walls. They'd hired a professional plumber and electrician, and the warehouse had been a hive of activity. It had been a couple of weeks since Noah had talked about their relationship growing beyond their friendship, but not much had changed. With the goal of opening the pie shop before the November buses rolled in, remodeling work consumed their lives. They had short moments to chat and share pie-related dreams of their future, but they hadn't found a good time to talk more about his past. Would there ever be a good time? It must be something truly horrible if he put off telling her. But what? She knew if she asked Mem she could find out. But she didn't want to hear it that way. She wanted to hear it from him—whatever "it" was.

Noah's booted footsteps echoed from the back office where he and the guys had just installed the new window air conditioning unit. She turned and watched him approach. He had an intense look on his face. Frustration? Resolution? Excitement? Maybe

227

a bit of all three. "Lovina, they were supposed deliver the rest of the kitchen equipment today. But they called and it won't be here until tomorrow."

Her eyes widened. "But does that put us behind? Do you think we can still open in time?" The muscles in her neck tightened, and she rubbed at them with fingers that were already sore from ripping open boxes and sorting through the boxes of restaurant supplies. Plates, mugs, glasses, linens, pie plates—who knew they'd need so much stuff! She didn't want to get tense, but they'd been working so hard. One missed deadline could hinder the rest of their plans.

Her stomach knotted too as she looked at Noah, wondering if there were other things he was hiding from her. More personal things. Perhaps the tension wasn't only because of the pie shop, but it was easier to blame it on that.

Noah reached a hand and stroked her face. "You look worried."

She wiped at the place he was touching her. "Do I have dirt there? Or paint?"

"No." The word was just a whisper. "You look beautiful, that's all."

She turned her head toward him, taking in the warm look on his face, his smile. All her tension seemed to melt under his gaze.

She'd never been told she was beautiful before, and she almost didn't believe him. But something in her heart told to believe the tender look that she saw in his gaze.

She lifted her hand to point out the area above the window. "If we put a shelf up there—"

"You didn't hear me, did you?"

"What?" Her cheeks warmed, and she looked to her feet. "Ja, of course I did."

His thumb gently stroked her wrist. "What did I say?"

"I'm...I'm..." She tried to repeat the word, but it wouldn't come out.

"You. Are. Beautiful." He spoke each word with conviction, and the words soaked into her soul. Tears rimmed her eyes, and she hoped she didn't look like a fool.

She dropped her eyes to their joined hands. "Thank you. I like hearing that."

"I hope so." His voice became solemn. "You'd better get used to me saying it. Because I intend to say it...often."

He turned her hand over and kissed her palm. His lips were warm and soft and a chill traveled up her arm and then raced down her spine. She thought back to that first time she'd seen him. It was the same day she saw this place. God had so much in store for her. So much planned for her. More than she could have imagined. She didn't know what to say...but she didn't need to say anything. A slow smile broke across her face.

Noah grinned. "You have been working very hard. And I have an idea. Why don't we skip work for the rest of the day and go to the beach?"

"To the beach?"

He chuckled. "By the way that you say that you'd think I was asking you to go to the moon."

"Sometimes it seems like going to the moon. My mind has just been so focused on this place. On getting everything just right."

"Well." He winked. "Maybe we should change that."

"Yes, Noah, I'd like that very much."

Twenty minutes later, they were riding their bikes down Bahia Vista Street to Tuttle Avenue. They parked their bikes there and took the #16 bus to the beach. There were a few other ladies in kapps on the bus—women Lovina didn't recognize. She'd noticed more and more tourists showing up every day. Most came down with hired drivers. A few Mennonite families flew on commercial flights. The colder it got up north the quicker they came. They still had three weeks before the first Pioneer Trails bus would arrive. Three weeks to finish getting everything ready.

Lovina sucked in a breath as all the things that needed to get done in the next three weeks filled her mind.

Noah turned from where he was looking out the window to face her. "Is something wrong?"

"Yes! Noah, I need to start working on the pies. Grace and I made a list a while ago, but there is so much to do. We need to start baking the shells. Those will freeze, but we need to start buying all the rest of the ingredients. And I need to figure out the food budget too."

Noah leaned close until his nose nearly touched hers. "Lovina, this is our afternoon off, remember? Can you just try to relax and enjoy it?"

She blew out a frustrated breath. "How can I? How will I be able to relax when there is so much to do?"

He took her hand in his and squeezed. "Well, I have a bit of wisdom to share that might help. My mem used to always say, 'The dearest things of life are most near at hand.'" He winked. "And today, Lovina, that is me."

She smiled at the gentle way he was leading her back to the present. Back to him. "Ja, well, my mem used to say, 'Half done is far from done.'"

He laughed. "That's a good one too, but why don't we focus on my mem's advice for today?"

She leaned against his shoulder, peering out the window and watching the cars pass. He smelled of wood shavings, sunshine, and bacon, most likely from breakfast. It was a homey, familiar smell. "I think I can do that. I'll try."

They arrived at the beach twenty minutes later. She took off her flip-flops as she walked on the sand. It was warm under her feet. Her hand easily slid into Noah's and she couldn't help but think back to the last time she was here. She had been with Thomas. Back then, she'd wanted nothing more than to leave, and now…well, she was looking forward to a beautiful day with Noah by her side.

Seagulls swooped and danced overhead. The ocean breeze was intoxicating. She'd always thought that her favorite aroma was pie cooking. It still was, but the ocean breeze was coming in a close second. Why hadn't she noticed it before? Why did today seem perfect—everything about it?

They walked hand in hand, strolling by those wearing bathing suits, shorts, and T-shirts. A woman strode by in a dark blue summer dress with a beach towel tucked under her arm. A man jogged up to her and wrapped his arm around her, and she was happy to see him. Then, without warning, he snatched the towel from her and she chased after him. They laughed as she chased him into the water. He tossed the towel to the dry sand and they splashed each other. Soon they were both soaking wet.

Lovina laughed, and then looked to Noah. He was watching her instead of them.

"What? What are you looking at?"

"Oh." He sighed. "I just like to see you smile. That's all."

He spread out a blanket, and they sat side by side. She wished he would say something. Wished he'd use this time to tell her the truth—whatever he'd worked so hard to keep hidden from her. She didn't want to ruin the moment, but all the things she'd imagined over the last few weeks were coming to a boiling point in her mind.

What was it about his past that bothered him so? Bothered Mem?

Instead, he talked about his parents coming down for Christmas. "I told my mem all about you, Lovina. She said she can't wait to meet the woman who's captured my heart." He ran his fingers through the sand and then focused on her. "My mem even asked about the future…our future. She wanted to know—"

"Noah." His name spouted from her lips. "I can guess…well, um." She lifted her face to the breeze, trying to gather her thoughts. "Why don't we talk about that…our relationship…after—"

"After the pie shop is done," he interrupted. He nodded with determination on his face, as if trying to agree that was the right thing to do.

That wasn't what she'd intended to say, but she couldn't correct him. Worry filled his eyes, and she didn't like it. She wanted to see the laughter and smiles of just moments ago. She forced a smile.

"Yes, after the pie shop is done," she agreed, telling herself there would be plenty of time to talk about other things. The pie shop would be opened in a few weeks if everything played out right.

Still the questions nagged her. Why wouldn't he just tell her? What was he hiding?

Noah pulled out their picnic lunch and took out two sandwiches from the bag. "My mem will be disappointed when I tell her we're not going to be published anytime soon."

Heat rose on her cheeks. So she wasn't the only one who thought about that. To be published was to tell the world that a wedding was coming, but again that wasn't something they needed to think about now. It was too soon. They had so much to learn about each other, more than their interest in the pie shop.

"There's only one way Mem's ever going to forgive me for telling her that we're taking things more slowly than she'd like."

"Oh, yes? What's that?" Lovina asked, pulling some homemade cookies from the bag.

"If you share your recipe for shoofly pie. She's been in search of the perfect recipe since I can remember. And Mem thinks you might have *the one*."

"I do make a good shoofly. Maybe I should make it for you some time."

"I'd like that, Lovina." He lifted her hand and kissed the tips of her fingers. "I love everything about you…and the pie is just a bonus. Remind me to write down the recipe when we get back, or I'll never hear the end of it."

Shoofly Pie

1 cup flour
⅔ cup brown sugar
1 tablespoon butter
1 teaspoon baking soda
¾ cup hot water
1 cup cane molasses
1 egg
1 unbaked pie shell

Preheat oven to 400°. Mix flour, brown sugar, and butter with a fork until crumbly. Measure out half the crumbs and set aside. Dissolve soda in water. Add molasses and egg, then stir into half of the crumbs. Pour into crust and sprinkle remaining crumbs on top. Bake 10 minutes, then reduce heat to 325° and bake an additional 30 minutes.

Twenty-Three

⚬

Lovina walked into the quilt shop and glanced around. She didn't see Joy and wondered if she was early. Instead, an older woman sat behind the counter. Although Lovina had never met her before, Lovina had heard enough about Elizabeth Beiler from Joy to feel as if she had.

Elizabeth waved her forward. "You must be Lovina. I can tell. You are so pretty like your sister."

"I—I am Lovina." She smiled as she walked up to the woman, certain the woman needed new glasses. "But I don't believe I look much like Joy." Joy had a beautiful face and the same honey blonde colored hair as Hope.

"Of course you do!" the woman insisted. "You have the same large, round brown eyes. And those cheekbones."

Lovina blushed. She opened her mouth and closed it again, not knowing what to say. Yes, she was certain now this woman needed to get her eyes checked.

"Now I know that we Plain people aren't supposed to be

prideful, but the Good Book also says we're supposed to speak the truth. I think it'll be a wonderful thing to have your pie shop open. It'll draw people together, like things used to be."

"Like things used to be?" Lovina asked.

"I've been coming to Pinecraft since I was just a *boppli*. There used to be a large boardinghouse just down the street. It was filled with small rooms and a common kitchen. I'd watch my mother and her friends cooking together and doing laundry together, but one of my favorite things was watching them make pies. Five or six women would be lined up at the long kitchen counter, rolling out the crusts. They'd be chatting with each other and chatting with all those gathered in the room watching. Joy said you were going to have an open area in your pie shop where the young women could do just that. It'll be a true blessing not only for those enjoying the pie, but those making it. In the Amish community, ladies sew together and cook together for weddings, but something just seems right about making pies side by side." Elizabeth's eyes twinkled as she spoke.

The bell on the door jingled and Joy strode in. "I'm so sorry I'm late, but I stopped by the pie shop. When I was looking over my figures, one of the window measurements looked off. *Gut* thing I checked. Atlee helped me, and I'd written the measurements down wrong. The curtains would have been far too—"

"Atlee, is it?" Elizabeth jumped in.

"Oh dear, Lizzy." Joy placed her notebook and pencil on the table and crossed her arms over her chest. "I know you'd like nothing more than to see me fall in love with a handsome Amish boy, but I'm afraid no one has caught my fancy yet." Joy leaned forward, placed her hands on the counter, and smiled. "But I'm going to volunteer to work in the pie shop at least a few days a week once it opens. It seems like the perfect place to meet a bachelor. And when I meet him I promise you'll be the first to know."

The older women laughed, and Lovina settled down on a chair next to Elizabeth. Lovina looked up at her sister. "So, are you going to tell me what the surprise is? I almost couldn't sleep last night from thinking about it." That was partly the truth. The other part was replaying her day at the beach with Noah.

"Ja, as soon as Grace shows up I'll tell you about it." Joy looked at the clock. "She's a little bit late. I think you're going to like what we've come up with."

They chatted about Joy's newest quilting project, and a few minutes later Grace strode in. Even though Grace was the youngest of them, she always carried herself with confidence. She wore a light pink dress today, and she held a binder pressed to her chest. Lovina noticed it was filled to the brim.

"I'm sorry I'm late! I'm so excited about what I have to show you." She settled in and flipped open the binder. "I've printed up a few articles about Pinecraft online at the library. *The New York Times* called it a time warp." Grace cleared her throat. "'White bungalows and honeybell orange trees line streets named after Amish families: Kaufman, Schrock, Yoder,'" she read.

Lovina nodded as she listened. She didn't know where Grace's mind was going with this, but her youngest sister was smart and capable. Lovina knew she'd get to the point.

"A few weeks ago, I was looking over some of the reclaimed furniture Noah is using and the plans he drew up, based on your ideas," Grace said. "As I did, the phrase *time-warp* kept running through my mind. I like the simple feel of many of the Amish restaurants and bakeries I've been to, but this is Pinecraft. People are a little bit more free here. I don't think you should shy away from decorations, like most Amish do. In fact, I think you should add more old items and more color. With a touch of vintage too."

"Vintage?" Lovina asked. "Are you talking about filling my new shop with old stuff?"

"Not just any old stuff, but good old stuff, like those lovely bowls Noah got you," Grace continued, turning to a page in her binder of vintage dishes. "I was talking to one of the librarians and I found out that Amish blue Pyrex bowls are very popular. People are collecting them, and look at the fabric we found." Grace looked over at Joy. Her eyes sparkled as they prepared for the big reveal.

Joy moved behind the store counter and pulled out a bag with fabric. She pulled out three bolts and laid them side by side. "This first is called Pyrex butterprint. The Amish butterprint design is on bowls, butter dishes, and all types of things. Just like on many of the dishes that Noah bought you. Isn't it beautiful?"

Lovina looked at the unbleached fabric that was made of white and teal alternating squares. In the squares were the same images on the bowl that Noah had given her: the stalks of wheat and wheat bundles, the rooster, and the Amish couple.

Lovina smiled. It seemed just right. "You found this for the pie shop?"

Joy clapped her hands together with excitement. "Ja, I thought that would make lovely tablecloths and linens for the display tables. And we found this for curtains."

Joy glanced over to Elizabeth as she put the second bolt on top. This one had a repeating pattern of aqua berries with teal leaves. The aqua was the same color as the Pyrex pattern. It was also the same color as the water on Siesta Key's beach.

Lovina sucked in a breath. "I love it. It's perfect!"

Grace nodded in agreement. "Yes, these are the same colors, but a different style. And then we'll make cloth napkins."

Lovina looked at Joy. "Cloth napkins?"

"Ja, doesn't that sound homey?" Joy said. She pointed to two more similar patterns on a second bolt, one of them with a spot of pink. "Cloth napkins remind one of home, and they're eco-friendly too."

Lovina looked at her sisters, seeing them differently than she'd ever seen them before. She'd always seen Joy hard at work on quilts or other sewing projects, but she'd never taken much time to ask what she was working on. She hadn't known her sister was so passionate about fabrics. She hadn't seen how creative and artistic she was.

She had also seen Grace reading the newspapers and business books, and now it was all making sense. Grace lived within an Amish community, but she also worked hard to understand the culture beyond.

Lovina knew that Grace's goal was to help Amish men and women get their handiwork into the larger marketplace, benefiting families—many of whom could no longer depend on farming for an income. And seeing her sister's excitement over connecting a business with the marketplace got Lovina excited too.

"I don't know what to say," Lovina gushed. "I think my customers are going to love it." Warmth filled her chest and flowed through her, and she realized again how God was providing for every one of her needs.

"Isn't this perfect?" Grace ran her hand over the fabric. "The teal and white are so popular around Pinecraft, and it matches the Amish motif on the dishes. It perfectly unites vintage with Amish, and the colors will make the place so inviting."

"I love how God uses all our talents for His common good," Elizabeth said, "don't you?"

Lovina nodded. For so long she'd dreamed alone, but not anymore. "I can't wait to see everything when it's done. It brings me such relief. It also makes me realize that this pie shop is so much bigger than just pie."

"God works in mysterious ways," Elizabeth said with joy in her voice, fingering the cloth. "God asked me to pray for that warehouse years ago. I'm thankful that He kept me around to see His good work. I'm reminded of a verse," Elizabeth continued. "'His compassions fail not. They are new every morning: great is thy faithfulness. The Lord *is* my portion, saith my soul; therefore will I hope in him.'"

The woman paused, and then looked to them. "That was from Lamentations."

Lovina smiled at the woman, and she couldn't help but think of her grandmother. She suspected that God Himself had given her those words.

Pyrex Amish Butterprint Pattern

The tradition of stamping butter started in the late nineteenth century. Butter makers marked their butter with their initials or an emblem such as a sheaf of wheat, a cow, or a beehive. After butter was measured to the right amount the stamp mold was dipped in cold water to prevent its sticking to the lump and then pressed firmly upon the butter, leaving a raised impression of the stamp.

Twenty-Four

To grow old gracefully you must start when you are young.

AMISH PROVERB

⟝⟞

The lights were dim when Lovina got to the warehouse the next morning—not the bright work lights she was used to. It was quiet too. Much too quiet. Her head tilted, and she hurried to the door.

Everything was clean. The sawdust and scraps of lumber had been picked up. The wooden pot rack for the kitchen that Noah had been working on leaned against the far wall. And there, in the middle of the floor, an old quilt was laid out, but no one was in sight.

"Noah?" she called out. She stepped closer to the blanket and noticed a picnic basket sitting beside a wooden box. A bow was on the top of the box, and suddenly she knew.

A smile curled on her lips. Somebody had spilled the beans on what today was.

Footsteps sounded behind her. Lovina turned as Noah hurried through the doorway. He held two forks in his right hand.

"I almost made it." He chuckled and held up the forks. "I almost remembered everything."

She twirled one of her kapp strings around her finger. "Everything?"

"Everything for your birthday breakfast." He stepped forward and reached for her hand. She placed her right hand in his left one. He gently squeezed it. "Happy birthday, Lovina."

Outside a gentle rain began to fall, splattering on the windows and on the sidewalk, but it just made the inside seem cozier. Noah moved to the quilt and sat cross-legged. He patted the blanket beside him.

Lovina walked to the quilt and sank to her knees. A sweet, yeasty aroma met her. "Is that what I think it is?"

He reached into a paper bag. "If you're thinking it's hot cinnamon rolls from Yoder's restaurant, you're right." He opened the bag and placed it before her. "And a little birdie told me your favorite drink is the raspberry sweet tea."

He handed her a Styrofoam cup, and she reached for it. "Ja, and I'll have to thank my sister Faith. It helps to have someone on the inside."

His smiled faded as she said those words. She laughed to let him know she was telling a joke.

"I was talking about inside Yoder's. Not inside like prison or anything."

"I didn't think you were talking about that…well, not completely." He opened his mouth as if to tell her something, and then he closed it again. "There's something I'd like to talk to you about…but later. Not today."

She studied his face. The smile was still there, but he wore a guarded expression. She could tell something was bothering him, but she didn't want to press.

Her stomach growled and she looked to the bag. "Do you mind?"

"Not at all." He reached into the bag, and she thought how this was the first birthday gift she'd ever received, other than home-made cards or small tokens from her family. She liked the thought of celebrating her birthdays with Noah. Of growing old together. In her mind's eye she pictured him older, but with the same wide, excited smile she saw now, and she liked the idea of that.

He took a napkin from the pile and placed a large cinnamon roll on it. It smelled heavenly. He lowered his head to say a silent prayer, and she followed his lead. She thanked God for this man sitting in front of her. Thanked Him for this chance to feel so special, so cared for.

She ate the roll with flourish and was licking off her fingers when she looked up to see Noah watching her.

"There's something else too, Lovina." He reached into the bag of cinnamon rolls and pulled out a small white box with a bow, handing it to her. "There are smudges of frosting on it. I hope you don't mind."

She wiped off the biggest clump of frosting with a swipe of her finger. "Not at all."

Gingerly she opened the box. Her breath caught as she noticed the small conch shell inside. She took it out and placed it on her open palm, holding it up.

"Do you remember where we got that?"

"Of course. At the beach."

"Ja, and then you tossed it aside. I rescued it because I wanted to remember."

"Remember?"

"The moment I realized I loved you."

She swallowed down her emotion and dared to look into his eyes. "You do?"

His gaze stayed on hers, and the slightest blush colored his cheeks. "In spite of what you think, Lovina, I'm doing this for more than just the pie. Even more than just a place to put these teens to good use and to show them the value of being part of a community." He shrugged. "Of course it didn't start that way."

She wagged a finger at him. "I know, I know. You saw me enter this place and knew you wanted to spend your life with me from the start." She let that word *love* swirl around in her mind and knew he meant it. All this—all he'd done for her on this picnic basket and in this place showed it. No, Noah wasn't just here for the pie.

She considered telling him that she loved him too. Or at least that was what her pounding heart and swirling thoughts told her. Still, she hesitated. How could she claim to love someone she didn't know completely? She wanted to confess her love, but Noah Yoder had some confessing to do first.

When is he going to tell me what's burdening his heart? And will it change things? Will it change us?

Noah rose up on his knees, and she was certain he was going to kiss her. He scooted forward and his arms wrapped around her, snuggling her close. His arms were strong, muscular around her, and tears pooled in the corners of her eyes. Tears of happiness. Tears of being accepted by him. She didn't even know that was possible. She expected this for her sisters, but never herself.

In a way, being held like this was even more powerful than a kiss. Her whole life she'd wondered what kissing a man would be like. She'd never realized how special it would be to be held in a loving embrace. His love was more than just a physical attraction. He was protecting her, holding her up. She snuggled closer and placed her cheek against his chest, hearing his heartbeat. The moment was intimate in a way she hadn't expected, and Lovina closed her eyes, taking it all in.

His head bent down, and he kissed her forehead. Noah's finger slid under her chin, and he pulled back. She knew what he wanted—for her to look up and then...

The sound of a truck's engine interrupted the moment. Lovina jerked back, remembering for the first time the large open window and the perfect view of them anyone would have from outside. The intimacy of the moment was replaced by embarrassment, and she quickly rose to her feet. Yes, she wanted to be close to Noah, and she wanted to be kissed, but that ought not to happen in such a public place.

Lovina bent down and bagged up the napkins. She set the shell to the side and hurriedly folded the blanket.

Noah waved at someone through the window, and she was afraid to turn.

"Who is it?"

"I'm not sure. Someone I haven't met before. An Englischer."

"I know it's an Englischer. He's driving." Her words were sharp, and she pressed her lips together.

The man knocked on the door. "I'm so sorry," she said as she hurried to the door. "I didn't mean my words to be so harsh."

He was right behind her, and she felt a hand on her shoulder.

"Lovina." The way he said her name was tender. "I was trying to do a nice thing, but I wasn't protecting you. I'm sorry. I won't be so inconsiderate with my actions in public again."

She felt her heartbeat slowing once again. She blew out a breath and moved to the door. "Thank you, Noah."

His words played on her thoughts as she opened the door. A real smile filled her lips as she did. A man stood there. He wore old jeans covered with paint and his T-shirt read *3J Construction*.

"Can I help you?"

"Yes, I'm looking for Noah Yoder. I hear he's your contractor."

Lovina's eyebrow cocked, and she turned, motioning Noah forward. Noah had a smudge of frosting on the corner of his mouth and she resisted the urge to reach up and wipe it.

"How can I help you?" Noah asked.

Lovina stepped out of the way as Noah walked out to talk to the man. She didn't mean to eavesdrop, but it sounded as if the man was asking Noah if he'd be interested in remodeling a building across town. Lovina smiled, realizing how Noah's name would no doubt get out after this project was complete, but then another thought hit her. Once it was done she'd be busy running a pie shop and Noah would be working on other projects.

They wouldn't be working together anymore. She wouldn't see him every day.

Lovina set to work cleaning the glass in the front window. With the door open she could hear the conversation. Would Noah take the man's offer?

"I'd like to hear more, but to be honest I'm hoping for more work in Pinecraft. It's easier sticking closer to home, and—well, I just want to make sure the community is taken care of first."

"That makes sense," the man said, but from the look on his face it didn't make sense at all. "Well, if you don't mind I'd love to come back in a few weeks with more details. At least you can see what we're doing. Look over our plans. Maybe you'll be interested in putting in a bid after all."

"Sure." Noah nodded. "I'll look forward to that." He shook the man's hand.

Lovina sprayed more glass cleaner. Noah had told the man that he was hoping for more work around Pinecraft, but was that even possible? Was there enough work here to sustain him and his teenage crew? Would he need to go back to Illinois? She hadn't let her mind move far beyond getting the pie shop set up, but maybe she needed to do that. Noah had been more than generous by working for her, but what was next?

"Don't waste your precious thoughts on worries that may never come to be." She could hear her grandmother's admonishment playing over in her mind. It was easier said than done, but Lovina knew those words to hold truth. If only she could make herself follow them.

Lovina looked at the clock. Faith would be by shortly to work on the menus, and she still had some cleaning today. She hurried to the back storage room to get more cleaning rags, and could almost imagine her grandma telling her that she needn't be so hard on herself.

She also knew her grandma would be smiling, because for the first time ever she was actually letting her mind wander about something else other than pie. Lovina had a feeling that Grandma would appreciate her new choice of daydreaming material.

Maybe this was really love? Lovina smiled as she pulled rags out of the cleaning cabinet. She loved Noah. The joy filling her inside declared that.

-- --

Cinnamon Rolls

⅔ cup sugar

1 cup warm water

2 packages yeast

2 teaspoons sugar

1 teaspoon salt

1 cup mashed potatoes

4 eggs, beaten

6 cups flour

⅔ cup vegetable oil

Filling
soft butter
brown sugar
cinnamon

Combine sugar, water, and yeast. Add the rest of roll ingredients and mix well. Let dough rise until double. Preheat oven to 350°. Break dough into two portions. Roll out dough one portion at a time and spread with soft butter, brown sugar, and cinnamon. Roll up from long side and cut into 1¾-inch slices. Place in pan. Let rise and bake until brown, about 15-20 minutes.

Twenty-Five

If there is a smile in your heart, your face will show it.

AMISH PROVERB

∽◦∾

Lovina heard the front door to the pie shop open, and she turned, expecting to see Faith. Instead, Grace strode into the warehouse alongside another woman—an Englischer, wearing tan slacks and a rosy red blouse.

Lovina paused from the list she'd been writing. She'd been pondering it for a week. It was a list of pies she would offer. Once she came up with the final list Faith was going to write them in calligraphy on a menu and they would make photocopies.

Lovina pushed the paper to the side and stood.

"Lovina," said Grace, "I'd like to introduce you to Cara Johnson from the *Sarasota Sun* newspaper. She was in Yoder's today interviewing Hank about the excitement of the new season. Cara's going to shoot a few photos now with the empty streets, and then a few next week after the buses arrive." Grace looked to the reporter, who was nodding enthusiastically. "I knew she'd want to hear about your shop."

"It'll make a great story," the reporter said. "I think people have a hard time believing there's an Amish community just a few miles down the road from million-dollar homes."

"When I overheard them talking I had to interrupt," Grace continued. "Ms. Johnson here was so excited, especially when I told her that an Amish bachelor and Amish teens were helping to remodel this old warehouse. She agreed that it made the perfect human interest story."

Lovina looked to her baby sister, her eyes growing wide. Grace had never been shy, but Lovina had never seen Grace in this element before. Grace's dark blonde hair was tucked neatly in her kapp and gave every appearance of being more comfortable in an Amish kitchen than talking to the media, but Lovina saw excitement in her little sister's eyes that gave her face a special glow.

"Yes, I'm so thankful your sister found me," the reporter jumped in. "Grace also said you wouldn't mind if I interviewed you." She pulled out a notebook and pen. "Can you start by telling me how this all got started?"

Lovina folded her hands in front of her. Her palms felt damp, and she wondered if the pounding of her heart was almost as loud as Noah's hammer pounding in the other room. She guessed it was. "Well, as a young girl I always enjoyed making pies. I think the first pumpkin pie I made was still runny in the middle, but my mem and dat just ate around the edges. I suppose one wants to continue what one gets praise for," Lovina chuckled. "Thankfully my pies got better over time."

"Food is a special part of Amish social life," Grace butted in. "It's served at potlucks, marriage services, fundraisers, and farewells. Families gather in homes for church, and they always eat together before they leave."

The reporter took notes and then turned her attention back

to Lovina. "And why did you want to open a pie shop? From that smile on your face I can see this means so much to you."

"Well." Lovina smiled bigger. "Food is also a way to connect people and reach out to a larger world. Offering a piece of pie makes a visitor, whether an old friend or a stranger, feel welcome. Like my sister said, we eat together as we gather, but it also is a sign of support when one's going through a hard time. It's a gesture of caring for each other. Sharing pie is loving another person in a caring way. And…it helps us to be reminded that God cares for us and offers us the gift of food and friends."

Lovina looked to her sister, hoping Grace wasn't upset that she'd been cut off. Instead, Grace's eyes shone with pride, and for a moment Lovina felt like she was the little sister getting the big sister's approval.

They continued to talk, and after a while Lovina forgot she was talking to a reporter. It was so natural to share about the pie shop. To express how important it was for people to sit face-to-face and enjoy the company of friends in the middle of a busy day.

Lovina showed the reporter the list of pies she'd selected. Cara took the list and began to read aloud. "Coconut cream, banana cream, peanut butter cream pie, key lime pie, strawberry rhubarb pie, cherry pie, lemon meringue, shoo-fly pie, apple skillet pie, and…orange pie? I've never heard of that one before."

"It's light and refreshing and perfect for Florida. I think it's going to be a wonderful taste of sunshine visitors will want to try during their stay. It's one of my favorites to make for church gatherings."

The woman asked a few more questions, and then she turned her attention to Noah and the teens, who were installing a large pan rack in the kitchen.

Cara pointed her pen. "And tell me about them."

"Oh, it's a lovely story," Grace gushed. "That handsome Amish bachelor is helping wayward youth by giving them job skills. He also does salvage work, repurposing cast-off items." Grace pointed to the large counter where the bakers were going to roll out the crusts. "Noah found that in an old house near the water. Can you believe someone was going to just throw that away?"

The woman scribbled notes, and a smile graced her lips. "This is great stuff. It'll make a nice story, but I have to ask one question."

"Ja. What is it?" Lovina asked.

"Well, no one has mentioned it, but is it just a coincidence that a handsome bachelor is so generously giving his time to help a beautiful young Amish woman opening a pie shop?" The reporter leaned forward with her pen poised over the page. "A romance like that seems so lovely and innocent, so different from what we read in the papers today."

"Well, I…it *is* a coincidence." Lovina felt heat rising to her cheeks. "I mean, God probably had something to do with it, but it wasn't in my plans." She touched her hand to her cheek. "I can't say too much, but I'm thankful…" She forced a smile. "Thankful that God brought Noah into my life."

Grace placed a hand over Lovina's. "I think what my sister is trying to say is 'no comment.'" Grace wrinkled her nose, as if realizing how strange this would all sound to an outsider. "You see, in the Amish community a couple only lets others know of a possible marriage a few weeks before the wedding. It's called 'getting published' when you let everyone know." Grace laughed. "And unless my sister is planning on getting married even before the shop is open, I doubt she wants any news of their relationship in the press."

Their relationship? The words replayed in Lovina's mind. "Ja, no comment." She released a breath with her words, realizing again how God was giving her more than she ever imagined. A pie shop and many people to share the joy with. And Noah, who not only shared the joy with her, but also the work. She couldn't help but look at him. And when she turned back she realized the reporter's eyes were on her.

"I won't write anything about it now, but maybe when I return." The woman offered a wistful smile. "It's stories like these our world needs to hear. Stories to let people know that not every place is corrupt with people wanting more power, more attention, more fame."

"When you return?" Lovina asked.

"Yes, when the pie shop is open." Cara Johnson stood, tucked a pen behind her ear, and held her notebook to her chest. "I can't wait to sample that orange pie." And then the reporter looked to Noah, still hard at work, and released a sigh. "And see how the rest of this project turns out. Sweet and happy, I'm certain. For both the shop and the baker."

There was a far-off look in Cara's eyes—one that Lovina didn't want to ignore. "Is it difficult being a reporter?" Lovina asked. "I'm sure you see so many hard things."

"I do." Cara nodded. "It is hard at times. Sometimes I've questioned why God lets bad things happen. But then I come to a place like this, and I'm reminded..." Her voice trailed off.

"Of what?" It was Grace who asked this time.

"I'm reminded that good things are happening too, and it may sound silly, but I can feel God here." The woman's eyes flickered to Lovina, but then she looked away, almost embarrassed. "I won't write it in the story...but I having a feeling you're going to serve up more than just pie, Lovina. I have a feeling you'll be serving faith and hope too."

A chill raced up Lovina's arms. She looked to Grace and

noticed her sister's smile. And deep down she had a feeling the woman was right. Maybe this place wasn't just about pie after all.

✎

Lovina sat on her bed running the brush down her long hair. She was tired and sore, but in a good way. She and Faith hadn't gotten around to working on the menus as she'd hoped, but she hadn't minded. Instead, after the reporter had left, she'd worked with Noah, sifting through a few more items from his storage area that he thought they could repurpose for the store.

She was amazed by Noah really. Once Lovina had relayed Grace's vision for the pie shop being a mix of Amish comfort and vintage, he'd found more items to repurpose. Her favorite item was an old, rusty metal stepladder that he'd used to display cookbooks. He'd set it up by the door, and joy bubbled up in Lovina as she imagined how delighted customers were going to be when they walked inside. There was so much to appreciate, to look at. Lovina released a contented sigh and lay back on her pillow.

On the next bed over, Hope twisted her strawberry blonde hair into a long braid. Out of all the sisters, Hope was the no-nonsense one. The sister more prone to practical ideas than wistful thoughts.

"Thinking of pies again? Have you narrowed down which ones you're going to have on your menu?" Hope asked.

"Uh, well..." Lovina couldn't help the smile that played on her lips.

Hope tied off her braid and then glanced over, waiting for Lovina's answer. Then she leaned forward and studied Lovina's face. "You're not thinking about pies at all!" Hope gasped. "You are thinking about a bachelor."

"Why would you think that?"

Hope's eyes widened. "Look at you. Your cheeks are all red. It's him, isn't it?"

"Him who? I don't know what you're talking about."

Hope pinned her sleeping handkerchief to her hair, a large smile on her face. "Who am I talking about?" She laughed. "As if you didn't know. Noah."

Lovina tried to hide her smile, but it didn't quite work. Hope reached over and placed a soft finger on Lovina's chin, urging her to look up.

Lovina did and the smile came.

"You like him!"

Out of all the sisters Hope had been around the pie shop the least, and Lovina knew that was why Hope was just now realizing how close she and Noah had become.

"Shhh…" Lovina placed her finger to her lips. "Of course I like him. He's a great worker. You should see him. He's become a favorite supplier at Sarasota Architectural Salvage, and just yesterday he traded some old wooden crates for some fencing pickets for the shop. He didn't have to do that. We agreed that he could have everything inside that he wanted, but he said he had a wonderful idea. He's going to create a white picket fence to separate the girls rolling pie crusts from the tables out front. I never would have come up with that, but I love the idea! I loved it from the first moment he showed it to me on a sketch. Grace loved it too." Lovina didn't tell Hope about the surprise birthday breakfast. She was cherishing that all to herself.

"So you're saying you're interested in him as a carpenter only?" Hope cocked one eyebrow. "I haven't seen him close up for myself, but I overheard one of the waitresses at Yoder's talking about how handsome he was."

A strange jealousy stirred in Lovina's chest. She swallowed hard. Which waitress was talking about him? Someone she knew?

"Look at you!" Hope chuckled. "I think you're going to have smoke escaping your ears."

"Why would I be concerned if other women think Noah handsome? It's not as if I have any ownership over the man. We've only gone on one real date." Yet even as she said those words, she knew they had an understanding. The way he'd held her...well, hadn't that meant something special?

Lovina put on her sleeping kapp and turned down the wick on their lantern. Even though they had electricity in their room, both she and Hope agreed that they loved the ambiance of lantern light at night when they read and talked in bed. They'd lived with lantern light their whole life. It seemed unnatural to fill their room with the harsh white light from the lightbulb now, no matter if they had electricity or not.

Hope chuckled. "And when would you have time to go on dates? You're at the shop from morning to night. Do you ever stop to eat?"

Lovina rolled to her side. "There's a lot to get done."

"Ja, and it helps things that your coworker is nice to look at too."

Lovina didn't say anything then. She didn't want to argue and she couldn't lie. Instead, she decided to change the subject.

"Noah found two large urns in the back storage area today. He said they'd look awful nice filled with flowers and sitting by the front door. Would you be interested in doing that for me?"

"Really?" Hope's voice rose, and there was shuffling in her bed as she propped herself up on her elbow and turned to face Lovina. "You'd let me do that?"

"Let you? I'd be honored. It would be helpful."

"Thank you." Hope's voice softened to a whisper. "It means a lot. It's just with everyone else helping—with the sewing, the art, the remodeling, and the business plans...I sort of felt left out."

"Left out?" She studied Hope's face in the low light and noticed tears rimming her eyes. "I just thought you weren't interested in helping. You've been spending so much time with friends at the beach. You always act like things don't bother you."

"Ja, well, then you have a lot to learn, don't you." Her sister tried to smile, but it was a sad affair. "Sometimes I feel the weakest. Sometimes I have to try to prove myself so I don't feel left out."

Lovina listened and nodded, trying to take it in. "I'm sorry, Hope, for leaving you out."

Hope shrugged. "I know you didn't mean to. But maybe you'll remember that for your future employees. When one of them is putting up a wall, remember that those with the hardest outer shell have the softest insides."

"Like that turtle you brought home the first week we lived here?"

Hope nodded. "Exactly."

Lovina lay there until her sister's soft snores told her that she slept. That was one thing about having four sisters—it seemed at least one of them was always feeling left out. Why hadn't she noticed? Mostly because of the pie shop, and also because Noah Yoder was filling all her thoughts. It was a lot to wrap her mind around, but as Lovina let her eyes flutter closed, she told herself to remember to pay attention to others too. God's dream wasn't just about her. What good would it do to open a pie shop—one that would bring people together—if it put a wedge between her and those she cared for most?

No good at all. That's what. As she drifted off to sleep she said a prayer for Hope. Prayed that Hope would find something good to smile about, just like Lovina had in not one, but in two ways.

- -

Orange Pie

One 9-inch baked pastry pie crust
2 cups water, divided
1 cup sugar
2 tablespoons cornstarch
1 teaspoon orange-flavored drink mix
3 oranges, peeled and chopped

Cream cheese mixture
4 ounces cream cheese, softened
2 cups powdered sugar
8 ounces whipped cream

To prepare orange topping: Bring 1½ cups of water to a boil in a saucepan. In a bowl, mix together sugar, cornstarch, and drink mix. Add remaining ½ cup of water into the sugar mixture and stir. Pour into boiling water and cook over medium heat, stirring constantly. Remove from heat when it begins to thicken a bit. Stir in orange pieces. Set aside until cool.

To prepare cream cheese mixture: Stir together cream cheese and powdered sugar until creamy. Add whipped cream to the mixture. Spread into baked pie crust and spoon orange topping over filling. Refrigerate overnight. Decorate the top of the pie with extra whipped cream, if desired.

Twenty-Six

ovina stepped into the morning, hoping for a cool breeze. She
heard a sound and noticed Hope sitting outside the back
door on the wooden bench that had been left by the previous
owners. At her side was a bucket of gardening tools. Hope was
glaring at the barren yard. Was she thinking about their large garden back in Walnut Creek? Of her old shed filled with rakes and
hoes, or garden stakes and a push tiller? Hope's garden had been
a sight to see. It had been appreciated by anyone who took a slow
ride by on a buggy.

Hope's head lifted as Lovina closed the door behind her. "Are
you heading to the pie shop?"

"Ja. Just heading there now. Want to join me? We can walk. It's
a beautiful day."

Hope picked up the bucket with gardening tools. "That
would be wunderbar. I'd like to look at those pots you were talking about." Hope smiled, and Lovina saw a light and joy in her

sister's eyes that she hadn't noticed in a while. "It'll give me something to focus on. Since I've been a complete failure at making vegetables grow in this yard, maybe I'll do better with flowers in pots." Hope shrugged. "You can't eat flowers, but it's a start."

They walked side by side to the pie shop, and nervous excitement stirred in Lovina's stomach as they approached. The outside had been painted and an awning had been put up. The teens had mowed the grassy area, and all the garbage had been cleared out of the small parking lot. It was starting to look like a real business now, and once the sign was up it would make it even more real.

Lovina showed Hope the pots, and her sister couldn't have looked more pleased as she headed to the nursery to get inspiration for what to put inside them. Lovina hurried toward the front door next, and she heard the pounding even before she reached it. *Bam, bam, bam-bam.* Two hammers, maybe three, worked together in a staccato beat. She listened a moment and then stepped inside. Boards leaned against the wall. Noah was on his knees erecting the white picket fence that would separate the long counter from the seating area. Gerald worked by his side, lining up the pickets for Noah. Noah was so focused on his task that he hadn't seen her come in. He smiled as he worked, and she was thankful. Thankful for so much—for him, for the good work he was doing, for his ideas, and…and for the love she saw in his eyes every time he looked at her.

She loved watching him work. Joy overwhelmed her. What did she do to deserve someone like Noah Yoder? Nothing. He was a gift, just as this place was a gift. She continued toward him, and then a sound rose and echoed through the warehouse, causing her to jump. A loud popping sound filled the air. Lovina's heart pounded inside her and she wondered if she needed to run. But where? She looked around, looked up…wondering where the noise had come from. The sound of small explosions echoed through the spacious building.

Noah was on his feet, hurrying toward her. "Are you all right?"

Lovina covered her ears with her hands. "Ja. It was something outside, I think."

Noah raced out the door and she followed. He scanned the parking lot and then turned toward his uncle's house. White, thin smoke curled from the shed and the odor of sulfur pricked her nostrils. Lovina gasped, spotting Mose and Atlee sprawled on the freshly cut grass in Roy's yard. Mose's body jerked, and Atlee lay as still as a board. One arm covered his eyes, and his hand lay splayed on his chest. A boulder grew in the pit of her stomach, and her feet seemed fixed to the ground. She wanted to hurry to them, to see what the problem was, but she was afraid of what she'd find.

"Mose!" Noah raced toward the yard, his boots pounding on the asphalt of the parking lot. "Atlee! Are you hurt?"

Feeling a rush of adrenaline, she raced behind him. Gerald hung back.

Entering the yard, Noah sunk down onto the grass and turned Mose over. Mose's face was red and distorted, and gurgling sounds emerged from his lips. Was this a seizure? Should she go inside and call 911? Lovina caught up, stopping just behind Noah.

"What's wrong? What happened?" Noah's voice was frantic.

A louder sound emerged from Mose's lips, and she stepped back, confused. It wasn't a moan of pain but laughter. She turned to Atlee then…and saw that he wasn't hurt. His shoulders trembled slightly and she guessed it was partly shock and partly an attempt at laughter.

Lovina stepped into the shed and understood where the loud noise had come from. A remote control car was hooked up to some type of ignition device. Next to it sat a small stack of smoldering, burnt-up fire crackers. Obviously Mose had created a device that caused the firecrackers to go off just as Atlee entered the shed.

"Noah, you need to come look at this," Lovina called to him.

Noah released his grip on Mose's shoulders, pushing him away and causing him to tumble to the grass in another fit of laughter.

"You should've...seen...his face. And...the...dancing jig..." Mose's words came out in gasps.

Noah paused next to Lovina, leaning forward slightly to get a better view of the device. He mumbled something under his breath that she couldn't make out, and his cheeks grew red. The redness moved down his face and onto his neck. Noah balled his hands at his sides, sucked in a deep breath, and then turned.

"Mose, you're laughing? Do you think this is funny?" he said through clenched teeth. He stomped over to him, standing above his nephew and looking down on him with disgust.

More laughter erupted from Mose. "You should've seen Atlee's face!"

Atlee dropped his arm, opened his eyes and sat up. He took a deep breath and then let it out, still trying to calm his nerves. "I went in the shed to get the weed eater to do the yard." There was the slightest tremor in his voice. "There was this explosion and the flashes of light. My ears are still ringing. I thought the whole shed was going up." He placed his hands to his ears and shook his head, trying to stop the ringing.

Gerald sauntered toward them, arms crossed over his chest, finally joining the group. He seemed neither surprised nor dismayed by the sight of his friends. Mose stood up to his full height and pointed to Gerald, his finger wagging. "It was his idea. He's the one who told me about it. Admit it, Gerald."

Gerald stood still, silent. He sheepishly peered down at his feet. The humor on Mose's face turned to anger.

Mose neared his friend, shoulders raised up, neck tight, and eyes narrowed. "You're not going to say anything? Not going to defend me? Gerald, you always try to be the perfect one. Don't try to get out of it and pretend it wasn't your idea. Admit it!"

Gerald placed his hands on his hips. "I didn't tell you to do it. I just told you how a friend did it." His eyes flickered up to Mose and he winced, as if almost expecting the barrage of words to come.

Instead, Mose reached out, grabbing up Gerald's shirt in his fist. Noah was in his face in two steps. He gripped Mose's arm, holding it tight. "Didn't I tell you I was done with your pranks? I said you could hurt someone. What if that shed had caught on fire? What if Atlee—"

"Hey, hey!" Mose pulled his arm away and held up his hands. "You told us no pranks at the *pie shop*. This isn't the pie shop, Noah. It's Roy's yard. And no one was hurt. Nothing was damaged. It was just a joke."

"I don't want to hear it. I don't want to talk to you." Noah turned, and then his eyes locked with Lovina's. They widened, as if for the first time realizing that she was there. "I...I'm sorry, Lovina."

She wanted to tell him it was all right. She wanted to laugh and say boys would be boys, but the thing was, these weren't boys. In the eyes of the world they were wayward youths, but their decisions were anything but innocent. This could have gone so wrong. The whole shed could have gone up. Atlee could have been seriously hurt, and he may have sustained damage to his hearing. And, if it had happened in her shop, well, so much more could have gone wrong. Damage to her shop would cost them. A lot.

There was so much at stake. Not only all her funds—her father's funds—and her reputation.

Instead of responding to Noah, she turned to Mose. "I wonder if I can trust you. Trust you in my shop. There's too much at stake." The words spilled from her mouth. "I can't risk letting anything happen. We have no insurance. And if my family loses everything…"

Mose's anger at Gerald changed to a look of worry. She could tell her words had finally penetrated, and Mose turned from Lovina back to Noah. "Yeah, of course. I—I guess I didn't think of that."

When Noah didn't respond, Mose looked back to Lovina. "It wasn't in your shop. I never would've done it in your shop," he said hurriedly. "I just thought it was funny, that's all."

Noah shook his head, not letting Mose get off that easy. "What you do affects every part of you. You can't be both a careless prankster and a dedicated, trustworthy employee. How you are seen in one area affects how others see you in all areas."

"Listen, it was just a joke…" Mose stated defensively again, and then paused. He crossed his arms over his chest. He lowered his head and his face fell. "I'd never do anything to hurt anyone." His tone was lower now. He looked to Lovina. "And I'd never do anything to hurt your shop."

"Not intentionally." The words were out before she could stop them. Hurt flashed on Mose's face, and he no longer looked so tough. She pictured him as a scared little boy. "I know you wouldn't cause damage on purpose, but it could happen more easily than you think."

Something flashed in his eyes, as if a memory replayed there, and all the cocky defenses he'd maintained a moment before melted away. There was a story there, she knew. It was clear from his gaze that he'd faced loss—of possessions, of his reputation. Why didn't teens learn?

Then again, what had she done to reach out to him? To any of them?

He'd been around, but she'd never really taken the time to talk to Mose. What was his childhood like? How did he like being in Florida? Did he think he'd stay Amish? She lowered her head, eyeing the freshly mowed grass. This was yet another person she'd pushed to the side in her desire to get the shop open. Had she let the goal of opening her shop get in the way of what really mattered?

Lovina opened her mouth to say something, but before she could, Noah stepped forward. He must have taken note of the same mournful look on Mose's face because his voice was gentle. "Listen, Mose, can we get away for a few minutes? Can we talk alone?"

Mose nodded, and Lovina knew she was no longer needed. She'd made her worries known. Now the rest was up to Noah.

She turned to the other two teens. By the curious looks on their faces, they also seemed to be wondering what they should do next. Lovina cleared her throat and they looked at her.

"I wanted to hang some antique pie plates. Gerald, Atlee, can you help me get the ladder?"

"Ja," Gerald answered.

"I can help," Atlee joined in.

With a small wave to Noah, she turned and walked toward the pie shop. She didn't envy him. Noah had his work cut out with these teens. And she guessed that dealing with them was harder than trying to remodel a warehouse into a pie shop. Wood and concrete could be molded without shrinking back. You didn't have to worry about the feelings of building materials. You didn't have to talk them into complying. They couldn't walk away.

Oh Lord, be with Noah and give him the words. She sent up a silent prayer. Mose needed to grow up. He needed to realize that his actions could be serious. But most of all he needed the grace that she herself had received more times than she could count.

❧

Noah took Mose to Yoder's for lunch. The place was busy, and he hoped the noise of the room would make it impossible for anyone to eavesdrop on their conversation. More than that, he hoped the food would help. He'd seen his parents use the tactic numerous times. Hard talks were easier to stomach when one had a good meal placed in front of them.

Lovina's sister Faith was working, and Noah caught the way she shyly eyed Mose as they walked to their table. She smiled, and Mose attempted to smile in return, but Noah knew she wouldn't be convinced. The cocky attitude that Mose had earlier had been replaced by a mournful look.

They both ordered the special—hand-breaded pork chops and creamy country gravy—and then Noah leaned forward, his elbows on the table, as conversations swirled around them.

"Listen, I'm sorry about today." Mose took a sip from his Coke. "It was stupid. I see that now." He lowered his gaze and fiddled with his fork. "And I know you'll have to talk to my parents…"

"I not going to tell them," Noah interrupted. "And I'll talk to Atlee and Gerald too."

"Really? So they're not going to find out?" Mose's eyebrows lifted, and he looked again like the twelve-year-old boy who used to tag along with Noah at the auction yard. In Amish families, when one has lots of brothers and sisters, attention was craved, and Noah could still see that in Mose now. The thing was, he often sought it in the wrong ways.

Mose let out a long breath. "I'd never hear the end of it."

Noah took a sip of his coffee and then nodded. "Do you think I don't understand? Growing up Amish, for your whole life you've lived by the rules. You've been told what to believe and how to act. You not only have your parents watching, but everyone in the whole community. One wrong move and everyone knows. Everyone."

Mose looked at him cautiously, as if wondering when the lecture was going to come. Instead Noah continued, trying to help the young man know that he understood, but wouldn't tolerate such actions again.

Noah ran his fingers through his hair. "One of my cousins talked me into trying a cigarette once. His older brother kept them stashed under the buggy cushions. We went behind the barn to smoke and we looked around. I was sure that no one could see us. No one.

"Well, it turned out a neighbor had been in the orchard behind his house, pruning some of the trees. He told his wife. His wife told someone in town. By the time I got home that night my mem already knew. I got sent to bed without supper."

Mose tossed his head so that his hair brushed against his forehead. Noah saw the hurt in his eyes. He also knew that even though Mose had messed up today, lecturing him would only push him further away. Besides, Lovina had already made her expectations known.

Their lunch arrived, and they both ate quickly as if it had been two days, instead of two hours, since breakfast. As Mose sopped up the last of his gravy with a roll, Noah cleared his throat, getting his attention.

"You know my whole plan in starting over in Florida was to keep you guys connected with the Amish community, but the longer this goes on the more I realize that maybe my focus has been too much on making the Amish life seem appealing. I've made a big mistake."

Mose paused his chewing. "What's that?"

"I'm afraid I haven't talked enough about God."

Mose put down his fork and shrugged. "I'm not sure I know what you mean."

The waitress approached to refill his coffee, and Noah waved her away. He didn't need coffee. He needed to share what was on his heart.

"I believe in our community. I appreciate the way we've chosen to live. But it's not being Amish that will get you to heaven. Eternity is about accepting what Jesus has done. We can try to be good all we want—to follow the rules of the community—but no one will ever get it right." Noah focused on Mose's eyes. "I know I give you guys a hard time, but I mess up too—and often. No one can do everything right. That's what we need God's grace for."

Mose nodded, but Noah could tell he was only half listening. He turned his attention to the pie menu. "Is it okay if I order pie to take back to Gerald and Atlee too?"

Noah released a heavy sigh. "Is that all?"

"Well, I don't think Lovina will want a piece. She makes her own pies, right?"

"I'm not talking about the pie, Mose. I'm talking about God, and about how we need Him. Have you been listening to anything I've been saying?"

Mose shrugged. "I've been listening. It makes sense. What else do you need me to say?"

"I don't need you to say anything, but I want you to come to me if you have questions. Living down here in Pinecraft I'm sure you've seen a lot of people not following the same Amish rules, and it may not make sense with how you've been raised, but what I've come to discover is that it's not the rules that matter. Rules don't save us. Grace does. It's not what we do but our trust in Jesus that determines where we will spend eternity."

Again Mose nodded, but it didn't seem as if Noah's words were truly sinking in.

Lovina's sister Faith approached with the bill. She tried to make small talk, but it was clear, even to her, that Mose wasn't in a talkative mood. Noah handed her cash for the ticket, not knowing what he could say. Faith took it, thanked him for the tip, and walked away disappointed.

Mose rose from the chair. Tension was clear on his face. Maybe the tension was from the prank earlier. Maybe the realization that Mose couldn't pull his old pranks was finally sinking in. Or maybe it was the conversation Noah just had with him. Did Noah's words battle within Mose's soul? It was hard to tell.

Noah rose from the seat, and they made their way through the restaurant. Mose held a paper bag with three slices of pie inside. When they got outside Mose paused and turned to Noah.

"Thanks for lunch, Noah, and before we get back to the warehouse there's something I need to tell you. I've been thinking about it for a while. After we finish the warehouse I'm going to head to Miami Beach. I've heard there are lots of good construction jobs there."

Noah's chest tightened, and it felt as if someone was trying to squeeze his heart. "I—I don't understand."

"I know you're trying to help me, I really do. But even if news of today's prank doesn't get back to my parents in the next few days, or even in a few months, they'll find out about that or about something else eventually. I'm just tired of trying to be perfect all the time. It seems like I can do one hundred things right and only one thing wrong, and everyone jumps down my throat about it."

Noah placed a hand on Mose's shoulder. "That's not what's happening. I hope you know how much I appreciate you guys. I—"

Mose shrugged off his touch. "Listen." He held up his hands. "I know you mean well, I really do. I just need some time on my own, to figure it out my own way. I thought I'd be doing that by coming to Florida, but this place is more connected to home than I thought. Everyone still knows everyone else's business."

Noah nodded. He wanted to bring up again how important God's grace was—not the opinions of men—but he knew that Mose wasn't in the right mind to receive it.

He'd known all along that if Mose decided not to stay there was nothing he could do to make him.

They continued walking back toward the pie shop and Noah dared to ask Mose one more question.

"What about Gerald and Atlee?"

Mose shrugged. "They don't know anything about my plans. I haven't mentioned it."

"Do you think they'll go with you?"

"Probably not. I heard both of them talking and they're looking forward to seeing their parents, who are coming down during the season. And I think they're still sweet on some Amish girls too. I figure with me out of the way there won't be anything that'll keep them from being baptized. I must be a bad influence or something."

"I hate to see you go off on your own like that."

"Yeah, well, just keep up the good work with Gerald and Atlee. I think you're close to roping them in…especially with Lovina's pretty sisters coming around all the time."

They neared the pie shop, and Noah could see there wasn't anything he could say that would change Mose's mind. He'd already checked out—if not with his body, then with his mind. If anything was going to get through to Mose it would have to be God's doing. Noah had done all he could, and it hadn't worked.

But Noah couldn't think about that now. He had the pie shop to finish up. He also had to make things right with Lovina. He'd given her his heart, but he hadn't fully revealed the truth of his past. Maybe he was more like Mose than he thought. Maybe he was afraid of everyone knowing the real him. Or at least he was afraid of Lovina knowing.

⤳

With a groan Noah sank onto the bed. For once the guys were silent in the other room. Their mood was somber tonight.

He leaned forward and clutched his forehead in both hands. His heart was still doing a double beat in his chest. *It's my fault... I don't seem to be getting through to them. And now Mose's leaving is my fault too.*

His whole goal in working on the pie shop was to help the guys. To spend time with them. To train them. To teach them the satisfaction of doing a job well. To mentor them in their relationships with God. And the truth was that he'd let his mind get caught up in other things.

At the thought of Lovina and her wide, brown eyes and her lips that so easily curled into a smile, his chest warmed with a love he'd never felt before.

That was the problem. He was letting his heart get in the way of his head. If he didn't keep his focus, the woman he loved would be hurt the most. If he kept letting his heart lead the way, her pie shop would suffer. Not to mention that he was already failing miserably with Mose, Gerald, and Atlee.

Lord, give me wisdom.

A Scripture verse filtered through his mind. If he'd heard the verse from his Aunt Karen's lips once, he'd heard it one hundred times. Aunt Karen had been from a Mennonite family, and had joined the Amish church when she'd fallen in love with Uncle Roy. She'd done her best to fit in with the Amish ways, but the people in their community—and even their family—thought she was too "Bible smart" for her own good.

"All that Bible knowledge just makes her think she's better than the rest of us. It's pride, I tell you," Noah's mem had said.

Yet even when others held her at arm's length, Noah found himself drawn to his aunt. With ten siblings he'd always felt like just another face around the dinner table, but Aunt Karen always took time to ask about him. She always took time to tell him stories and to remind him of God's love.

He'd thought of her words during his darkest moments, sitting alone in the jail cell. When his mind cleared after the accident, he liked to think that the gracious God his aunt talked about was more accurate than the God the Amish minister spoke of. The God who kept track of all his rights and wrongs and would one day weigh them on his entry into heaven.

Aunt Karen had been one of the first to visit him when he got out of jail. She'd gone with him to see the damage the accident had done to the shop too. And it was her words that had sent him in the right direction.

"Noah, *you* can choose the type of person you're remembered for. Wrongs can be made right. But remember you can't do it alone."

He'd clung to those words back then. "Wrongs can be made

right." He'd done that to the best of his ability. He'd rebuilt the gift shop, and he'd set his mind and heart on working with the teens. But now, as he sat in the dark of his room, he thought of those words again. *You can't do it alone.* Was that what he'd been doing? He knew it was. And what had he been trying to prove?

He thought about his words to Mose earlier in the day. He'd told Mose that the most important thing was one's relationship with God, but had he lived like that was the truth? Not really. The weight of all he'd said and done—and hadn't said and done—weighed like a ton of bricks on his shoulders.

God, I've failed. Failed You. Failed them.

He picked up his Bible from his nightstand and pressed it to his chest. He didn't need to figure everything out on his own. He couldn't save the teens. He couldn't save Mose. "God, I want to invite You back in. I'm sorry I've been trying to figure it out myself."

He thought about the distant look in Mose's face, and it broke his heart. He knew that if Mose accepted God, all his human relationships would work themselves out.

"Whatever it takes, Lord. Do what You need to capture their hearts."

He hated to think what that might mean. Too many people had to get to their lowest point before they turned to God—just like he had. Yet outside comfort mattered little compared to inner peace.

"Do whatever it takes," he whispered again. It was a hard prayer to pray, but the only one that would make any difference. Only God could help Mose now. And a peace settled over Noah's heart.

Hand-Breaded Pork Chops and Creamy Country Gravy

2 tablespoons butter
½ cup vegetable oil, divided
6 thick pork chops
1 cup milk or cream
2 cups all-purpose flour
salt and pepper
½ onion, sliced

Creamy Country Gravy
meat drippings
1 tablespoon butter
3 tablespoons all-purpose flour (more may be used)
1½ cups milk (I use hot milk)
salt and pepper

Heat cast iron skillet with butter and ¼ cup oil. Dip pork chops one at a time in a bowl of milk. Dredge in flour. Season chops with salt and pepper. Place in heated pan along with onion slices. Cook until browned on each side and meat is no longer pink. Add more butter and remaining oil as needed until the last pork chop is cooked. Remove chops and onions and arrange on platter. To the drippings in pan, add butter and 3 tablespoons flour and slowly stir in milk. Now, take a little taste with a spoon. If it's not quite perfect add more salt and pepper. Those are all the spices needed for this pork chop dinner. The only thing that makes this dish better is to serve it with homemade creamy, red-skin mashed potatoes.

Red-Skin Mashed Potatoes

8 medium red potatoes
1 stick butter
1 clove garlic, minced
1-2 cups milk—depending on size of potatoes
salt and pepper to taste

Boil potatoes with skin on until soft. Melt butter in a saucepan with garlic. Lightly simmer until butter is melted and garlic is lightly browned. In a mixer (or by hand), mix potatoes with garlic butter, adding the milk slowly until potatoes reach desired consistency. Season with salt and pepper.

Twenty-Seven

Be life long or short, its completeness
depends on what it was lived for.

AMISH PROVERB

⤳

Lovina pulled off her soiled apron and tossed it into the hamper in the laundry room. She touched her kapp, making sure it was still in place, and then hurried into the kitchen where fifteen pies were lined up. She'd made her final decisions for the menu and had baked all day. Now they were going to taste them. They'd had a simple dinner of split pea soup, knowing that their bellies would soon be full of pie.

Hope and Faith were finishing washing the dishes. Joy stood next to an ironing board set up next to the dining room table. She was painstakingly ironing the curtain valances that would soon be hung in the large windows of the pie shop.

Grace had set out Mem's good dishes and had taken some photos of the pies lined up on the counter. She'd purchased the camera with the money she'd been saving. Dat still didn't like the idea of Grace owning a camera, but he'd come to terms with it since his youngest daughter was using it for business. Maintaining

Amish ways was important, but so was making sure Lovina's pie shop succeeded.

Mem was eying the pies. She held a knife in one hand, stopping next to a sweet potato pie. Lovina had changed the recipe a little and it looked perfectly golden and delicious. It smelled fantastic too. All the pies did.

Mem licked her lips. "Can I cut into this one now? I smelled this baking this morning, and I've wanted to taste it all day."

"Not yet." Lovina placed a soft hand on her mother's arm. "We have one more guest who should be coming." She moved to the window and looked out, but she didn't see Noah. It was already twenty minutes later than she'd told him to come, and she knew that she wouldn't be able to hold everyone back much longer.

Lovina smiled to herself at the thought of seeing him again. After the incident with Mose yesterday he'd been distracted all afternoon. Now she couldn't wait to see him smiling and enjoying her pies. She'd baked them thinking of him.

Lovina glanced back from the window and noticed Mem's eyes on her. Her smile fell.

"So Noah Yoder is coming over? You should have warned us."

"Warned you?" Lovina placed a hand on her hip and turned to face her mother. "Why would you need a *warning*? You are delighted when any of our other Amish neighbors stop by—expected or not."

"There are things about Noah Yoder you do not know. Have you ever asked what he's hiding from you?" Mem cocked her head to the side and raised an eyebrow. Lovina didn't look away. Faith and Hope paused their washing and rinsing and turned. Grace put down her camera, and from the corner of her eye Lovina could see that Joy had stopped ironing too. Everyone seemed to be waiting.

Lovina pressed her lips together, trying to figure out how to respond. Mem had made it clear that Noah had a questionable past, and she too wondered why he hadn't told her about it, but Lovina had faith he would. When the time was right he would.

"I trust Noah, Mem. We've been busy with the pie shop. The day will come soon when we'll have the chance to talk about everything that needs to be discussed."

"That may be so, Lovina, but it seems too late to me. From the look on your face you've already given the young man more of your heart than you should have. I just hate to see your heart broken—that's all."

"But don't you want us to get married, Mem?" It was Hope who jumped in now. Her voice was sweet, but Lovina could tell that Hope was holding back. "Hasn't that been your wish—that we fall in love? That we get married? We know how hard it must be to have so many unmarried daughters."

"Of course I want my daughters to get married." Mem jutted out her chin. "But it matters who our daughters marry, right John?" She turned to her husband.

Lovina's dat looked up, and she could tell from the look on his face that this wasn't a conversation he wanted to be pulled into. He just nodded, but offered no comment.

"Noah's a *gut* man, Mem. He's a hard worker. He's thoughtful and kind…" Lovina's words spilled out. They were things she'd wanted to say for so long, and she could no longer hold them back. "I think you'd really appreciate him if you took the chance to get to know him."

Mem's eyebrow lifted skeptically. "He fixes up things, Lovina. He hauls old junk. Do you really think he'll be able to provide for a family like that?"

"He'll do his best. He always does his best." Lovina's lower lip trembled. "And his work is a beautiful thing. He finds worth in things that have been cast away. He sees value in things others overlook." *Like me,* she wanted to add.

"Yes, well, maybe I'd believe you if he showed up when he said he would. I've seen you watching the clock for the last thirty minutes." Mem put down the knife and moved to the table to sit by Dat. "A lot can be said by how one lives his daily life, Lovina. How one handles his responsibilities."

Lovina didn't know what to say to that. She didn't want to argue, and she was also frustrated that Noah was late. She wanted him to impress her parents. She wanted them to like him. Had he forgotten? Had something happened at the pie shop? She hoped not.

She picked up the knife Mem had put down and moved to the sweet potato pie. She didn't know what was keeping Noah, but she did know how to sweeten Mem up before his arrival.

"You're right, Mem. I'm not sure what's keeping Noah, but it shouldn't keep us from celebrating. It's time to start sampling the pies." And with a forced smile, Lovina cut a large slice of sweet potato pie for Mem. And then an equally large piece for herself. At least it would keep her occupied until Noah showed up.

If Noah showed up.

⁓

Noah took a deep breath and knocked on the door. He hated that he'd lost track of time. He was supposed to be here an hour ago for pie tasting. He and the guys had been so busy setting up all the tables and chairs that he hadn't noticed the sun sinking lower in the horizon. Noah heard shuffling footsteps on the other side of the door. Slowly it opened.

"Noah, glad you could make it. I imagine you put in a long day at the pie shop. Come in." John Miller opened the front door, but the living room was dim. Behind him two lanterns lit the kitchen, and the sound of women's voices chirped, rising every now and then with laughter.

"Sorry, Mr. Miller—I lost track of time." Noah removed his hat and turned it over in his hands.

"I imagined that was what happened." John smiled. "I never look down on a man who's busy at work."

Noah studied the older man's face in the shadows. His face was thin—evidence of his illness—but his eyes were large and brown, just like Lovina's. There was no blame or accusation there, but still Noah's squared shoulders had a hard time relaxing.

"I didn't mean to come so late and keep you up."

"You think you're the one keeping me up?" He pointed a thumb behind him. "Come. Lovina has made pie. Lots of pie." He turned to move to the kitchen.

"No, wait." Noah cleared his throat. "Can I talk to you first?"

"Ja." Instead of going to the kitchen, John Miller stepped outside. He motioned to the two rockers on the front porch. Noah sat in one and faced the older man.

"Sir, we could talk about the weather or the progress on the shop, but I just need to get it out. You may have guessed that I have feelings for Lovina. I've never enjoyed spending time with anyone as much as I've enjoyed spending time with her, but I am afraid."

"Afraid?" John asked.

Noah hesitated, wondering how to say what he needed to. Noah didn't want to talk too highly of himself, declaring that all his mistakes were far behind him. But neither did he want to condemn himself too much and destroy any chance of a life with Lovina. Noah took a deep breath and then released it, determined to tell the truth—about his past and about God's work in his life—the best he could.

"Sir, there are things I need to tell you. Things I haven't told Lovina yet. Things that happened back in my hometown in Illinois."

"Son, are you talking about the car accident? And the big mess you made of that building?"

Noah's jaw dropped. He didn't know how to answer.

"If my daughters were to tell you something about me, they'd tell you I like to read. I read *The Budget* religiously. I remember when I first heard about that story. An Amish young man on his rumspringa racing another car, losing control, and crashing. That's a hard story to forget."

"It is. I wish I didn't have to try to explain how I got into that state. How my life was back then. I didn't have a relationship with God. And I don't have any excuses. I just wanted to get it all out on the table. I've been wanting to tell Lovina for a while, but I'm afraid."

"Son, if you're going to talk to her, I want you to tell her the whole truth."

"I will, even though some of the events of that night are fuzzy."

John Miller shook his head. "I'm not only talking about the accident. I'm talking about the restitution."

"Sir?" Noah asked, unsure what he was leading to.

"You made a mistake, son, yes. But you also made it right." John's eyes twinkled in the moonlight. "I followed that story too." John pointed to the door as if telling Noah to go ahead and get it all out before he thought twice.

Noah nodded, relief flooding over him. He shook the man's hand and stood.

"And son…" John's voice trailed after him.

Noah turned. "Yes?"

"I need to apologize too."

Noah rubbed his furrowed brow. "For what?"

John stood slowly. "Months and months ago you came by looking for work. We talked about your working on my roof, but I never hired you. I'm sorry to say that at the time I was just trying to keep peace with my wife." He offered a humorless smile. "She gets her own idea about things…"

"I understand. Everything has worked out as it should. God has seen to that."

"Yes, well, I also want you to know that Anna does get bent out of shape about some things, but she's not unreasonable. Once she gets to know you, she will come around. Just love my daughter as you already do and my wife will soon see what everyone else does. You're a *gut* man, Noah. A *gut* man."

Noah smiled. He'd wanted to come to some type of agreement about pursuing Lovina, but from the sound of her father's words Noah was getting more than that. He was getting the man's blessing. "Thank you, sir. I'll do my best. I promise. Lovina is an easy person to love."

John Miller chuckled. "No one is easy to love all the time, son, but I know you'll do your best. She has a strong will, that one. Most people don't see it. She's soft as velvet on the outside with a spine tough as iron underneath."

"And that's how she's been able to come this far with the pie shop. You need a strong will to tackle that."

"I'm glad you've seen that too. Just know that even those with iron wills need gentleness at times. Do your best, Noah, to give her soft care and understanding…even when you think she doesn't need it. It'll take you far." His eyes twinkled. "And that's from a man who's been married more years than you are old."

Sweet Potato Pie

One 9-inch unbaked pie crust
⅓ cup butter
½ cup firmly packed brown sugar
2 large eggs, beaten
¾ cup heavy cream
2 cups sweet potato, cooked and mashed
1 teaspoon vanilla extract
½ teaspoon ground cinnamon
¼ teaspoon ground ginger
¼ teaspoon salt
dash ground nutmeg (optional)
whipped cream (optional)

Preheat oven to 425°. Mix all ingredients together thoroughly in a bowl. Pour into the pie crust. Bake 15 minutes, then reduce heat to 350° and bake 40 minutes longer, being careful not to burn the crust. Remove from the oven and let cool. Refrigerate until ready to serve. Top with sweetened whipped cream and a dash of nutmeg if desired.

Twenty-Eight

Swallowing pride rarely gives you indigestion.

AMISH PROVERB

⌐☞

Noah took two steps into the kitchen and all the conversation stopped. Six sets of eyes turned to him, and he forced a smile. He scanned the faces and then settled his gaze on Lovina. Her eyes were full of questions and worry. He released a slow breath.

"I'm so sorry I'm late. We were setting up tables and chairs. I lost track of time."

He looked to her mem next, who was eyeing him with curiosity. "Ma'am, please forgive me. I hope it's not too late."

"Too late for pie? Never!" Hope called out. And then the laughter of her sisters followed.

"Which one would you like a piece of first?" Faith asked. "So far my favorite has been the pecan, but all of them are delicious."

"I'd love a piece...well, a small bite of each." He cleared his throat. "But first, may I have a moment alone with Lovina?"

He looked first to her and then to her mem. Her mem offered a soft nod. "It's a perfectly lovely night, and I smell gardenias on the air. There will be plenty of pie when you're done talking."

Lovina moved to the back door and he followed. She sat on a bench by the back fence and patted the space beside her. He sat down, and even in the moonlight he could see the worry clear on her face.

"You have bad news, don't you?" She bit her lower lip.

"Why would you say that?"

Lovina pointed. "Your ears are red. They always turn red when you're angry or upset...or if you have bad news."

"Well, I—"

The slam of the window closing interrupted his words. Noah glanced up to see that Hope had shut it.

Laughter spilled from Lovina's lips, breaking the tension. "I'm so thankful for Hope. Her no-nonsense attitude keeps us all in line."

"It's good to see you smile. And I'm thankful for the way you care. And..." Noah's heart pounded in his chest. He'd do anything not to disappoint her, but he knew that in the next few minutes, that was exactly what he was going to do.

"I have to tell you about my past, Lovina. I wish I didn't have it trailing behind me, but ignoring it isn't going to make it go away."

Lovina didn't seem surprised. She nodded and waited.

Noah tilted his head. "Do you know? I mean...has someone already told you about what happened?"

"I don't know what happened. But my mem has let me know that something did." She lowered her head and looked to her lap. "I've considered all types of things. Maybe you were married before. Or have a child. Maybe..."

"Oh, nothing like that!" He lifted her face with the gentle nudge of his finger under her chin. She looked up at him, seemingly relieved.

Noah swallowed and then started in. "When I turned sixteen

I couldn't wait to get a car and drive. There were plenty lying around the auction yard, and I'd been eyeing them for a while. I did all kinds of salvage work and worked odd jobs to save money, and just a few months after my sixteenth birthday I bought an old Chevy Nova. It was a piece of junk, but it ran. Around the same time my brother Leonard bought an old Mustang. I can't tell you how many summer nights we worked on those cars…much to our parents' dismay."

"I can only imagine." Lovina listened, her full attention on him. "I've seen it happen in our community. I've seen the heartbroken parents."

"That's not the worse of it." He leaned forward and took her hand in his, as if wanting to hold on. Wanting to gain strength from her love. "It took a few years, but we finally got the cars up and running. And we did the stupidest thing we could do. We started racing."

Lovina lifted an eyebrow. "Like on a race track?"

"No." He shook his head. "With each other. On the weekends mostly. We'd find a lonely stretch of road and drive as fast as we could. I loved it…the speed. The adrenaline. I almost felt as if I was flying. Sometimes others asked to race us too, but some guys were too dangerous. They drank as they drove." He let out a harsh laugh. "We thought we were safe because we were sober. But we couldn't have been more wrong."

She studied his face, trying to picture him as the wayward teen. "And then…"

"And then one night we were racing, and I still don't know what happened. We were going around a corner by an Amish gift shop. It was winter and either I hit ice or my tire went off the pavement. Next thing I know my car was sailing through the air."

Lovina gasped and covered her mouth with her hand.

"It went right through the front windows into the shop. By the time my car stopped, only the rear bumper wasn't in the store. The place was a total loss."

"Were you hurt?"

"I broke my nose and a few of my ribs on the steering wheel. It was a miracle I wasn't hurt more."

"And the shop?"

"Oh, you know how the Amish are. They set up a new shop for her in town. They thought it was easier to build a new one on a piece of property in town. They demolished the old place. Only a few things were salvageable. Of course I learned about all that while sitting in prison."

"Prison?" Lovina swallowed hard.

"Yes, I was in there over a year. My dat didn't post bail. I got cited for reckless driving, but my defense attorney was able to get me out since the police report stated that ice on the road was most likely a factor. But..." Tears pooled in Noah's eyes, and his guilt piled upon guilt. "But while I was locked up Leonard kept on racing. And he started drinking with those other guys too. He was a passenger in the car of an Englisch kid one night. They hit a tree."

Lovina gasped. "And was he okay?"

"The driver walked away but Leonard was killed instantly." Noah lowered his head. "I always told myself that if I hadn't been in jail I could have watched over him."

"Oh, Noah." She placed a hand on his arm. "It's not your fault. Leonard made those decisions. And maybe God was protecting you...who knows if you would have been in that car too."

He nodded. He'd thought about that. The accident had been a wakeup call. Would he have continued down the same destructive path as Leonard if he hadn't been stopped? Noah had no doubt that would have been the case.

"One of the chaplains in the jail gave me a Bible, and I began to read it—something I'd never done growing up. I began to seek after God. I dedicated my life to Him. I started to understand grace. And when I got out I knew I needed to do what I could to make things right."

"What do you mean?"

His heel kicked against the leg of the bench, and for some reason it seemed just as hard to tell her what had come next. Maybe because, from the earliest age, one was taught not to be prideful.

"Even though the Amish community built a new shop in town, every time I passed the demolished shop my heart sank. And that was when I knew I had to do something. I worked for a year, saved up all my money, and then spent two years rebuilding her shop."

Lovina's eyes widened. "By yourself?"

"Well, mostly. Halfway through a friend pitched in, but it was good for me to do it. I built it from the ground up, and that's where I learned most of my carpentry skills. To save money I bought odds and ends from the auction yard, and I also salvaged job sites. That friend who helped…he was my dat's cousin, and he became a mentor. He'd messed up at a young age too, and he was impressed by my decision to rebuild the shop. I turned to him for advice on carpentry and life. He made such a difference to me that I wanted to do the same for Mose and his friends." Noah's voice trailed off. He couldn't tell her the rest. The wound was too fresh to tell Lovina about Mose's decision to leave. But he would in good time.

Lovina opened her mouth to speak, and then she closed it again.

"What, Lovina? What were you going to say?"

She squeezed his hand tighter and ran her thumb over the back of his hand. "It seems silly, but I was going to say that I'm thankful."

"Thankful?"

"Ja. Don't you see, Noah? Everything that's happened to you—the good and the bad—it's all brought you here today. To Pinecraft. To the shop. To me."

Lovina's eyes were wide as she looked at him, her expression one of deep love. Noah had heard of a person's life flashing before his eyes, and listening to her that was exactly what happened.

He pictured himself as a little kid, walking through the aisles of salvage materials at his dat's auction yard. He saw the wayward teenager, trying to run away from conformity…and getting lost in the process. He pictured the set of his chin when he picked up the hammer and decided to rebuild the destroyed gift shop one nail at a time. He also remembered the forlorn look in Mose's eyes as he sat in the county jail four years after Noah had sat in that same cell. Noah had known then that he had to get Mose out of there before his nephew's heart hardened completely. And that was why he'd brought them here. Each image was like a piece of a puzzle, and as they clicked into place in his mind, it formed a picture of *now*. Of this place. Of Lovina.

Amazement and joy somersaulted through him.

"What are you thinking about?" she asked in a whisper.

"This feels right. Us. Together. It's as you said—everything fits."

"It's God-designed and right." The words escaped in a sigh. She smiled. "He meant for us to be together like this now."

"Yes." Noah didn't know what else to say. Thankfulness to God flooded his heart as he realized what a great gift God had planned for him.

Lovina's lips parted slightly, and he imagined kissing her. His heartbeat quickened and he felt his pulse in his neck. Thankfulness, joy, and desire rose up within him. He wanted to be with Lovina their whole lives long. He wanted to be with her completely. He wanted to help her fulfill her dreams in this season and in every season to come.

He reached over and took her hand, weaving her fingers through his. "I love you, Lovina. I want to spend my life with you."

He watched as she swallowed hard and smiled. But instead of the uncertainty there was only peace in her eyes.

Noah tightened his grip. "You don't seem surprised."

"Well, is it wrong to say that I was hoping?" She gazed up at him with such admiration that he thought he'd burst. And though he waited for her to declare her love, she didn't say it. Even though he could see the love in her eyes, the words didn't come.

Don't rush her. Give her time. Everything is happening at once, he told himself. Still, he couldn't hold back his heart. He bent down and kissed the top of her head where her hair met her temple. He wanted to kiss her lips, but not until she told him she loved him too. He wanted Lovina to say it. To mean it.

They sat there for another minute, enjoying the sweet-smelling evening breeze.

"Are you ready for some pie?" she finally dared to ask.

"Today and every day from now on." He chuckled, but as soon as he said it he wished that he hadn't. For instead of joy on Lovina's face there was worry. Didn't she have the same desire—to grow in their relationship? To allow herself to fall in love?

There was no smile on Lovina's face as she rose, still holding his hand. "I think we can arrange that, Noah Yoder…but first we have a pie shop to open." She tried to smile, but Noah could see that he'd pushed too far. Lovina cared for him. He knew she did. Now he just needed her to realize that for herself.

In God's good time, he told himself, hoping he wasn't just setting himself up for heartbreak. Because no matter how he looked at it, helping her open her pie shop was no longer enough. Noah knew he had Lovina's respect, but now he wanted her heart.

༄

Lovina couldn't believe how late it was when Noah finally left. In his hand was a plastic container filled with pie, but his stomach held even more. The old-fashioned buttermilk pie had been his favorite, and Lovina wasn't surprised. Noah appreciated things with a heritage—things that weren't too fussy or pretentious.

Lovina hummed to herself as she put away the rest of the pie and washed the plates and forks. Her sisters had all gone to bed, but she couldn't sleep. She sat at the kitchen table and folded the cloth napkins as her mind replayed Noah confessing his love and telling her how he wanted to spend his life with her. She wanted to hear that, didn't she? So why did those words make her as nervous as they did excited?

"Still up?" Mem's voice caused Lovina to jump. Mem looked around the corner and Lovina had a hard time reading the expression on her face. Was that worry? Resignation?

"Ja. Just finishing up a few things before heading to bed."

Mem entered the kitchen and pulled up the chair next to Lovina. "Is that your excuse?"

"Excuse?"

"When I was your age I was infatuated with a young man, and I had a hard time sleeping too."

Lovina folded the teal blue napkin and placed it in the pile. "It's more than infatuation, Mem." Yet she couldn't even say it then. Couldn't say the word *love*.

Mem let out a sigh. "Lovina, it seems you always have to do things the hard way. Noah seems to be a nice man, I'll admit that now, but marrying him will not give you an easy life. And this pie shop...do you see how much time it's consuming already? And not just your time, but everybody's. It's a lot for a young woman to take on. You can sell it now and get ahead. I'm sure there's an older Amish woman who would like such a venture. It's still not too late."

Pained emotion rose in Lovina's throat, but she swallowed it down. "Do you think I'm making the wrong choice?"

"It's not that you're doing anything wrong…but I learned growing up that it isn't right for a woman to run a business. Besides…" Mem pursed her lips. "Now that you are building a relationship with Noah you no longer have need of a backup plan."

Lovina gasped. She placed a hand over her heart, wishing it didn't sting so. "It's not a backup plan, Mem. This is my dream. And Noah is becoming part of that dream."

"So it seems." Mem rubbed her eyes, as if the weariness of this conversation was becoming too much for her. "But if we had stayed in Ohio you would have been married by now, and I wouldn't have to worry so much about this shop. About you…"

And about our whole life savings, Lovina knew her mem wanted to say.

"But God brought us to Pinecraft for a reason," Lovina said. "I'm using my God-given talent. I'm building connections between families and friends."

"It's just pie," Mem muttered under her breath, rising.

That comment stung her heart more than any ever had, and Lovina closed her eyes. It may just have been pie to Mem, but to her it meant everything. Didn't it?

"Maybe so. But maybe God put the pie shop on my heart to bring Noah and me together. Maybe it's His plans I'm chasing, not only my own."

Mem took two steps toward the hall and then looked back over her shoulder. "It seems a bit prideful to think that God has unique plans for you, don't you think? You're not the only daughter in this family, Lovina. And you're not God's only child. He loves you—He does. Just like I love you. But you must think of more than yourself. You must realize how much this dream is costing all of us. Daughter, would you take time to think of that?"

⟡

Anna walked with heavy steps to her bedroom. The lantern light was still on, but John was fast asleep. Her heart felt heavy from the words she'd just said. Not because she didn't believe them. She did. She was honestly worried that Lovina was getting in over her head.

If she had to choose, she'd settle for Lovina falling in love with Noah. John seemed to think the young man had changed. She'd take that any day over her daughter chaining herself—her future—to a pie shop. But Anna knew she didn't have a choice. Would anyone ever listen to what she thought?

Anna pulled back the covers, preparing to climb into bed, when an envelope on her nightstand caught her eye. It was a letter from Regina. Someone must have collected the mail and placed it there. Without hesitation Anna opened it, looking forward to some bright news that would take away the dour feeling after her conversation with Lovina.

Dear Anna,

Greetings in the name of our Lord. Isn't it wonderful that we have a God we can trust completely with our lives? How hard for all those who do not have Jesus to turn to for wisdom and strength!

I've read your recent note about Lovina's pie shop with interest. But I was especially intrigued by this young man you mentioned. I remember years ago when the accident happened. An accident like that is hard to forget. But when I was talking to Abe about it I learned what happened in more recent years. It seems Noah Yoder rebuilt the owner's gift shop from the ground up, even though he didn't have to, since the community already built a new one. Abe seems to think the young man has a gut reputation now. I thought that might settle your heart. I know how you worry about these things, dear friend.

This is going to be a short note since I have so much to do, but I did want to mention something else I learned. I asked a friend about Thomas Chupp. It seems he has a girlfriend and she's moving to Somerset soon!

Of course Sarah from Sugarcreek didn't know this when she moved there and took the schoolteacher job. She met Thomas early in the year when she was visiting a cousin from Somerset. It seems that Thomas used his charm to bring in a teacher for their school. Now Sarah is brokenhearted. Everyone is guessing who Thomas's love might be, but no one knows. Maybe it's someone he met in Pinecraft?

Oh, and the reason why I have so little time to write is that Abe and I are winterizing the house since we're planning on coming to Pinecraft for the season! I've been so eager to write and tell you!

Abe found a rental and was waiting until my birthday to tell me the surprise. I'll be hugging your neck soon, friend! I cannot wait to see the girlies and the new pie shop! Anna, I know you'll be the best tour guide.

Love, Regina

Anna folded the letter and returned it to the envelope. A sinking feeling hit her stomach…and it wasn't from the pie. Had she been wrong not once, but twice? She'd been so sure that Thomas Chupp was the right fit for Lovina…and so sure that Noah Yoder wasn't.

She adjusted her sleeping kerchief and turned off the lamp. She'd have to be more open-minded about Noah…and maybe about the pie shop too. Lovina felt certain God had done this for her. He'd helped her find a man to care for and fulfill a dream. Anna hadn't seen God in that way before, as Someone so intimately concerned with one's life. But maybe God was. After all, Regina was coming to Pinecraft! Butterflies danced in her stomach to think of it. And if God answered that prayer, maybe He was answering Lovina's prayers too.

Old-Fashioned Buttermilk Pie

4 eggs
1 cup sugar
1½ cups buttermilk
¼ cup butter, melted
2 teaspoons vanilla extract
½ teaspoon ground nutmeg
whipped cream (optional)

Preheat oven to 400°. In a large bowl, beat eggs and sugar together. Add flour and mix together. Slowly add buttermilk, butter, and vanilla until thoroughly incorporated. Pour into unbaked pie crust. Dust top with ground nutmeg. Place on a baking sheet and bake 20 minutes. Reduce heat to 350° and continue baking for 30-40 minutes, or until pie is set. Serve with whipped cream, if desired.

Twenty-Nine

◅◦◦

"Okay, Lovina. Close your eyes." Noah whispered close to her ear as she stood in front of the door to Me, Myself, and Pie.

It had been two weeks since Noah had declared he wanted to spend his life with her. And that had consumed her thoughts, but not in a happy way. More than once Noah had said he loved her, but why couldn't she respond the same? What was holding her back?

She took Noah's hand and squeezed it, closing her eyes. "Can you believe tomorrow's the opening day?"

"Finally, whew. I thought we'd never get here." He chuckled.

She reached her hand forward and let him lead her. When she felt herself step onto the concrete floor she paused.

"Okay, go ahead and open them."

Lovina opened her eyes and looked around. "Oh, Noah," she sucked in a breath. For the last two days she'd been allowed into the kitchen only as he worked in front. She'd been led through blindfolded because Noah had wanted the final reveal to be special. And it was.

A new archway had been built, leading from the pie-making station to the kitchen in the back. The countertop waited for the bakers to do their work, and a white picket fence separated the baking area from the customers.

The cash register was set up on the long wooden counter, and Hoosier cupboards held cookbooks and Lovina's display of Pyrex bowls. Vintage pie plates and antique eggbeaters hung on the wall. An old metal ladder displayed more cookbooks. Seats were clustered near the front door for waiting guests, and the tables and chairs with colorful paint, fresh flowers, and fabric napkins looked so inviting.

"It's more than I ever dreamed." She turned to Noah, seeing pride in his eyes. "I can't wait to thank the guys as well. All three of them have done so much for this shop."

"Ja." Noah smiled, but she noticed the brightness in his eyes dim slightly. "And there is another surprise too." He pointed behind her.

Lovina turned to see Joy hurrying up the walkway with a pile of fabric in hand. She smiled and waved as she entered.

"What's that?" Lovina asked.

Joy's cheeks were red and rosy. "Are you ready for this? It's a gift."

She placed the pile on the countertop and unfolded the top one. It was a white apron with a quilted pattern on the pocket. Neat stitching on the front read *Me, Myself, and Pie.*

Lovina clasped her hands together. "Aprons! But that wasn't in the budget. How did you accomplish that?"

"I didn't." Joy giggled. "Elizabeth Beiler from the quilt store did. It was a gift from her and some of her friends. I'm not sure how many hours she spent on this." Joy's face glowed. "Elizabeth said it was the least she could do since God had so graciously answered her prayers."

Lovina took the apron Joy handed her and slipped it on. She tied it and wanted to squeal. "I need to go thank Elizabeth." She turned to Noah. "You don't need me around here, do you?"

"The guys are stocking the fridges with the supplies that were delivered just a bit ago. Why don't you go see your friend, and we can do a walk-through when you get back."

Lovina turned to Joy. "Can you go with me?"

Joy shook her head. "I wish I could, but I want to go iron these. They need to be perfect for tomorrow."

Lovina clasped her sister's shoulders, emotion overwhelming her. "Thank you." Tears filled her eyes as she remembered her mother's words. "I hope all of this hasn't been too much trouble."

"Trouble?" Joy shook her head, blue eyes widening. "It's so fun…and I hope it does what Faith believes—brings around all types of bachelors!"

Noah laughed out loud at that one. "Oh, is that the real ploy? Now I know!" he teased.

Lovina softly slugged his arm. "Well, it worked, didn't it?"

"I think so." Noah winked at her. "I'm just hoping you'll want to keep me around awhile."

Lovina felt heat flush her face, and Joy's eyes grew wide.

"Well, that *did* work, didn't it?" Joy giggled.

Lovina looked to her sister and then to Noah, unsure of what to say. She wanted to open her heart up to him, but every time she thought of it fear held her back. Blowing out a deep breath, Lovina wagged her finger at Noah. "Mr. Yoder, we promised to discuss this after the opening of the shop, remember?"

"How can I forget?" he winked. "And why do you think I've been working so hard?"

Lovina grinned. "I'm going to go thank Elizabeth Beiler, and then we'll be ready for the walkthrough."

Noah nodded. Lovina could tell that he wanted to say more, but thankfully he held his tongue. Joy would relay this conversation to their sisters as it was, and her sisters were quick to blow every small comment out of proportion.

With a small wave she left the pie shop, thankful for the breeze that blew outside. She was at the quilt shop before she knew it, and still her heart pounded. Tomorrow the store would open. She couldn't be more excited. But after that…was she really ready to commit to Noah completely?

"Well, there you are! Just the young woman I've been hoping to see! I want to thank you," Elizabeth called out as Lovina entered the quilt shop. Her voice held age and wisdom. Lovina looked around to see if Elizabeth was talking to someone else, but the shop was empty.

"Elizabeth, I came to thank *you*." Lovina approached and gave the old woman a hug.

"Oh, but I want to thank you too. I'm excited about your shop. I'm excited about what it's going to do to spread the Good News."

"Spread the Good News?" Lovina asked.

"Oh, yes." Elizabeth patted the stool next to her and Lovina sat. She knew she needed to get back to the pie shop, but she could tell from the older woman's eyes that Elizabeth had something important to share.

"Have you ever taken time to talk to the Englisch?" Elizabeth asked.

It wasn't the question Lovina had been expecting.

"I really haven't thought about doing that before. Almost everyone I know is Amish or Mennonite."

"It's one of my favorite things about living here in Pinecraft." The wrinkles around Elizabeth's eyes grew with her smile. "The good Lord says to go out into the world to spread the Good News. I used to worry and fret about that—fret that I wasn't going out to all the places around here, telling them about Jesus. I even prayed, 'Lord, does that mean I need to go into those fancy neighborhoods near the beach?'"

Elizabeth smiled and then continued. "Then, as I was thinking about that one day, two women walked in. They had so many jewels on their fingers and neck, but as we talked it was almost as if they envied me. They envied my simpler life. I talked about quilting patterns—one woman was planning to buy a quilt for her mother in a rest home. But I also talked about the hope we Amish and Mennonites have in Jesus, and it was as if the Lord told me I didn't need to worry about going out into the world. I simply had to love those He brought to me."

As they talked, two women walked by, peering in the front window of the quilt shop. They wore Englisch clothes, and Lovina could tell they were from out of town. They pointed and smiled as they watched an Amish woman in one of the cottage rentals nearby hanging her laundry on the line.

"And sometimes choosing to love one person is a wonderful first step. It makes it easier to love everyone after that—after you open your heart."

Loving one person first? Chills ran up Lovina's arms.

She thought of Noah. He'd worked so hard over the last few months. The old broken pieces of the warehouse had been stripped down, but he'd lovingly built it back up. He'd made everything new, fresh, and bright. Because of Noah, Lovina's dream ended up being so much more than she ever thought, yet she also knew she was holding back. She hadn't allowed herself to open her heart. Was that what God was asking her to do? To start by loving the one person He'd brought into her life? And then…would she find it easier to love others too? Love the customers who came into her pie shop?

Lovina had locked herself up tight, fearful of what would happen if she let Noah in completely. But now she had a feeling that God was asking her to do the thing that was hardest of all. To dare to place her heart in the hands of another.

In the months she'd known Elizabeth, the older woman had said things that had inspired Lovina's own relationship with God. Lovina had changed as she'd watched the pie shop transform, but was that just the beginning? Did God have *gut* plans for her customers too? Could she serve up a slice of hope along with pie? She'd never really considered that before, but from the peace and joy she saw in Elizabeth's eyes, she had no doubt it could be so.

Elizabeth pointed to the apron Lovina was wearing. "Do you know Jesus put on an apron? He was the Son of God and yet He wrapped a towel around His waist and kneeled to wash His disciples' feet. You're serving up pie, but knowing you there's going to be a lot of love served up too. Every day when you put on that apron ask God to show you the one person to extend extra love to."

Tears rimmed Lovina's eyes as she pictured that. She nodded. "I will. Starting tomorrow."

"Oh, no." Elizabeth wagged a finger at her. "Not starting tomorrow. You're wearing that apron today, aren't you? I think you already have someone in mind. Someone you need to love first."

Lovina nodded. Noah's smiling face filled her mind. "How did you know?"

Elizabeth tapped her temple. "When you get to be my age you know and see many things…and now I know it's time for you to go." She patted Lovina's arm. "But don't worry. I'll see you tomorrow when I come in for my slice of pie."

It was already past noon by the time Lovina left the quilt shop, and when she got to the pie shop it was empty and locked. She wondered if Noah had gone out to lunch. No, knowing him he'd probably gone home to get something quick to eat.

With quickened steps she walked to Roy Yoder's house. The sun was high, casting a warm glow over the neighborhood. She started to walk up the sidewalk and then paused. What if she was interrupting his lunch? Maybe she should come back later. She turned back toward the pie shop when she heard the sound of a door opening behind her.

"Lovina…"

She paused at the sound of his voice.

"Everything all right?"

She turned and saw that he was dressed in the familiar homemade jeans and a work shirt. His hair was damp and rumpled, as if he'd been working up a sweat. It clung to his face at his temples, and her heart jumped to her throat as she focused on his blue eyes. She could no longer keep the truth of her love inside her. She glanced down at the apron. He was the one she needed to love first…and love in a different way than she ever had.

"Noah, I don't want you to say anything. Please…just let me say what I have to say. Then tomorrow—after the opening—we can talk about what it means."

Noah nodded. "All right."

"I love you, Noah Yoder. More than I ever thought I could love a man. I've been holding you at bay, and that's been foolish. And once the pie shop is open, I don't want that to be the end of spending my days with you. Instead, I want that to be the beginning. Of us."

"Lovina," Noah started, but Lovina put a finger on his lips. She could see all the emotion in his gaze. She knew how he felt. She didn't need to hear his response. He'd told her everything already.

"Shhh, not now. Tomorrow we'll talk about it. After the first day."

Noah smiled, and it was only then that Lovina noticed three guys standing in the doorway behind them. They were smiling, all of them. Even Mose.

Noah took her hand and they began to walk, away from listening ears.

"I'm sorry. Maybe I should have waited, but I had to talk to you now. I needed you to know how I really feel."

"Lovina, I thought I knew what I was here for." He glanced back at the pie shop. "To give you your dream. And I'm so glad I was able to give you what you want most..."

"What I used to want most." She grinned.

"Used to?" He cocked an eyebrow. "Is it something different now?"

"I knew about making pies. I knew about the joy that a community could bring, when they gathered together, sitting face-to-face. But Noah." She paused looking up at him. She bit her lower lip and her eyelashes fluttered softly as she considered her words. "But Noah, that's because I hadn't met you yet. How could I have known what I'd wanted most if I'd never known it before?"

She squeezed his hand, and she saw that he was smiling.

"I still want a pie shop, yes, but it's not my biggest dream now."

"Does your biggest dream have to do with me, Lovina? With the rest of our lives?" He leaned above her, kissing her hair. Lovina released a small gasp and her eyes drifted closed.

"Ja."

"I like to hear that. I want nothing more. But I need you to do something for me."

She opened her eyes and looked to him again. "What is that?"

"Enjoy the opening tomorrow. Soak in every moment."

"Of course. I'll make sure I do. You have a way of bringing my dreams to life. I'm ready for that walkthrough now. I can't wait to see the finished product."

"Finished?" Noah's eyebrow lifted. And then he reached down with both hands and entwined his fingers in hers. "Don't think of this as a finish, Love, but just the beginning."

Noah moved forward to kiss her lips. The touch was light at first, but then she lifted onto her toes, leaning in. Her movement surprised him, and he released her hands and grasped her shoulders, pulling her forward. Her hand rested on his chest, keeping space between them, but the kiss lingered, and Lovina wondered what it would be like to be married to this man and kiss every day like this.

Finally she pulled back and glanced over her shoulder, remembering where she was—in the middle of Roy Yoder's yard.

She breathed out a sigh. "Can you come over for lunch—if you haven't eaten yet? I promised Mem I'd be there, but I want you to be there to celebrate with us."

"Ja, but can you give me twenty minutes? I was teaching the guys how to make turkey biscuit skillet. Then they need to finish up some work in the office area before the walkthrough. Only then can we officially say we've marked everything off our to-do list."

Lovina placed a hand on her hip. "Turkey biscuit skillet. I'm impressed."

"We got tired of eating cereal, so I wrote home and asked Mem for some recipes. That was one of the easiest to make."

"I'll hurry home and tell them to expect you. I know Dat will be excited to see you."

"And your mem?" Noah asked.

Lovina shrugged. "She'll warm up. I know she will. God's doing a *gut* work in her, I feel it."

- -

Turkey Biscuit Skillet

¾ cup butter

1½ cups chopped celery

1½ cups chopped carrots

1 chopped onion

1-2 cups chopped potato

1 cup all-purpose flour

4½ cups chicken broth

1-2 teaspoons salt (based on taste)

1 tablespoon pepper

1 tablespoon fresh dill, chopped

1 tablespoon fresh sage, chopped

2 bay leaves

3 cups heavy cream

5-6 cups leftover turkey pieces cut into chunks

2 cups fresh or frozen peas

1 cup fresh or frozen yellow corn kernels

Preheat the oven to 375°. In a large saucepan, melt the butter and then add celery, carrots, onion, and potato pieces. Sauté for 5-8 minutes and then sprinkle flour over the vegetables and stir until the mixture starts to bubble in the pan. Using a large whisk, add chicken broth, stirring until the sauce is smooth. Season with salt, pepper, and spices. Heat to a simmer on stovetop. Add the cream, turkey, peas, and corn and cook on a slow simmer until the sauce is thickened. Always taste and adjust your seasonings to your preferences. Place the filling in an extra-large cast iron skillet (this filling recipe makes enough for 2 large skillets.) Top with fresh-made biscuit dough and bake in oven until biscuits are browned and the filling is bubbling.

You may also use the same filling recipe to make pot pie in a pie pan or casserole dish using your favorite pie dough recipe. If you make a pie, wrap the outside of your pie pan with foil to keep the crust from burning. Bake until center is almost brown and then remove the foil to continue to cook the outer edges.

Thirty

It's better to suffer wrong than to commit wrong.

AMISH PROVERB

～⌒⌒

Lovina hurried home, and her heart felt light, full. Mem was at the stove, cooking up her famous quiche.

Lovina took a big whiff when she walked through the door. "Mem, that smells delicious!"

Mem's smile was large—something Lovina hadn't seen in a while.

"Ja. You aren't the only one who knows how to make pie."

Lovina placed an arm around Mem's shoulders. "Is there enough for company?"

"Company?" Mem glanced up at her. "It wouldn't be a handsome bachelor, would it?"

"I invited Noah."

Lovina waited for the disappointing look, but instead her mem smiled. "Ja, there will be enough. Serving him lunch is the least I can do for all the work he's done." Mem placed the knife on the counter and reached for the plates in the cupboard. "I made a few extra quiches for tomorrow. I thought Regina would enjoy not having to cook on her first day."

"I nearly forgot. How exciting to have your best friend here tomorrow."

"Just in time for the opening of the shop. We're both so excited to be there."

Lovina paused, taking in the moment. It had taken Mem time to come around, and she had no doubt Regina had helped with that. Regina always was a positive influence on Mem. Something Lovina was thankful for.

A knock sounded at the door, and Lovina's heart skipped a beat. "That should be Noah."

"Perfect timing." Mem placed the quiche on the kitchen table. "I'll just go out back and get your dat."

Lovina hurried to the front door and swung it open. "If you like pie—" Her words stopped short when she saw that it wasn't Noah who stood there. It was a police officer. His car was parked out front.

"Are you Miss Miller?" The police officer looked down at his notepad.

"One of them." Dread spread through her chest. Had one of her sisters gotten hurt?

"Miss Lovina Miller?" he asked.

"Yes." She stood there frozen.

"I'm sorry to say there's been a fire at your pie shop."

"A fire?" Her knees trembled and her mind raced. "I don't understand. I was just there twenty minutes ago."

"The fire department is still there. If you'd like to come with me …"

She followed him, not knowing what to do or what to think. "Lovina!"

Dat was at the door behind her. When she turned to look at him the worry on his face overwhelmed her. "Dat…there's been a fire. At the shop." With her words the tears came. Had the whole thing gone up? How bad was the damage? She was afraid to ask. Instead, she just opened her arms and allowed Mem and Dat to come to her, grabbing her up in an embrace.

"We'll go with you," Mem said. "We'll help in any way we can."

But as Lovina looked to her father's ashen face she knew two things for certain. First, that there was no insurance. Everything lost was lost for good. And second, she knew deep down what had caused the fire. She'd witnessed enough of Mose's pranks not to have any doubt about that.

I should have put an end to it. I shouldn't have let them into the shop, she thought as she climbed into the front seat of the cop car.

With her heart pounding she turned to the police officer, almost afraid to confirm her fears.

"Can you t-tell me"—her voice trembled—"tell me where the fire started?"

"From what we can tell it started in the office. The fire was caught early, but I'm afraid there's fire damage throughout."

Lovina nodded but didn't say a word as the officer drove her to the pie shop. And only when she saw the smoke rising did she realize what the visitors coming off the Pioneer Trails bus would see. They wouldn't see a place to gather, but a scorched building.

Why, Lord, why?

She'd given it her all. She'd dared to dream, and what good did it do? Not only had her dream gone up in smoke, but her father's investment too. She was too trusting…and where did that leave her now?

The police car parked in front of the pie shop, and Lovina hurried to the door. Smoke filled the air, stinging her eyes. It poured from the back of the shop and from the front window she'd left open this morning. She tried to rush in—to see the damage—but a fireman stopped her. "I'm sorry, miss. You can't go in there. It's not safe. We're still checking for hot spots. We have to make sure the structure is safe before we let anyone in."

The tears came then, and she couldn't hold them back. "Lovina." It was Dat's voice. "Let's get you back to the car. You need to sit. This is too much for you to take."

She followed him, and Mem stood by the open door. Her eyes welled with tears. "Oh, Love, I'm so, so sorry." Mem rarely used her pet name, and hearing it made it even more real.

"Lovina…" Another voice broke through the fog of her emotions. *Noah.*

She covered her face with her hands. Gone was the joy she'd felt just half an hour earlier. Hot anger replaced it. She looked up, narrowing her eyes. Noah's face was red. Soot smudged his face. Had he gone into the fire? Had he tried to fight it? She didn't see the teens, and that was a good thing.

"You." She pointed a finger at his chest. "You were supposed to control them. You told me no more pranks. I knew—deep down I *knew* something like this was going to happen."

She lowered her head, suddenly ashamed of her words. The Amish way was to forgive. To extend grace. But at this moment there was no grace in her. Lovina pinched her lips together and turned away.

"I don't think…" Noah started and then stopped. She felt his hand on her shoulder. "I'll find out what happened, Lovina. I promise I will."

Lovina nodded, and suddenly she knew she couldn't stay here. She couldn't listen to the shouts of the firemen. She couldn't see her beautiful shop destroyed. She needed to leave. She needed to get away. She had to put space between herself and her shop before her heart broke into a million pieces.

She moved away from the police car and headed for home.

"I'll go with you." Noah was at her side.

"No." She crossed her arms over her chest. "Not now. Don't." The word came out as a hiss. She continued on, thankful he didn't follow. Instead her company was the words that replayed in her mind.

It's gone. The shop's gone. Dat's money is gone. And it's all my fault for being too trusting.

Whatever would her family do now? How would they survive?

As she strode away she realized there was something worse than never chasing one's dream. It was coming so close only to see it destroyed. And her hopes of happiness—of a future—with it.

Thirty-One

A man is happier to be sometimes
cheated than to never trust.

AMISH PROVERB

⁓

It was dark before Noah made it back to Roy's house. He staggered inside covered in soot and dirt and smelling of smoke. He'd stayed at the scene of the fire all afternoon. The volunteer fire department had put it out and checked for hot spots. And all day long it had seemed like a bad dream. If only he could wake up. If only he could open his eyes and the pie shop could return to the way it had been this morning.

Noah's eyes were burning, partly from the sting of the smoke and partly from the tears threatening to break through. Guilt burdened him down like a physical weight. He hadn't started the fire, but he might as well have. He thought he'd made himself clear— no more pranks. And now not only was the pie shop damaged, but when the cause of the fire was discovered Mose, Gerald, and Atlee would end up where he'd found them: in prison. And then all of this—every last bit of his effort—would come to nothing.

Emotion caught in his throat and he tried to swallow it away. Another pang of guilt shot through his heart.

The image of Lovina's face, distorted in pain and horror, filled his mind. He'd worked so hard to make her dream happen. He'd given his everything, but it wasn't enough. Not only was the pie shop destroyed by water and smoke, but it was his fault. He was the one who'd trusted Mose one more time. He'd seen the panicked look on Mose's face when he ran to tell Noah about the fire. He, Gerald, and Atlee had come upon it—or so they said. They'd tried to put it out, but they claimed it had already spread from the office to the pie shop storage room before they got there.

Fear had filled Mose's gaze. Not fear of the fire, but fear of Noah's response. Then, once the crowd had gathered and started speculating about the cause of the fire, the young men had disappeared. Of course they would run from responsibility. Maybe they hoped no one would figure out they'd been the cause.

Noah coughed out a smoky breath and then opened his eyes. No one was in the kitchen, and an empty pizza box sat on the table. Seeing that box, new anger bubbled up in him. *They couldn't step out this door to help—to face responsibility—but they could step out to buy a pizza?*

More coughs erupted from Noah's chest. They tasted like the thick smoke. He quickly moved to the kitchen to get a drink of water. His hand trembled as he lifted the glass to his lips, and it took everything within him not to let the tears come.

In addition to worrying that the teens would end up behind bars, he worried about himself too. He remembered the stench of the cell, the humiliation of being told when to eat, when to sleep, when to use the toilet—and being watched. Always watched. Would they point a finger at him for negligence?

Even as Noah had helped to clear out some of the least

damaged items—carrying them to the lawn to prevent more smoke damage—he'd heard the comments shared by the observers. They'd come up with every conceivable idea for the fire, from messing up the wiring to leaving combustible liquids unattended. But instead of placing the blame on the teens, they all looked at him with suspicion.

Noah took another long drink, and then he sat at the kitchen table and slowly removed his boots. The fire examiner would be there early in the morning. And then everyone would know the truth. But how would that help Lovina? And what would it mean for them?

Finally, after weeks of waiting for a confession of her love, he'd heard it. And the emotional high of the moment made the pain of her tears, her accusations, even more painful. She was right. He should have done more. He should have protected her.

He could hear low talking from the teens' bedroom, and Noah couldn't hold back anymore. Anger balled up in his gut, and he strode in that direction. They'd disappeared from the scene of the fire, and Noah guessed why. They didn't want to face up to their mistake. They didn't want to be asked any questions. Not that it would keep them from trouble. Not this time.

Noah pushed the door open without knocking. Mose and Gerald sat on their beds, and Atlee sat on the one chair in the room. All of them looked up in surprise as he entered. He scanned their faces, and each set of eyes fixed on him, waiting for his words.

"So, tell me how the fire started." Noah spoke the words through clenched teeth.

"What do you mean?" It was Mose who answered for the group. He tried to give Noah an innocent look, but Noah wasn't buying it.

"I mean, which prank was it? More firecrackers? The welder?

You can tell me now or I can wait to hear it from the fire examiner. If I were you, I'd tell me now. Things might be easier on you if you confess to the authorities."

Mose stood, straightening his shoulders. His brow wrinkled in confusion, and then anger flashed in his gaze. "Wait, you—you think we did this?"

"I don't *think* you did it. I *know* you did. I told you to finish up cleaning the office and hang the clock—the surprise for Lovina. You were the last ones in the office, and I want to know what you were doing."

"Noah, we hung the clock and then we left." Gerald raised his hands in defense. "I swear that's all that happened."

"We weren't even there. We—" Atlee started, but Mose cut off his words.

"Don't try to explain, Atlee. Noah's not gonna listen." Mose crossed his arms and cocked his chin. "Noah says he wants to help us, but now we know different. I'm glad I was already planning to get out of here. The truth is, he just wanted to make himself look good…isn't that right, Noah? Show off some good deeds to win yourself a wife. Seems to me Lovina bought it…or at least that's what she said earlier." Mose clicked his tongue. "I'd hate to see how she feels about that now. I bet she blames you. That's why you're so angry, right?"

Noah's eyes narrowed, and he wanted nothing more than to defend his actions. He had been doing everything for them. But from the look in his eyes it would do no good. Mose's opinion was set, just as his was set.

"Listen." Gerald's voice was low. "We're telling you the truth, Noah. Things were fine when we were in the office. We came home for lunch, and that's when we saw the smoke. Mose is telling you the truth."

He studied Gerald's face, wishing that *was* the truth. Noah let out a sigh. "I suppose we'll find out in the morning, won't we?"

Noah stepped back and shut the door. The last of his energy drained from him. He headed to the shower and knew that he'd failed them. More than that, now he'd failed Lovina. He'd tried to do everything right, but now all was lost. Another shop was destroyed, and he had no money to fix it. History was repeating itself, only this time there was more than his reputation at stake—there also was his heart.

Everything was gone now—his good name, the pie shop, his work with the boys, and now Lovina. He'd worked so hard, and this was how he was rewarded? And just think, he'd been the one to talk to Mose about a loving, grace-filled God. God felt far, far away.

Noah took a quick shower and then slumped into bed. He wanted to pray but no words came. Ever since working on this project he'd been eager to start the new day. But now…now he wished the night would last. He didn't want to wake up. He didn't want to know how the teens had caused the fire. And he didn't want to see the disappointment on Lovina's face.

Where was God in all this? None of it made sense.

⌒

A loud knock on the front door woke Noah, and he struggled for consciousness. The first thing he realized was that the whole room smelled of smoke because of the filthy clothes he'd been wearing yesterday. The second—that the sunlight streamed through the windows.

Noah looked at the clock. It was already eight o'clock. He couldn't remember the last time he'd slept that long. He hurriedly put on clean clothes and rushed to the front door.

He opened it to see the fire marshal there, and his heart sank. "We determined the cause of the fire," the man said. "I'd like to take you to see what I found. And I need to talk to those teens from your work crew too."

"Of course." Noah turned to go get them, and the three emerged from the kitchen. Dark circles rimmed their eyes, and he wondered if any of them had slept. At first Noah felt pity for them, but the anger quickly returned.

All four walked silently as they made their way around the back side of the building. John Miller stood there watching Noah approach, and Noah's heart sank even lower. The man's life work had been invested in this pie shop. John had trusted him...and now it came to this. Tears filled Noah's eyes to see the burned wall, the burned-out office, and the charred mess.

Noah paused before it, and then turned to John. "I'm so sorry. I—"

John held up his hand, cutting off Noah's words. "Don't say a word, son. Wait until you see what we found inside."

The fire marshal cleared his throat. "I got here early, and in my gut I knew what I'd find," the man said. "I've seen more fires like this than I care to tell you about." The man looked from Noah to the teens, and then he pointed to the window air-conditioning unit. It lay on the ground, completely burned.

"In these parts people use those window units a lot, but they have no idea of the fire danger. In this county alone I've seen three fires caused by these units in the last six months. When the air handler leaks it short-circuits the electrical equipment underneath, causing sparks. Usually a fire ignites before anyone even sees the leak."

Noah opened his mouth in disbelief. "So...it was the air-conditioning unit?"

John Miller placed his hand on Noah's shoulder. "There was nothing different you could have done, son. These things just happen."

Noah turned to the teens. Relief was clear on Atlee and Gerald's faces, but before he could say a word Mose turned and sauntered away. Was Mose relieved too? No doubt he was. But the anger was evident. Noah had accused them. He'd pointed a finger. Noah remembered what it was like, and he lowered his head. The fire had destroyed more than the shop. It had destroyed any relationship he'd managed to build with Mose…and that came not from the flames, but from his own words.

Thirty-Two

A friend is like a rainbow, always
there for you after a storm.

AMISH PROVERB

~⌾~

Lovina didn't know how long she'd been sleeping, but the sun was bright in the windows when she awoke. She sat up and opened her eyes. They felt puffy and scratchy, as if they'd been rubbed with sand. How late was it now? She didn't have a clock in her bedroom, but from the brightness of the sun streaming through the windows it must have been after eight. The only time she slept in was when she was sick. This time she was heartbroken.

Her dream was gone. Worse than that, so were her father's life-savings. He'd worked his whole life to save up that money. The farm in Ohio had been his inheritance.

Outside the window, a gaggle of teen girls walked by with bags that held their lawn chairs, towels, and lunch. Why had she been so focused on this dream? Why couldn't she just have been happy spending time at the beach with friends?

Lovina pressed her head against her pillow and squeezed her eyes shut, wishing she didn't have to wake up. She thought back to the first moments when she'd focused on her dream. It seemed to have always been there. Making pies had given her value. Provided her worth.

As she lay there, a memory fluttered in her mind—one she hadn't thought about in a while. She'd been just a girl and one of her aunts had been visiting. It had been a cooler winter day, and instead of being outside her sisters had been in the living room.

Joy had been sewing, of course, and the other three had been taking turns playing checkers. Aunt Irma had lived far away in New York, but Lovina had been so excited to meet her.

Lovina could still hear her aunt's voice in her mind. "Look at those blonde curls and light blue eyes. I thought since John has such dark coloring that all your children would be darker too. You'll have no trouble finding *gut* husbands for them."

"I've always loved Lovina's dark hair," Mem had said, pulling her back into the conversation.

Even though Lovina hadn't turned her head she'd felt her aunt's gaze on her. "Ja, well." Her aunt's voice had been low. "Lovina is rather plain, but she does make lovely pies. At least she has that going for her."

Lovina snuggled deeper into her covers. The tears came quick and unexpected. Lovina tried to wipe them away with the backs of her knuckles, but it did no good.

Remembering that moment, so much about Lovina's life now made sense. She'd believed Aunt Irma. She'd thought herself to be the homely one of the sisters. Honestly, deep down, Lovina had never thought she'd ever get married.

A dozen smaller moments fought for attention in her mind. The moment she was sewing dishtowels and messed up and didn't fix the mistake, because she really couldn't picture herself getting married and needing the towels. The times she'd been approached by a young man at a singing who tried to strike up a conversation, but she made an excuse to leave, because deep down she thought it would be easier to walk away from a conversation than be left behind later.

She thought again about the phrase that her grandmother had shared. "It is always a good thing to trust an unknown future to a God who holds each person in His palm." Yet the truth was that even from her younger days she'd thought she'd known what her future would be. Lovina hadn't needed to trust an unknown future to God because she had believed she'd known it. The worst thing an Amish woman could be was prideful, yet hadn't she been full of pride by deciding she'd already figured out what lie ahead?

She'd thought that because she was not as lovely as her sisters she would never get married. But had that been God's plan? Had her poor self-image, planted by the hurtful words of an aunt she barely knew, set her on a path to closing her heart to love?

A sob erupted from her throat as she thought about more recent struggles, like the four days last year where she tried fourteen different recipes for key lime pie, trying to find the best one. After all, who'd ever be able to open a pie shop if they hadn't figured out the best key lime?

And somehow that coincided with the large volleyball tournament, attend by dozens of Amish bachelors who'd come on Pioneer Trails at the end of last season. Every time one of her sisters came home, urging her to join them because they'd found the perfect date for her, she'd pull out another pie recipe. Making pie was easier than meeting someone new. The benefit was almost every neighbor on their street had enjoyed key lime pie after their dinner, but she'd been the one who'd missed out on new friendships.

And then she'd found the truth. In pursuit of her dream she'd fallen in love with someone who was more wonderful than she'd ever known a man could be. She'd been so excited that Noah was helping her follow her dream, she'd let down her guard.

Conversation by conversation, and dream shared by dream shared, she'd opened up the door to her heart a little more. She'd been so busy opening her pie shop that she hadn't worried about not ever being chosen to be someone's wife. And as she let her guard down, Noah stepped in. He loved her. Or at least he had. Did he still? She thought of her display yesterday and the terrible words she'd said. She'd been awful to him, blaming his negligence for the fire. How could he ever love her after that?

What good would love do for her now?

Lovina sucked in a breath, and the air that filled her lungs seemed to be made of lead. The burden of trying to shield her heart and pursue her dream had been so heavy. She was tired of attempting to figure it out. She was tired of trying to hold back the longing and the dreaming of one day being a wife and having children.

Lovina climbed out of bed and sank to her knees. The wood of the floor was cool through the fabric of her skirt and her body slumped forward. She wanted to pray but didn't know how to start. She didn't know how to express the sadness she'd brought upon herself by believing she'd figured out her bleak future herself.

"Lord, help." They were the only words that escaped.

She dropped her head, and her silent cries shook her shoulders. She was tired of carrying this burden. She'd been up most of the night trying to figure out how to pay Dat back. She didn't want to think about the pie shop or the fire. And for that moment she didn't want to think about Noah either. Her thoughts centered on God alone. For so many years she'd learned about Him. Her grandmother had been an example of reading God's Word, and she'd tried to understand all she could, but this whole time Lovina had never thought to ask God what He thought of her.

Lovina sank down lower, almost being afraid to be seen in His gaze. That was silly. She knew God reigned over all and saw everything. He'd been there the whole time, reaching out His hands and wanting her to pursue Him. God had been waiting…for her.

Instead of turning to Him, she had run from her fears of being alone her whole life. Instead, she had pursued her dream. Because how could one ever truly be alone if they were busy from sunup to sundown running a pie shop? When would one ever have to worry about being alone with one's thoughts if they were surrounded by customers—both Amish and Englisch?

And the thing that broke her heart the most was that by trying to figure it out herself, Lovina had taken God off the throne of her heart and had put the pie shop there. She swallowed that truth and blinked twice, attempting to hold back the tears, but they refused to be tucked inside.

She leaned back, removing her hands from the floor. She sat straighter and turned them over, lifting them up with open palms. *This*, she told the Lord. *This is all I have. Myself. I'm tired of trying to figure it out. I'm tired of pursuing a dream. I long to pursue You, God. Show me how to do that better. I know You've seen me. You've seen me from before the creation of the world, and I am beauti…*

Even the words playing through her thoughts had a hard time saying it. Her heart had a hard time believing it.

I am beautiful in Your sight. She forced the words through her mind. *Wherever I go, You will be with me. And even if I lose everything in this world, Your love will not waver. Your love that stems not from what I do, but who I am: Your daughter.*

Why had it taken her so long to get to this place of surrender? Why had she been holding on to her dreams so hard? It had taken losing everything—her family's inheritance, her dream, and most likely Noah—for her to realize that she'd always had all that she needed in God. She had His favor. And no matter what happened in her life, as His child, she always would.

Knowing Noah, loving Noah, had opened up parts of her heart that she'd tucked away. And in a way she didn't understand, seeing the love in his eyes had helped her to understand God's love. Maybe the fact of knowing Noah found her beautiful helped her know that God did too.

A familiar old German hymn that they often sang in church flowed through her mind. She was used to repeating the German words. Or even more so, the German syllables. Because each word was strung out in the slow way they sang, she hadn't thought much about what the words meant to her personally. But now she just focused on this moment, trying to let the familiar words speak to her.

Where shall I go? I am so ignorant. Only to God can I go, because God alone will be my helper. I trust in You, God, in all my distress. You will not forsake me. You will stand with me, even in death. I have committed myself to Your Word. That is why I have lost favor in all places. But by losing the world's favor, I gained Yours. Therefore I say to the world: Away with you! I will follow Christ.

"Away with you," Lovina whispered to her ideas of what true beauty looked like.

"Away with you," she whispered to her dream of a pie shop.

"Away with you," she whispered to the idea that she had to figure her life out herself.

"Away with you," she said to the idea that she'd live her whole life alone. She'd been cruel to Noah. She'd said hurtful things, things that had cut him to the core. She questioned if he could still love her after that, but she wasn't going to give up hope.

Lovina closed her eyes and let her mind go places it had never gone before. She pictured a simple house that she shared with her husband. She pictured a pie baking in the oven. She pictured the laughter of children in the other room and a baby resting on her left hip as she stirred ingredients with a spoon in her right. She pictured a bedroom with a man's boots at the foot of the bed and a man's shirts hanging neatly beside her colorful dresses on hangers. She smiled as she pictured her wedding. Standing in front of friends and family, with her hand in Noah's.

Her leg began to fall asleep, and that was when she remembered why she was on the floor. She'd been prostrate before God, submitting her life to Him, and here she was letting her mind wander again. Would she ever get it right?

She felt shameful thoughts try to push into her mind, and that was when the peace came as a flood. She'd lifted up her hands, palms open to God, and told Him she was giving Him everything. Would it be too much for Him to give something back? A *gut* man like Noah?

Maybe God had given Lovina the dream of a pie shop in order to bring into her life the gift of a husband.

She'd lost the pie shop. She'd lost her father's money. But maybe she hadn't lost Noah's love. She'd said mean words, hurtful ones, and she'd seen pain as she'd walked away. She'd seen something else last night too. Compassion. And love in Noah's gaze.

Lovina washed up and dressed as quickly as she could. It was only as she exited the bathroom that she realized the house was quiet. She tried to remember if she'd heard any noise after she woke up, and she realized she hadn't. Had everyone in her family been gone all morning? If so, where had they gone?

She moved to the kitchen and cut herself a slice of wheat bread, wrapping it up in a napkin to eat on the way. Then she hurried to the back porch and slipped on her flip-flops. Her only guess was that they'd gone to meet the first Pioneer Trails bus. The first of the season was always exciting. The first thing those exiting the bus would see was the burned shell of her dream…but Lovina held her head high. She knew God was holding her close.

Thirty-Three

Every spiritual investment will bear eternal interest.

AMISH PROVERB

⤳

Lovina turned down the street toward the pie shop and hesitated. She wondered if more than one bus had come, for there was a huge crowd gathering in the front of the Tourist Church. She picked up her pace and hurried down the street. She knew exactly what they'd be seeing across the street. Her heart ached remembering the damage from the fire and water.

But as Lovina neared, her steps slowed. The crowd wasn't circled around the parking lot of the Tourist Church. Instead they were gathered around Me, Myself, and Pie. Her friends and neighbors would most likely be curious about the fire, but frustration pumped through her too. Had they all come to gawk? To give evidence that she'd been a fool for allowing Mose, Atlee, and Gerald to work on the building? For trusting Noah to watch them?

Lovina moved to the side of the road, clinging to a white, wooden fence, remembering how nice the picket fence in the pie shop had looked. Remembering how everything had been so…perfect.

God, why did You let this happen? Why did You call me to failure? Why…why did we have to lose everything?

A wind picked up, rustling her dress and brushing it on her legs. The aroma of gardenias was carried on the breeze, just like on that first day when she'd seen the warehouse. The first day that she saw Noah. She was mad at him, yes, but she still loved him…which only made things worse. She remembered walking into the warehouse for the first time. It had been dark, full of junk, and dirty. How had she ever seen the potential? It was as if God had given her the eyes to see.

"I thought it was God's dream even before it was mine," she whispered to the wind. But if that was the case why did the fire happen? Why did she have to look like a fool now?

Lovina closed her eyes, not caring that she was on a public street. Not caring that someone might see the tears that had just begun to fall. And she remembered what she knew to be true: The pie shop was God's to give and God's to take away. More than that…it was His dream that He'd birthed in her heart. Now it was time to give it back to Him and see what He would do with it.

Lord, it's not my dream, but Yours, she prayed silently. *This doesn't surprise You. None of it.*

No, God wasn't surprised that she'd fallen in love with Noah Yoder. He wasn't surprised that she'd lost so much. He wasn't surprised by her questions or her pain. And still He'd placed that dream in her heart…so why?

Lovina thought about the newspaper reporter. Yes, it had been *gut* of the woman to be interested in the bakery, but even more exciting were the questions she had asked afterward—about God, about faith. Cara Johnson had said the pie shop would be about more than just pie…and the woman's faith had been renewed.

"Letting go of earthly possessions enables us to take hold of heavenly treasures," her grandmother used to say. And without a doubt Lovina knew that was what God was asking her to do now.

God hadn't called her to be successful. He'd called her to follow Him, even if it meant walking down the dark valley where she found herself now. Because maybe someone else going through a dark time would be able to see her light that came from God alone.

Lovina breathed in slowly and continued on. Yes, a fire caused by careless youths had taken away something she'd worked so hard for, but nothing could take away her faith in God.

It was Grace who spotted her first. Grace lifted a hand and waved her forward. A moment later Lovina recognized the woman standing next to her—the newspaper reporter. Her heart sank. It would be hard enough to have to face the people of Pinecraft, but did she have to face this so soon?

Lovina squared her shoulders and approached the woman. She tried to force a smile, but she knew it was no good.

"Oh, Lovina, I was so sorry to hear about the fire. My editor told me as soon as I got into the office this morning. I knew I had to come over. But"—the woman's eyes widened—"I never expected to see this!" The words gushed from her mouth, and only then did Lovina turn to look at the pie shop. Her breath caught in her throat to see that the people weren't there gawking. They were working.

Tears filled her eyes when she saw a group of women carrying out all the linens. The curtains, tablecloths, and napkins were being placed into laundry baskets. Beyond them a group of men were hauling out pieces of furniture. There was a pile for pieces that were partially burned, but even more seemed to have little or no damage.

"What—what are they doing?"

Grace touched her arm. "Why don't you go up there and look?"

Lovina excused herself and walked to the front of the building. Jason Schlabach stood there.

"What's going on?"

"Well, do you remember how I talked to you about liability? We bankers know that Amish don't carry insurance. We still work with them because we know one thing. The Amish take care of their own."

"So they're…"

"The bishop stopped by this morning. A fund has been set up at the bank. Donations have already come in. But more than just giving money, the people have decided to do as much as they can themselves. They're dividing up the work. Everyone is doing what he or she can."

A click sounded behind her, and Lovina turned. It was the reporter. Cara had followed her and was snapping photos. "Honestly, in all my years covering the news I haven't seen anything like this." She turned to Grace. "Remember how I told you I've been thinking a lot about God lately? Well, I think this pushed me over. If this is how God's people care for each other, then it's clear to me He must be real."

Joy mounted in Lovina's heart, and she didn't think she could contain all the emotions she was holding inside. Her shoulders trembled slightly, and in her mind she said a silent prayer to God. *Thank You. You knew all along. You knew.*

A truck pulled up, and she recognized Daniel from the window company. He climbed out of the truck and walked to…

…to Noah. He stood at a table filled with food and jugs of water. Love filled Lovina's heart seeing him there. Her heart also ached as she remembered her harsh words. Noah was here because he was an honorable man. Just like he'd made it right with the gift shop owner, he'd make this right too. After all, it was the teens who'd caused all the trouble.

Another truck followed. This one had *Sarasota Salvage* on the side. Lovina gasped to see furniture in the back. Tables and chairs. She couldn't stop the tears now. Instead of picking up, they were dropping off.

Jason pointed to the truck. "Those are donations. Can you believe it?"

"They're doing all this…for me?"

"For you and the community, Lovina. It seems people caught on to your dream and they don't want to let go."

And then something else caught her attention. Suitcases and boxes lined the roadway in front of Roy Yoder's place. She placed her hand on Jason's arm and pointed. "What's all that?"

Jason smiled. "Well, can you imagine getting off the Pioneers Trails bus and seeing all this?" He swept a hand across the view. "They heard what was happening and wanted to help. The first busload of people never did make it to their rentals to drop off their things. They just left everything there and decided to pitch in."

"Lovina." It was Dat's voice. Lovina turned, and what she saw surprised her. He stood erect and in charge—stronger than she'd seen him in a while.

"Dat." She put her arms around him, not caring if anyone saw their hug. She pulled back and took note of his smile. Even with all the loss her father smiled.

"I wanted to tell you what the fire marshal found. They discovered the cause of the fire."

Lovina braced herself. She needed to hear this. And then she knew her next step would be to work toward forgiving the teens.

"It turns out it was the air conditioning unit. It developed a leak and then shorted out the wiring, causing sparks. The fire chief says it happens often. I'm just so sorry that it happened here."

"The…the air conditioning unit?" A gasp escaped her lips. She was both thankful to hear the news and horrified at the way she'd jumped to conclusions. "Does Noah know?"

Dat nodded. "Ja, and I think you should go talk to him. He's been asking about you. Asking if you're alright."

Lovina didn't have to be told twice. She moved through the crowd, making a beeline to Noah. He turned to her, almost as if sensing she approached, and he smiled. It was a weary smile. She wanted nothing more than to rush into his arms, but she held back. She felt a gentle peace wash over her to see the forgiveness in his gaze. Her cheeks grew warm remembering yesterday's kiss.

"Lovina, did you hear…"

"The air-conditioning. I'm so sorry I blamed the teens. I'm so sorry I blamed you. I'm so, so sorry."

The noise of people at work continued around them, but Lovina only wanted to focus on him. On making up for what she'd done and how she'd treated him.

"I hope that's the first of many spats." He grinned.

"What?"

"Don't you see, Love? I want you in my life for a very long time. More spats means more time together…and then of course we'll get to make up."

She chuckled and realized even more why she loved Noah Yoder.

Then his face grew serious. "I can't lose you. I want to be with you for the rest of my life."

"And I with you," she said over the noise of another truck pulling up. She reached for his hand as she turned back to him. "Just as long as you realize we won't have to tackle life alone, Noah. Not with this community…and not with God. We'll never have to carry our burdens alone."

"No. And we're not the only ones figuring it out."

Lovina turned and warmth streamed in her heart to see a group of their neighbors gathering around the teens, who were standing not too far away. The teens seemed to be surprised by how everyone was pitching in. They seemed especially surprised by the way the men approached.

"Young men, I've been watching you work," one of the men said to Mose. "Not only today, but through this whole project. I was wondering if the three of you would be interested in helping me remodel my guest cabin. It's a big project that will last a few months."

A smile filled Mose's face, and then he looked back over his shoulder as if seeking Noah's approval. Noah nodded, and then Mose stretched his hand toward the man. "It's a deal. We'd love to help." Gerald and Atlee nodded in agreement.

"And what about you?" Lovina asked, leaning close to Noah. "How are you going to work with your crew gone?"

Noah rubbed his chin. "Well, Lovina, I was going to ask you about that. You see, there is no damage to the back half of the building. And there are still plenty of items we need to sell. What do you think of me opening a salvage shop back there?"

Lovina smiled big, feeling the last of God's puzzle pieces slipping into place. "Does it mean I'll get to see you during the day?"

"A dozen times at least."

Lovina extended her hand as she had seen Mose do just a moment before. "Then it's a deal."

Noah took it and grasped it, holding it tight. "*Gut*, because I can't think of anything nicer than seeing your face throughout the day…especially as you serve up pie."

"Is that what this is about, Noah Yoder? About the pie?"

"To start with, Love, to start with…and then God seemed to take it from there."

Epilogue

❧

Every Thursday during the winter season Henry Wise met the Pioneer Trails bus and pulled off two large bundles of *The Budget* newspaper. Folks who came to meet the bus lined up to get their copy. Henry glanced around, knowing they'd be especially interested in this week's issue for a few reasons. He opened the paper and read the first entry by Grace Miller:

> Many of you have been following the story of the new pie shop opening here in Pinecraft. As Lovina Miller's youngest sister, I've had a firsthand view. Because of the fire you've read about, the grand opening of *Me, Myself and Pie* happened three weeks later than Lovina had planned. But she discovered that her plan didn't matter nearly as much as God's did. By 7:30 on opening day there was a line of customers in front of the door. Those who didn't get a seat at the tables sat in the waiting area. And still others brought lawn chairs and sat out front.
>
> The pie display was full of pies. Thankfully, even in the

fire, the pie shells in the large, walk-in freezer had been saved. Still, that supply only lasted so long. The six bakers that Lovina hired worked as fast as they could. Everyone loved being able to see the bakers roll out the crusts. Some Englischers even took pictures. And if you have a chance to see one of the photos in the press, you might see one baker who had a few years on the others.

Lovina's mem (my mem too!) might have looked out of place to everyone else as she stood at the end of the line rolling out crusts, but she's the one who started the whole thing by teaching Lovina how to make pie. Our mem's best friend, Regina Schwartz, was there too. She wore a *Me, Myself and Pie* apron, freshly washed and pressed, and she stood by the door taking orders.

Each of us sisters played a part that day, and in addition to the beautiful menus our sister Faith created, she also presented Lovina with folded tent cards. *Made with Love,* they read. These tent cards were placed in front of each pie in the display. A lot of love went into them for certain—by the bakers and by the Amish community who made sure the burned building was made good as new in record time.

The first piece of pie of the day went to Noah Yoder, who was the lead contractor on the project. The second to Daniel from the glass company. And the next slices went to all those who'd helped with the remodel.

As for Noah Yoder, he's already received calls from some of the best designers in town. The calls weren't for remodel work, but for specialty items—unique pieces that most people throw away. Pieces that Noah salvages and resells. For this will be his main work from now on. Just last week, Noah's family came into town. They'll be staying the rest of the season, maybe longer. Noah's dat is helping Noah set up Pinecraft Salvage in the second half of Lovina's warehouse. And many folks from the community are excited about this second business opening up.

Noah's ability to turn trash into treasure is a gift indeed. But Noah is always quick to point out that finding true value in each and every person is even more important.

So if you visit Pinecraft please stop by. Nothing will make the bride and groom happier than to meet you. Yes, you read that right—bride and groom. Lovina Miller and Noah Yoder's wedding has recently been published. They'll be getting married the first week in January.

We have a lot to celebrate, as you can see. And we've discovered the best way to celebrate is with a piece of pie. Won't you join us?

Grace Yoder
Pinecraft's newest scribe

Reader's Guide

∽

1. Lovina Miller wants one thing more than any other…to open an Amish bakery of her own. Why was this such an important dream for Lovina?

2. Noah Yoder longed to help out three wayward teens. Why was this so important to Noah?

3. Why did Noah choose Pinecraft as the place to help the young men start a new life?

4. How is Pinecraft different from other Amish communities you've read about or visited?

5. Lovina found the perfect location for her pie shop. How did the warehouse benefit both her and Noah?

6. Lovina's mother, Anna, has her own dreams for her oldest daughter. How did Anna's desires affect Lovina?

7. What were some of the risks Lovina took to follow her dream? What were some of the risks her family took?

8. Lovina is one of five sisters. What things did you appreciate most about their relationship? What hopes do you have for Lovina's sisters in future books?

9. Noah liked to salvage discarded things. In what ways did Noah display this calling in the book?

10. Regina was a sounding board for Anna. How did Regina's letters affect Anna?

11. How did working on the remodel with Noah open Lovina's heart to him?

12. What things was Noah drawn to in Lovina? Why did he feel she was the one to pursue?

13. Thomas Chupp seemed to be a wonderful catch. How do you think things would have worked out if Lovina had listened to her mother and allowed herself to be wooed by Thomas?

14. How did others' opinions from both Lovina's and Noah's pasts nearly keep them from opening themselves up to love?

15. What did the remodeled warehouse mean to the community?

16. How did the challenge of almost losing the pie shop turn out to be a blessing in disguise?

17. What is the one pie you'd most like to try?

18. How were both Lovina and Noah's dreams fulfilled in the end? Were they as they expected or better than they expected? How?

List of Recipes

~

Connect with Tricia Goyer and Sherry Gore online!

 facebook.com/AuthorTriciaGoyer
facebook.com/AuthorSherryGore

 @TriciaGoyer
@SherryGore

 @TriciaGoyer
@MyLovelyPieAndI

 pinterest.com/TriciaGoyer
pinterest.com/100books

And be sure to visit
TriciaGoyer.com and **SherryGoreBooks.com**
for the latest news, blog posts, recipes, and more!

not quite AMISH

Maybe you'd like to be Amish...but not quite. You want more peace in your life, in your home, in your family, and in your heart. You want to try a new recipe and pick up a needle and thread. You want to learn to simplify and care for God's green earth (and teach your children to do the same).

You're not alone in your quest. Visit NotQuiteAmishLiving .com and discover like-minded people who find inspiration in all things Amish. With homestyle recipes, tips on frugal living, and ideas for everything from sewing to cleaning, you'll take joy in creating a simpler, more wholesome life!

Tricia Goyer is a busy wife, mom of six, and grandmother of two. A *USA Today* bestselling author, Tricia has published over 50 books and has written more than 500 articles. She's well-known for her Big Sky and Seven Brides for Seven Bachelors Amish series. For more information visit Tricia at www.Tri ciaGoyer.com. Tricia, along with a group of friends, also runs www.NotQuiteAmishLiving.com, sharing ideas about simplifying life.

Sherry Gore is the author of *Simply Delicious Amish Cooking* and *Me, Myself and Pie* and is a weekly scribe for the national edition of the Amish newspaper *The Budget*. Sherry's culinary adventures have been seen on NBC Daytime, Today.com, and Mr. Food Test Kitchen. Sherry is a resident of Sarasota, Florida, the vacation paradise of the Plain People. She has three children and is a member of a Beachy Amish Mennonite church.

To learn more about books by Tricia Goyer and Sherry Gore
or to read sample chapters, log on to our website:

www.harvesthousepublishers.com

HARVEST HOUSE PUBLISHERS
EUGENE, OREGON